"You don't have to be so cross."

Finn ducked to look her in the eyes. "Seriously? How old are you? You sound like you're sixty-five when you say that."

Olivia gasped, offended. "I can't believe you just said that to me."

"I can't believe I'm the only one who ever has. Some friends you've got."

"I have very good friends, thank you very much. And maybe they don't say anything because, first, it's unbelievably rude, and second, you are probably the only person I've said it to because you are the only person who ever gets cross…ticked at me."

"Really? That surprises me. Because, Sweet Cheeks, you can be annoying."

Primrose Lane

DEBBIE MASON

FOREVER

NEW YORK BOSTON

Copyright © 2017 by Debbie Mazzuca
Excerpt from *Starlight Bridge* © 2017 by Debbie Mazzuca

Cover design by Elizabeth Turner.
Cover illustration by Tom Hallman.
Cover copyright © 2017 by Hachette Book Group, Inc.

Forever
Hachette Book Group
1290 Avenue of the Americas, New York, NY 10104
forever-romance.com
twitter.com/foreverromance

First Edition: June 2017

Forever is an imprint of Grand Central Publishing. The Forever name and logo are trademarks of Hachette Book Group, Inc.

The publisher is not responsible for websites (or their content) that are not owned by the publisher.

The Hachette Speakers Bureau provides a wide range of authors for speaking events. To find out more, go to www.hachettespeakersbureau.com or call (866) 376-6591.

ISBNs: 978-1-4555-3723-5 (Mass Market), 978-1-4555-3724-2 (ebook)
Printed in the United States of America

OPM

10 9 8 7 6 5 4 3 2 1

Chapter One

♥

Gardening had once been Olivia Davenport's favorite pastime. Her mother and grandmother had both been avid gardeners. They'd passed on their love of flowers to Olivia and taught her to appreciate the simple pleasure of being at one with nature.

But Olivia hadn't picked up a trowel or hoe in more than two years. She'd lost the desire to carefully tend the tender shoots and bulbs only to have them blossom and then die. Yet here she was, sitting in the middle of an overgrown garden on the Gallaghers' estate with her trusty trowel in hand.

As the event planner for Greystone Manor, she took care of all the details—nothing was too big or too small. Including ensuring that the gardens were shipshape for the upcoming outdoor wedding season.

She looked up from under her wide-brimmed sunhat

at the imposing granite mansion casting a shadow over the fragrant garden. Eight months before, on a dark and dreary September night, a thick fog rolling off the Atlantic had forced her to seek shelter in the coastal town of Harmony Harbor. Little did she know then, as she'd spied the fairy-tale castle rising from the mist, that Greystone Manor would become her home. The place where she'd reinvent herself. The place where she'd become Dana Templeton.

No one here knew she was missing Boston socialite Olivia Davenport. No one knew she'd once been a mother and a wife. No one knew that for the past week the memories had been threatening to bring her to her knees.

She never knew when they would strike. Sometimes they were like a thief in the night, coming out of the darkness to pounce on her, stealing her breath and the tiny bit of contentment she'd managed to carve out for herself in her new life. At other times, they were like a warm, all-encompassing hug that she never wanted to end.

But it didn't seem to matter if the memories were good or bad; they had one thing in common: the power to send her to that dark place she'd escaped from not so very long ago. She supposed it said something that she actually cared whether she ended up back there or not. There'd been a time when she hadn't.

It was the anniversaries. They were piling up on one another. Today was difficult. Tomorrow would be far worse. Even so, Olivia had no choice but to do her job.

That wasn't entirely true. She had a choice; there was always a choice. It wasn't like she had to work for a living. But in some ways, she credited her job for saving her life. Staying busy, filling her mind and time with work, helped her cope.

Her job as Greystone's event planner had given her a sense of purpose, a sense of accomplishment and fulfillment. And the Gallagher women had given her something even more precious—their friendship.

So, no matter how tempting it was to stay in bed tomorrow with the blankets pulled over her head, Olivia would do her best to make the day special for both her friends and the other mothers staying at the manor. She'd keep the crippling memories at bay the same way she had for the past week—antianxiety pills and sleeping pills.

They were the same weapons she'd used in the past. However, now she was using them not only to help with the pain of remembering, but also to fight the feeling of impending doom. She didn't worry she'd become addicted. She just needed a little help to get through the next thirty-six hours. Admittedly, she'd doubled up on that help today.

Her nerves were frayed because of the phone calls. The ones she wouldn't answer because she recognized his number. She'd have to answer, eventually. Stanley Morton wasn't a man who gave up. But he couldn't hurt her anymore. He'd already done his worst. Now it was probably something as mundane as changing the ownership on the brownstone. Except, in her mind, even something that small could grow like a tenacious weed and suck her back into her old life.

Tossing a clump of yellowtail into the growing pile beside her, she did her best to push thoughts of Stanley and his phone calls out of her head. She couldn't afford to be paralyzed by worry today. Her schedule wouldn't permit it.

At three that afternoon, fifteen children between the ages of four and ten were scheduled to gather in the conference room to paint miniature flowerpots. Each pot would hold one of the pink tulips Olivia was now trying to carefully dislodge from the greedy hands of the spring soil. She was determined that the mothers would enjoy their flowers for more than a few days and did her best to keep the roots intact.

Smiling when she lifted the entire flower, bulb and all, from the ground, she transferred it into one of the small pots. The tulip symbolized happiness and good wishes, which, in her opinion, made them the perfect choice for the children to give to their mothers. No sooner had the thought passed through her mind than a memory from three years earlier sprang to life right before her eyes. She clearly saw her little boy carrying a white wicker breakfast tray to where she sat in a canopied bed. Noting how he struggled under the weight of the tray, she reached out to help him. Cooper lifted his determined little chin.

He was six, pale and skinny from another round of treatment for leukemia, and it made it next to impossible not to try and help him. Worrying her bottom lip between her teeth, she clasped her hands tightly on her lap to keep from doing so. From beneath his Boston Red Sox hat, he rewarded her with a proud smile that reached his blue eyes as he placed the tray on the bed.

He'd made her breakfast, a juicy orange peeled and torn into segments and a bowl of his favorite cereal, Cocoa Puffs. He held up a painted pot that contained a perfect pink tulip. He'd remembered the meaning. She reached out to hug him. Instead she grabbed thin air.

Her eyes grew wet, the grounds a blurred blob of green and blue as she checked to be sure no one had witnessed the moment. She lowered her empty arms to her sides. Two years ago tomorrow, she'd buried her son. This year, the anniversary fell on Mother's Day.

She didn't know who she'd been trying to fool. Herself, obviously. Because no matter how much medication she'd taken today or would take tomorrow, it wouldn't be enough to keep the memories at bay or her emotions in check. And wouldn't that be embarrassing…and possibly terrifying for the children. Maybe her good friend and boss, Sophie Gallagher, would take over the craft session for her.

No sooner had the idea popped into Olivia's head than she heard Sophie's voice coming from the patio on the other side of the boxwood hedge. Olivia took it as a good omen and was pushing to her feet to wave her friend over when another voice joined Sophie's, deep and rich with a seductive rumble that Olivia felt straight down to her rubber-boot-encased toes. She immediately dropped to her knees to hide, wincing when she landed on the edge of the trowel.

Ridiculously handsome, dark-haired, blue-eyed men didn't typically send Olivia to the ground, but this particular one did. And it wasn't because of the temptation of his alluring face and seductive voice or that lately he'd played a starring role in her dreams—for which she put the entire blame on her medication. No, it was because, when Finn Gallagher looked at her, she had an uncomfortable feeling he saw past her disguise and knew exactly what she was hiding.

There was another reason for her discomfort. But she didn't want to acknowledge it because, once she did, she'd have to face her feelings.

"Have you seen Dana?" asked the man with the sea-blue eyes that seemed to see through to Olivia's very soul. "Grams is worried about her. She thinks Dana's coming down with something."

At the sarcastic edge in Finn's voice, Olivia stiffened while her traitorous heart picked up speed. It seemed the universe wouldn't be happy until she faced every uncomfortable and worrisome thought and feeling today. Any hope of achieving a Zenlike state in the garden was shot thanks to Finn's matchmaking grandmother.

Oh yes, Olivia knew exactly what Kitty Gallagher was up to. The seventysomething woman was hardly secretive about her determination to find her grandson a wife.

And sadly, Kitty's recent successes with Finn's older and younger brothers led the older woman to believe she had a gift.

She was also highly motivated. A wife would keep Finn from returning to the Congo to serve with Doctors Without Borders. He'd been badly injured in March when rebels attacked the hospital where he'd been working.

"I just saw her a little while ago," Sophie said. "She seemed fine to me."

Olivia heard the frown in Sophie's voice. Four months pregnant, head over heels in love with her husband, Liam, an extremely hot and sweet firefighter, and busy raising their adorable eight-year-old Mia and managing the manor, Sophie wouldn't have a clue what Kitty was up to.

"Come on, you can't seriously think the woman is fine, Soph."

And there it was, the thing Olivia didn't want to examine too closely—Finn and his resemblance to her late husband, Nathan. Not so much in looks despite them both having dark hair and blue eyes; Nathan had been handsome but Finn was stop-and-stare gorgeous.

It was the way Finn spoke about her, the scorn in his voice that reminded her of Nathan. Admittedly, she hadn't spent much time in Finn's company. Intentional on his part, she thought. He did his best to hide his feelings, but she could tell he'd judged her and found her lacking.

Not that anyone else would notice because Finn was unfailingly polite whenever they crossed paths. But he would be, wouldn't he? He was a Gallagher after all. One of the good guys, men who were raised to serve and protect.

"Well, I did think she was fine, Finn, but obviously you think I'm missing something," Olivia heard Sophie say. Her friend sounded ticked with Finn too. Which Olivia found somewhat gratifying.

"Sorry, I didn't mean for it to come out that way. Blame Grams. I'm running a little low on patience these days thanks to her."

"You can't blame Kitty for trying to keep you here. She's worried about you, Finn. So are Liam and your dad. Are you sure you're not rushing things? It hasn't been that long since you were in a wheelchair."

"Your days must go a lot faster than mine. I've been out of the chair for more than six weeks, Soph. I've booked my flight. I leave the day after Griff and Ava get back," he said, referring to his oldest brother and his wife. The couple were honeymooning in Italy.

"You haven't told them yet, have you?"

"No, I've been putting it off."

Olivia felt sorry for Finn. Yes, he was judgmental and not overly friendly toward her, but she knew how much he loved his family. It would be difficult for him to say goodbye, especially knowing how much they wanted him to stay.

"They'll miss you. We all will." There was a smile in Sophie's voice when she added, "So will Miller. He's gotten used to having someone at home with him all day. Here, go fetch, boy."

Miller, the Gallaghers' golden retriever, gave a happy bark, his paws scrabbling on the flagstone patio as he went after whatever Sophie had thrown.

"Jeez, you're almost as good as Grams and Dad with the guilt thing."

"Sorry, I didn't mean to make you feel guilty. So, tell me what you think is wrong with Dana."

Oh no, it sounded like they were walking toward the other end of the patio—the end that would lead them onto the garden path on which Olivia was currently kneeling. She awkwardly got to her feet and then crouched low to walk to the back of the garden. Branches and dried-out stems from the overgrown perennials got caught on her hat as she made her way to the back hedges to stay out of view.

She was reaching up to pull off the leaves when Finn said, "What I think or what Grams thinks?"

"It's not the same?"

"Nope. Grams thinks her precious Dana has migraines. I don't know what it is about that woman, but to hear Grams tell it, Dana Templeton is a saint."

If Olivia didn't know what Kitty was up to, she might have smiled. But the sarcasm in Finn's voice would have immediately wiped it away. He really didn't like her. She didn't know what she'd ever done to him. He certainly didn't take after his grandmother and great-grandmother, who were kind and welcoming. Olivia didn't know where she'd be right now if not for Kitty and Colleen Gallagher.

"I don't know what your problem with Dana is, Finn. She's one of the sweetest women I know. She's been a wonderful friend to me and everyone at the manor. She's tireless. She'd give you the shirt off her back if you asked."

Take that, Finn Gallagher, Olivia thought, her lips lifting in a grateful smile.

"Well, if I'm not mistaken, the sweetest woman you know is using, Soph."

Olivia lifted her hand to cover her outraged gasp. *Using*? How on earth did he come to the conclusion she was doing drugs? Just before her hand reached her mouth, her eyes dropped to the palm-shaped leaf attached to the glove. She must have removed it from her straw hat. Distracted by the conversation between Sophie and Finn, she hadn't realized she'd crumpled it in her gloved hand.

She recognized the leaf's shape almost immediately—monkshood. A member of the buttercup family, its showy blue flowers would bloom midsummer. And while it was a tall and lovely perennial that would grow beautifully in the shady spot at the back of the garden, there was one problem. It was poisonous. In the language of flowers, monkshood symbolized a warning that a deadly foe was near.

Finn's voice penetrated her panic. "You don't seem surprised."

"I'm not. But she's not using illegal drugs. She would never do that. I think she's hiding from someone, Finn. I just wish she'd open up to us and let us help her."

"You might want to find a way to get her to do that sooner rather than later, because I have a feeling your friend is in more trouble than you know."

She wasn't in trouble. She'd been getting better. As soon as Finn left, she'd be fine. Kitty would stop trying to match her with her grandson and the most difficult anniversary would have passed. And somehow Olivia would find a way to deal with Stanley. As she carefully removed the gardening gloves, she wondered if it was her late husband's best friend or Finn Gallagher who was her deadly foe.

An animal brushed against her back, and she released a startled yelp, throwing the gloves in the air—one almost hitting a black cat as he came around to sit at her side. She pressed a hand to her chest and bowed her head. "A meow would have been nice, Simon. You scared the life out of me." He meowed. "A little late," she informed him.

She glanced at Simon, following the direction of his bright blue gaze. A fortysomething woman strode toward them carrying a broom. She had a silver streak in the front of her dark hair and wore a short-sleeve black uniform dress with a black and white apron. It was a woman from housekeeping. Ivy, Olivia thought her name was. She helped out at the events too. Olivia noticed her lips turn down when she spotted Simon, her hand tightening around the broom.

"What have you been up to, Simon? She doesn't look happy with you." Olivia put a protective arm around him. She wasn't really a cat person, but she'd grown fond of Simon. He had an odd habit of showing up whenever Olivia needed a friend.

Like Colleen, he knew all her secrets. At least Olivia didn't have to worry about the truth getting out. Although, she did have a small fright when she'd discovered Colleen had written everyone's stories in a leather-bound book—*The Secret Keeper of Harmony Harbor*—and it had gone missing.

Since the manor had been extensively searched, Olivia's fears had been somewhat alleviated. Even if there was a book, she assumed it had gone missing long before Colleen died. So the Gallagher matriarch wouldn't have had the opportunity to write down the secrets Olivia had shared not long after she'd arrived at the manor.

"Is there a problem, Ivy?" she asked when the woman approached. At the sound of Finn and Sophie calling to Miller, Olivia scooped up Simon and came to her feet.

The woman sucked on her teeth, lifting her chin at Simon. "Is he your cat?"

"In a way, I suppose he is. We've all adopted him. He belongs to the manor, something of a mascot." Olivia smiled.

The woman didn't return her smile. Her eyes flicked beyond Olivia, then back to her. "I'd suggest you all find yourself a new mascot before this one lands you in hot water with the Health Department."

That's all they needed. "Was he in the kitchen? He's a very good mouser, so perhaps—"

"There weren't any mice around. He was—"

At the sound of Miller barking, Simon hissed and jumped from Olivia's arms. She turned to see retriever galloping down the path toward her, his tongue lolling happily out of his mouth. Then he veered off the path and into the garden, tromping on the pink tulips and anything else that got in his way.

"Miller, come out of the garden this—" Olivia began, but the friendly retriever gave her a playful bark and then picked up...her glove. "Miller, no, drop the glove. Drop it now!"

Chapter Two

♥

Finn Gallagher stood on the garden path calling after the willowy redhead running after his dog. "Dana, don't chase him! He thinks you want to play!"

If he wasn't concerned about Miller getting lost in the woods because some crazy woman wouldn't listen, Finn might take the time to figure out what it said about Dana Templeton that she was gardening in a pink shirt and a pair of khaki slacks stuffed into beige rubber boots decorated with pink flowers. He thought it was seriously weird that someone coordinated their wardrobe to dig in the dirt.

She whipped around, the pink floppy hat falling off her head. If he didn't know better, it appeared her shoulder-length red hair was about to do the same.

"You don't understand. He has my gardening gloves!"

"Good God, woman, I'll buy you another pair! Just

stop running after him." He blew out an annoyed breath when she ignored him and continued to sprint down the path. He didn't know what ticked him off more—that she wouldn't listen to him or that he now had to chase after her and his dog.

"It's okay. Don't strain your leg, Finn. I'll go," his sister-in-law offered.

Huh, he didn't think anything could have ticked him off more than Dana and his inability to run like he used to, but his sister-in-law had just proved him wrong.

He started after Dana. "Thanks, but I've got this. I'm not an invalid, you know," he said to Sophie. Then realizing he was being hypersensitive, he added over his shoulder, "My overprotective baby brother would have my head if he knew I let you run a five-mile marathon when you're pregnant and not feeling well. Go home and put your feet up, have a nap."

Sophie called after him, sounding a little sheepish, "It was just an excuse. I'm feeling fine. I didn't want Kitty and Tina to know we're having an early Mother's Day celebration with Rosa today."

Their grandmothers had a long-standing feud. He didn't know what it was about or if they'd just taken up where their DiRossi and Gallagher ancestors had left off. According to local folklore, the original feud had started sometime in the seventeen hundreds. Apparently his grandmother had started this one by insisting that Sophie's mother, Tina, stay at the manor. A move that was guaranteed to tick off Rosa, who wasn't exactly her former daughter-in-law's number one fan.

"I've got your back, but you might want to…" He

lifted his chin at the dark-haired woman crouched on the path picking up the flowerpots that Miller had bowled over. Because he wasn't paying attention, Finn's foot landed awkwardly on the uneven woodland trail. His pained grimace turned into an eye roll when he heard Miller's playful bark and Dana's panicked cries for his dog to stop before he dies.

Talk about a drama queen. Then again, maybe it was a reaction to whatever drug she was on. She might be delusional, but she was also fast. He was running full-out...He shook his head at his assessment.

His full-out was equivalent to someone jogging. Finn ignored the voice in his head that said he had to accept his limitations, that he was lucky to have survived the rebels' attack. The voice sounded a lot like his old man's.

Finn grimaced, and this time it wasn't due to the twisting pain in his leg. It was because Sophie was right; the family wouldn't be happy about him leaving. Grams, never one to let the grass grow under her feet, as his great-grandmother Colleen used to say, had already come up with what she seemed to believe was a winning strategy.

First, she and her fellow members of the Widows Club had decided he should take over for Doc Bishop, the local family physician, who was retiring next week. Not that it was going to happen, because the last thing Finn wanted was to move back home and have his every move dissected, discussed, and evaluated.

He loved his family, but really, what thirty-four-year-old guy would subject himself to 24/7 surveillance and interference? Grams had proven him right when she suggested Dana would make a wonderful wife. *Wife*? He barely knew the woman. But he'd seen and heard enough to know that she wasn't his type, even when she wasn't wasted.

Up ahead, he caught a glimpse of pink through the trees. They were closing in on the footbridge that arched over the tide pools. The bridge connected the estate to the windswept spit of land his oldest brother, Griff, a former Navy SEAL, had recently purchased. Griff and his wife, Sophie's cousin, were renovating the lighthouse.

They'd be back in a few days from their honeymoon… and he'd break the news he was leaving the next day. He'd put off telling his family. Mostly because he hated goodbyes. And it was tough to hold his ground in the face of their sorrow. He hoped none of them cried. Tears got to him every time. There was a part of him that wanted to sneak off in the middle of the night without saying goodbye.

"Miller, stop this instant!"

The image of what his family would do to him if he left without saying goodbye faded at the sound of Dana's voice. Her tone was all proper and superior. He thought of it as her high-society voice. Come to think of it, that might have been the reason he'd taken an almost instant dislike to Dana.

It wasn't her fault. She reminded him of Amber, a woman he'd dated while doing his residency. Amber and her mother, who lunched and raised funds for the hospital like the rest of their moneyed friends. Women who had no idea how the other half lived and had no interest in knowing. The only thing they were concerned about was their social standing, having a wing named after the family, and the preferential treatment they felt they were entitled to due to their connections and their husband's or daddy's bank accounts.

But even if Dana were his type, the last thing Finn wanted was a wife. He didn't do long-term relationships. He liked his women fun and fleeting. Did he have issues? Sure he did, and he'd made friends with his issues years before. And if his grandmother thought that was going to change anytime soon, she was as delusional as the woman she was trying to set him up with. The one who was currently on her knees and elbows, her backside in the air, playing tug-of-war with Miller.

Now, Finn might not have any interest in the woman, but he had to admit she had one great-looking ass. He wondered how he'd failed to notice that. Probably because her conservative wardrobe was classy and not sexy or the least bit revealing. He couldn't help but wonder what else she'd been hiding, because that was one sweet…

As though his matchmaking grandmother could see that particular thought bubble over his head, Finn quickly burst it by reminding himself that Dana was the reason for the persistent throb in his leg.

He limped to the small hill in the clearing where the tug-of-war continued. Miller was winning, and Dana was…Oh hell, she was sobbing. "Please, I don't want you to die. Please let me have the glove."

"Hey, come on, don't cry. Miller isn't going to die because he ate your garden glove." He had to work to keep the sarcasm from his voice. Beige with pink flowers, the glove matched her gardening outfit to a T. His leg screaming in protest as he crouched beside her, he bit back a curse and rested a hand on her shoulder. "Seriously, if you saw what he eats, you wouldn't be worried about a little—"

She looked up at him, a tear slipping from eyes that almost looked black. "No, you don't understand. The glove came in contact with a monkshood leaf. They're highly poisonous." A sob broke in her voice. "Does...does he look dizzy or confused to you?"

The slivers of bright blue that ringed her dilated pupils reminded him that he was dealing with a woman whose feelings and thoughts may not exactly be grounded in reality.

"Let go of the glove, okay? I'll handle it from here." He spoke to her in low, soothing tones, smiling to let her know he wasn't mad and everything was good.

Her eyes narrowed. "I am not high, so don't speak to me like I am. If you want to save your dog, call a vet and then pry his mouth open while I get the glove." She tossed him her phone.

He felt bad that she'd obviously overheard his conversation with Sophie, but her clipped and proper tone took his guilt down a notch or two. And maybe because it did, and his kneecap felt like it was tearing through his skin, he said, "Your dilated pupils and glazed eyes say you're high and so does the way you're enunciating your words. You're trying not to slur. And FYI, I'm a doctor, and"—he pointed at the dog—"Miller is not dying." He swore under his breath when the retriever rolled on his back and pretended to be dead. It's a trick they'd taught him when he was a puppy. But he only did it when Finn or his brothers used the word *dead* or when they shot him with their fingers.

Finn only had a moment to wonder whether Miller was confused by the word *dying* or the hand gesture before Olivia threw herself at the dog. It looked like she was about to give Miller mouth-to-mouth. Finn had to admit that his opinion of her went up a couple of notches at that.

But it went down when she turned on him. "What is wrong with you? Don't just sit there—do something. Call the vet, do chest compressions, just do something!" she cried, tears sliding down her cheeks.

Finn sighed, leaned over, and picked up the infamous glove Miller had dropped when he rolled over. "Miller, buddy, go fetch," Finn said, pretending to throw the glove.

Miller rolled over so fast that he took out Dana. Finn assumed it was either because her rubber boots slid on the grass or because her balance was impaired due to the fact that she was high.

She lay flat on her back, blinking, and then slowly turned her head to look at him. "He's not dying?"

He bit back a smile. She looked pretty cute lying there, and he wasn't going to kick her when she was down. With a hint of pink tinting her pale cheeks, it was obvious she was embarrassed for overreacting. Miller had galloped toward the white wooden footbridge in search of the elusive glove, snuffling the patches of clover. Before he gave up and came back, Finn examined the glove, lifting it to his nose. "It smells like—"

She made a grab for the glove. "No, don't, there could still be— Oh!" she gasped, and began rolling down the hill.

He stared at her, kind of in shock and then positive that she'd realize all she had to do was put out a hand or a foot and stop her downward momentum. But no, apparently, she was just going to roll right on down the hill and into the—

"Dana!" he yelled, lunging in an effort to reach her. At the same time he made a grab for her, she lifted her head, and his fingers got tangled in her hair. Figuring the pain of him tearing a hunk of hair from her scalp would be worse than her landing in the tide pool, he was about to let go when she jerked away, leaving him holding an entire head of hair. He didn't have time to wonder why she was wearing a wig because at that moment he realized *he* was in trouble.

Dana's jarring movement had not only left him holding a fistful of red hair, but it'd also thrown him completely off balance. Over his grunts of pain as he repeatedly rolled over his bad leg, he heard a splash and a shriek. Then a *whoomph* when he landed on top of her in the tide pool.

It was a surprisingly soft landing. Her boringly expensive wardrobe did a good job of concealing not only a nicely rounded backside, but some other intriguing curves as well. And for the first time—since they were practically nose to nose—he noticed her features were softer than he expected.

Her creamy skin was flawless, the defined bow of her full upper lip sexy, and her blue eyes…were not blue. Well, the left one was but the right one was brown. Okay, that was a little weird; he could have sworn…He didn't have time to contemplate why the woman was in disguise because, at that moment, she made a funny sound in her throat.

After a quick visual search ensured that she wasn't outwardly injured or lying on a rock, he realized he was probably responsible for her distress. He wasn't exactly a lightweight. "Sorry, just give me a sec, and I'll get—" He bit down a pained groan. His leg had locked. He wasn't sure how to break it to Dana that they might be stuck in this position for a while. He looked over his shoulder to see Miller sitting at the top of the hill with his head cocked as if to say, *Stupid humans.*

"Hurry! There's something biting…Ow!" Dana yelped, pushing against Finn's chest while trying to move out from under him.

His brain flashed a warning: *Do not react to the soft, tantalizing body parts rubbing against you.* The warning proved unnecessary when her knee slammed into his. Hers was sharp and bony, and his had only recently recovered from knee surgery. "Dammit, woman, are you trying to ensure I never walk again?" he asked through clenched teeth as he let go of her wig to grab his leg.

"Sorry, I'm so sorry. I didn't mean to hurt you. But you really need to get off me. Something bit me and…," she babbled, and then howled, "Ow!"

"I'm trying, and it's probably a minnow. So could you just relax and stop yelling in my ear?" he shouted, and then felt bad for doing so because, for all he knew, she was hallucinating.

"You don't have to be so cross. It's not my fault something is biting me."

Cross? Seriously, who talked like that? Oh right, she

did. Somehow, despite lying in a pool of stagnant water, she still managed to pull off her superior act. He supposed he was being unfair. She'd never been anything but nice to him.

Unfair or not, Dana was the reason they were currently in the position they were in. And if the crippling pain in his leg was any indication, she had more than likely set his recovery back by a couple of weeks. So maybe he was *cross* after all. Because she'd just ensured he wouldn't be leaving Harmony Harbor next week as he had planned.

He scowled down at her as he admitted the embarrassing truth. "My leg locked. Just give me a minute."

A flash of panic and then frustration crossed her face, but both were quickly replaced with sympathy. He'd prefer the frustration, which obviously he wasn't going to get now. He shouldn't have opened his big mouth.

"I'm so sorry. Let me see if I can just move…" She wrapped her arms around him and bit her bottom lip to stifle an *ouch* from what he imagined was another nip from her pal the minnow.

At that moment, he kind of envied the minnow. Just a normal guy reaction, he assured himself. It had nothing to do with…She lifted her hips, and he stifled a groan. Good God, he had to get off her. "Miller! Come on, boy. Come play." He hoped Dana didn't pick up on the desperation in his voice.

It didn't seem like she noticed, or maybe she did and thought it would be fun to torture him, because she kept lifting her hips while yelling, "Get off me. Oh, please get off me."

As Miller galloped to their rescue, latching on to the

back of Finn's shirt with his teeth to drag him off Dana, he realized she'd been saying *it*. And he knew this because when she jumped from the tide pool and began dancing in a circle, she cried, "Get it off me. Please, get it off me."

He winced. It wasn't a minnow after all. She had a green crab clinging to her backside.

Chapter Three

♥

Olivia glanced over her shoulder and yelped at the sight of a green crab hanging onto her butt. She shook and wiggled in an effort to shake the crab loose. It didn't work out as she had hoped. As though the crustacean were holding on for dear life, its slime-green pincers sank deeper into her butt cheek. Watching Finn struggling to his feet, Olivia felt bad for being unable to contain a tortured whimper.

"Okay, I realize you have a problem taking my advice, but I'm going to try one more time," Finn said. "Stop shaking your ass."

"That's so rude!"

"Yeah, well, if you haven't noticed, I'm having a hard time standing on my own two feet." He leaned heavily on Miller, who seemed to sense Finn needed him and didn't move from his side. "So forgive me if I'm not feeling overly sympathetic at the moment. But my advice still stands—stop shaking your butt, woman."

"I…" She was going to say *wasn't* but caught herself midwiggle. "Fine, but please stop calling me *woman*." She yelped. "It's moving."

"Come here." Finn gestured to the spot in front of him.

She shuffled her way toward him in an effort not to jostle the crab. Finn glanced at her and then looked away. There was something about the expression on his face that made her drop her gaze. Lovely, the water had left her pink shirt and white lace bra virtually transparent. And while it was a warm spring day with the temperatures hovering in the midseventies, her nipples were acting as though they were in the middle of a deep freeze. And now the man had to touch her backside with his big, beautifully formed hand.

She turned around and walked backward.

When she stopped in front of him, Finn cleared his throat. "Could you, ah, maybe bend down?"

"Like this…" She bumped into something hard. "Oh, I'm so sorry," she said, reaching back to steady him. "Maybe if I bend over first and then shuffle back toward you. Would that work?"

"Yeah, why don't you do that," he said, sounding as though it took some effort to get the words out.

She thought maybe he was laughing at her and glanced over her shoulder. Definitely no sign of amusement on his too-gorgeous face. The man was staring at her butt. She rolled her eyes at herself. *Of course, he isn't staring at your butt.* Obviously, he was trying to decide how to remove the crab without also removing a chunk of her cheek. The thought of him stitching her bare backside had her scrambling for another solution.

"I've got a better idea. Why don't I sit in the tide pool? I'm sure he'd much rather be swimming with his friends than being stuck on me. Maybe then you could just push him off?"

Finn said something under his breath that sounded suspiciously like, *Not a very bright crab if he does.*

"Excuse me, did you say something?"

"Huh? No, nothing." He raised his gaze. "Just bend over and wrap your hands around your ankles. It should loosen his hold—"

"My ankles? I don't think that's a good idea. How about my knees?"

"Are you always this contrary?"

She was going to ask if he was always this cranky, but given that she could clearly see the pain etched on his face, she thought it might be best to keep quiet and do what he asked. If she could. She hadn't given any time or thought to exercise over the past few years. She'd been consumed with helping Cooper get well. When she'd lost him, she'd been lost too. And then, just as she managed to claw her way out of the bottomless pit of grief, she got the news about her late husband Nathan.

She'd known nothing of his secret life until the call from Stanley that rainy September night. She didn't get the opportunity to ask Nathan why, why he'd married another woman when he was still married to her, why he fought to save children in a faraway place and not their own son. So many questions that would never be answered. Nathan had died half a world away on a bright blue September day.

"Hey now, don't cry. I promise I'm going to get it off you right…Looks like Miller is enjoying his role of hero today. Good job, buddy."

Sniffing back tears, she reached behind her. She had no idea how Finn knew she'd been crying—they were silent tears. Sometimes like the memories, they just snuck up on her. At least she had a good excuse.

"It's gone?" she asked, patting her backside, though the throbbing as the blood rushed to the pincer sites should have been her first indication she was crab-free. She straightened to see Finn prying the crustacean from the retriever's mouth. "Don't let Miller eat him."

Finn bowed his head, took a deep breath as though searching for patience, and then hobbled to the tide pool with the crab gingerly in hand.

Olivia's stomach somersaulted to the soles of her feet. "You're really hurt, aren't you?" It was more of an observation than a question. There was no denying that he'd been reinjured and that she bore the brunt of the responsibility. "I'm so sorry. I—"

"I'll live. But I think this is a goner." He held up her wig.

Fig Newton, she forgot about that. She waved her hand like him finding out she wore a wig wasn't a big deal. "We can just leave it for the birds to nest in. I have others. I like to experiment with my look."

"Is that right? So you have one blue eye and one brown eye on purpose?"

She touched the corner of her eye and caught the twitch of his lips. "One of my contacts must have fallen out."

"You wear glasses?"

The man was annoying because apparently he could

tell she was lying. But he was also hurt. Because of her, she reminded herself. "Here, let me help you." She put an arm around his waist. Tucked in close to his warm body, she got a whiff of a delectable scent—bergamot and sandalwood. She angled her head to take a careful sniff. It was him. He smelled amazing, which made it hard for her not to keep sniffing him. Which would look really odd if he caught her. Instead, she drew his heavy arm over her shoulders. "Lean on me."

He didn't move. She glanced up and got caught in his sea-blue gaze. Without his square jaw and the hard angles of his face to balance his ridiculously long eyelashes and that sumptuous mane of dark brown hair, the man would be too perfect.

His eyebrow was raised. He'd caught her blatant stare. She wished she could see what she looked like right now. Could he tell she'd been devouring him with her eyes?

Break eye contact and do it now before you embarrass yourself, said a forceful voice in her head. At least part of her was thinking clearly. She managed a weak smile for Finn, praying he couldn't tell she'd been moments away from fantasizing about kissing his sensuous lips, of being wrapped around his tall, muscular frame.

Where are these crazy thoughts coming from? she wondered, and decided they were a result of doubling up on her medication. That'll teach her. She wouldn't do that again: oh no, she wouldn't.

"All right, how about we…," she began, and then noticed he hadn't moved. He was still looking down at her. "What's wrong?" She prayed the conversation she'd been having with herself had been in her head.

"What are you on?"

"Pardon me?"

"Come on, Dana. I'm not judging you. I just want to help if I can."

She had no idea where it came from—she barely knew the man—but all of a sudden, she had an almost overwhelming urge to tell him everything. To unburden herself and get it all out in the open. Maybe because, like Nathan, Finn was a doctor and worked with an international aid organization. They had something in common. Somehow, she felt like she could trust him to keep her confidence. She didn't know why, but she did.

Maybe because Finn was strong and courageous, a hero. A man who'd faced down armed rebels to get his team and his patients to safety. Maybe he'd be able to show her how to face her own fears. Her fear of what would happen once she worked up the courage to return Stanley's call.

"You know what, if you don't want to open up to me, that's your business. I get it, okay. But you're working for my family, and if you're involved in anything that could create problems for—"

His voice was clipped and judgmental, and all she could think was thank God she hadn't confided in him. She was usually a good judge of character. It went to show how rattled she was. She was angry too. Angry that he could think she'd do anything to hurt his family. Given that he planned to leave in a few days' time and break his grandmother's and father's hearts, she didn't think he had a right to judge.

As quickly as her temper flared to life, it dissipated.

All he was trying to do was look out for the people he loved. She respected him for that. She wished Nathan had looked out for Cooper, for her.

She pushed aside thoughts of Nathan to reassure Finn. "I'm taking prescription drugs, not illegal ones. I realize you have no reason to trust me, but I'd never do anything to hurt your family." An emotion darkened his eyes. She didn't think it was anger. His face didn't harden; it softened. She thought maybe he could tell how much his family meant to her.

"I don't know about that. My family cares about you, Dana. As I've recently come to learn, they care about you a lot. So, if you're doing something that will hurt yourself, indirectly it will hurt them."

"I haven't been sleeping. I forgot I'd taken a pill in the middle of the night and took another one this morning. I'm just a little groggy. It was an accident. It won't happen again." She kept focused on her rubber boots as she helped him up the hill.

Miller walked on the other side, keeping an eye on his master. Dana could feel the tension in Finn's body, hear the catch in his breath. She was a bit breathless herself. The man was at least six inches taller than she was and must outweigh her by a good hundred pounds. She wouldn't make it to the manor, but as she'd witnessed, Finn had his pride and was probably stubborn enough to try and make the trek himself. Olivia was pretty sure he'd end up facedown on the path.

"What are you taking?"

"I thought it was your brother Aidan who was the cop?" she said, annoyed that he wouldn't let up.

A couple years older than Finn, Aidan was actually an undercover DEA agent. Olivia probably shouldn't have mentioned him. She knew Kitty and Finn's father were worried about Aidan. No one had heard from him since March.

"All right, I won't pry. But if you ever want to go the natural route, I can suggest a few things for you to try. See if they help with the insomnia."

"Thank you. I'll keep that in mind." She glanced to the left, where a white-brick lighthouse with a red roof jutted out toward the sea. "You wouldn't happen to have a key for Ava and Griffin's, would you?"

He nodded. "I've been keeping an eye on the place for them. Why?"

"If it's okay with you, I wouldn't mind cleaning up before we go back to the manor. My top…" She trailed off, positive he'd know what she was alluding to without her spelling it out.

"No problem. I wouldn't mind getting cleaned up myself. We can borrow a change of clothes from Griff and Ava. I'm sure they won't—"

The sun glinted off something metallic and caught her eye. It was her phone, lying on the ground. Her phone that she'd handed to Finn when…She jerked to a stop. Finn groaned. "Sorry, but this is really important. Where's my glove?"

"Come on, not this again. Look, Miller's fine."

"I know, and I'm glad. But we still have to be careful. I picked up the leaf with my right hand. Maybe Miller got the left-hand glove?"

He reached behind him.

She leaned back, slapping a hand on the bulge in his pocket.

His eyebrow went up, and she fought back a blush because she was sort of touching his butt. She lowered her hand. "No, to be safe, don't touch it again. We'll just throw out your jeans and the glove, but we'll have to hunt the other one down."

"Hey, I like these jeans. You're not throwing them out."

She leaned down to scoop her phone off the ground. No sooner had she picked it up than it rang. She recognized the number. Her finger trembled when she rejected the call. She should answer and get it over with. It might be something as simple as sending her copies of her divorce papers. But she didn't believe that was all Stanley wanted.

Because every time she saw his number, the small hairs on the back of her neck stood on end, and she was overcome by a heavy sense of foreboding. Given the last time they spoke and the reason for the call, it's possible her overreaction was due to a form of PTSD.

Strong fingers closed around her wrist. "Dana, relax. Take slow, even breaths or you'll hyperventilate. That's a girl," he said when she did as he suggested, his other hand going to the nape of her neck. He gently massaged the tight muscles there, murmuring his encouragement as she got herself under control. There was no judgment in his voice. Just kindness and concern.

She'd heard Finn was well loved and respected by the people he served in the Congo. She now had a better understanding why. Leaning against him, she was en-

veloped by the strength and warmth of his body and the
seductive scent of his cologne. She felt him take an awkward step back and realized she was resting too much of
her weight on him.

"Thank you." She self-consciously pulled away. "We
should probably get going. I have to be back at the manor
by two to get organized for the children's craft session.
They're going to paint flowerpots for their mothers. I was
going to use pink tulips but Miller trampled them, so
maybe I'll go with hyacinths. I think there'll be enough.
They're pretty, and they mean constant love and fertility.
That should work, don't you think?"

"I have no idea what you're talking about. And not to
be rude, but I really don't care. What I do care about is
who's trying to contact you. It's obvious that they frighten
you, Dana. Why don't you let me help?"

"No, it's not what you think. I'm fine, honestly."

"Sure you are, because perfectly fine people have
panic attacks when they get a call in the middle of the
afternoon, take too many sleeping pills, and wear a disguise. Come on, what do you take me for? At least do me
the courtesy of being honest."

All she could do was blink up at him, the warm feelings of moments ago shriveling up in response to his
Arctic-cold words. She'd been right the day she met him.
He probably did have a God complex. He might be ten
years younger than Nathan, but he was just as sanctimonious and judgmental.

Finn didn't know what it was about Dana, but she managed to bring out the worst in him. She got under his skin.

And because she did, he'd overstepped and said things he shouldn't and in a way that he shouldn't have. "I'm sorry. I had no business getting on your case like that. In my defense, I was worried about you. Occupational hazard, I guess. It won't happen again."

It wouldn't because, after today, he planned to stay well away from Dana Templeton. She was dangerous. And vulnerable, and dammit, the haunted look in her eyes when she'd looked at her phone wasn't easy to forget.

He put his arm around her slender shoulders, leaning on her as he maneuvered her toward the footbridge that arched over the tide pools. After how he'd called her out, he was afraid she'd want to head directly back to the manor. He didn't know if he could make it, and he wanted one last chance to find out what was going on with her. If he couldn't break past her defenses, he'd let someone else try. Because one way or another, he was getting to the bottom of this. And then he'd be done, finished, out of her life for good.

"Are you giving me the silent treatment?" he asked as they walked across the bridge and onto a path bordered by tall, rustling grasses.

"No, I had to concentrate while we were walking over the bridge. You may not have noticed, but some of the boards were loose. I didn't want you to trip. This isn't much better. Be careful." She nodded at a rock at the edge of the path.

If anyone else coddled him like she was, he'd probably bite off their head. For some reason, it didn't bother him when she did. But he didn't want her to make a habit of it, so he said, "You know that I just have my arm around you to keep you warm, right? I don't want you to catch a chill."

"You don't seriously think I buy that, do you?" she asked, then gave an involuntary shiver when a strong wind blew off the Atlantic, dampening their faces with sea spray.

"Believe me now?"

"No, but I'll take you up on that offer." She snuggled in a little closer. "Would it be okay if I grab a shower?"

"I was going to suggest that you do. You were lying in stagnant water and no doubt have open wounds. They'll need to be disinfected."

She jerked back, throwing him off balance. "You don't have to take care of them. I can."

"Would you stop moving like that?" he snapped, more from frustration than anger. It wasn't solely related to the zing of pain that shot up his leg in response to the aggressive movement. The conversation had inspired an image from earlier to pop into his head. He tried his best to erase the memory of her bending over in front of him, bumping into his groin. His mind wasn't cooperating. It immediately replaced that image with the one of her standing in front of him in her see-through shirt and bra.

He cleared his throat. "I wasn't planning to take care of your wounds. You can put an antibacterial cream on them yourself. But you do realize I'm a professional, right? It's not like you have anything I haven't seen before."

He should have shut up while he was ahead. But he didn't want her to think the thought of stripping her bare was turning him on. Whoa, where the hell had that come from?

She looked up at him.

He pretended he didn't notice and hurried her along the path to the lighthouse, gritting his teeth the entire way.

Opening the red wooden door, he ushered her inside. "Chase and his crew have been doing the renovations while Griff and Ava are away, so be careful. They're mostly working in the kitchen though." Which was fairly obvious since it had been gutted. "You can take the shower off the master. Everything you need should be in there."

"You're sure you don't mind? I can—"

"No, go ahead." And he hoped she did it quickly because her top and bra were still wet and see-through. He looked away to pull out a chair at the rustic, rough-hewn wooden table. "I should sit for a while anyway."

"Wouldn't it be better if you lie down? You can prop your leg on some pillows."

It would be. But there was a problem, and it was a fairly substantial one. "They're redoing the other bedrooms. There's only the one bed. It's in the master."

"Right, I remember Ava saying something about that now." Dana chewed on her bottom lip while glancing at his leg, then lifted a shoulder. "It's not like…I'll be in the shower, and you'll be dressed. You will be dressed, won't you?"

He looked down at his wet jeans and kept his gaze there.

"Oh my gosh, your jeans. I completely forgot. You have to get out of them now."

"You want me to strip right here, right this minute?"

She nodded. "I'll look for a garbage bag. You better

have your shower first. You don't want to contaminate Griffin and Ava's bed with monkshood."

As Finn soon learned, the woman's willowy frame and delicate features hid an iron will. She was a force of nature. She wouldn't let up until he'd handed over his jeans, showered for ten minutes longer than he thought was necessary, changed into his brother's T-shirt and sweatpants, propped his leg on two pillows, and then shoved a best-selling psychological thriller in his hands, all in under twenty minutes.

Miller lay at the end of the bed snoring while Finn stared unseeing at the page, listening to the water running in the shower. He rubbed his eyes and tried to refocus on the book. Maybe there was something with this monks-hood thing after all. There had to be a logical explanation for him being unable to get an image of Dana in the shower out of his head.

Her cell phone rang. It was on the nightstand within easy reach. It rang again. He glanced from the phone to the closed bathroom door. He remembered the haunted look on her face, the panic attack when she saw the number on the screen. She was lying. Whoever had been on the other end terrified her.

Finn didn't want to invade Dana's privacy, but for her sake, he needed to know what she was dealing with. Because whether she'd admit it or not, she needed his help. On the third ring, he picked up the phone.

Chapter Four

♥

Finn disconnected from Stanley Morton and stared at the phone in his hand, trying to come to terms with what he'd just learned. Dana Templeton was actually Olivia Davenport.

The door to the bathroom opened, and he turned his head to see her standing inside the door frame enveloped in a cloud of steam. She no longer looked like the woman he thought he knew, or sort of knew, because he'd had no real interest in getting to know her.

Thick, honey-blond hair fell softly to her narrow shoulders, framing her flawless, oval face; her pretty, pink mouth; and her big, whiskey-colored eyes. Her fine-boned hand clutched the terry-cloth bathrobe to her throat. An oversized plain white robe shouldn't be sexy, but it was. Maybe because her skin was damp and flushed and her feet were bare.

He returned his gaze to her face. The woman he'd once thought gave off a cold and superior vibe looked warm and vulnerable.

He almost laughed at the thought. From the first time he'd laid eyes on her, he'd written Dana Templeton off as a snob, someone like his ex, Amber, who thought the world revolved around her and had no interest in how the other half lived. And now that he knew who Dana really was…Yeah, the irony didn't escape him.

Because this was a woman who, with a simple phone call, had one of the leading oncologists in the country drop what he was doing to take over the care of Griffin's ex-wife, Lexi. A woman who Finn also knew had a hospital wing named after the son she'd lost to leukemia two years before. She hadn't needed her late father's or husband's money to pay for it. Socialite Olivia Davenport was a wealthy woman in her own right.

At the sound of a muffled gasp, he refocused on her face. She stared at the phone in his hand with her fingers pressed to her mouth.

"I can explain." He wasn't sure if there was any explanation that made up for him invading her privacy. But he'd known that going in. If he could alleviate even a small measure of the fear he'd seen on her face earlier, he'd be fine with her never speaking to him again.

"You answered my phone?" Her voice was little more than a whisper.

"Yeah, it was Sophie. She wanted to make sure you were okay and to let you know you didn't have to worry about the kids' craft session. It's handled. I told her about the other glove too. They'll search for it and handle it with care." But he hadn't left it at that. He'd scrolled down and hit redial on the number below Sophie's.

As though the tension stringing her muscles tight released all at once, Olivia lost the pinched look on her face and practically sagged against the door frame. For a minute, Finn considered not telling her he'd uncovered her secret. But that was the whole point of picking up the phone, wasn't it? The only way he could help her was letting her know that he knew the truth. She didn't have to hide it from him. Maybe then she'd open up and tell him why she was living a lie.

He returned the phone to the nightstand while easing his legs over the side of the bed to sit up. "There's something else I have to tell—" Finn broke off when Miller lifted his head and looked toward the open bedroom door with his ears perked.

"Why is Miller—" Olivia began, only to have the sound of a woman's voice calling out Finn's name stop her cold. Her eyes went wide. "Please tell me Chase has an older woman working for him who sounds like your grandmother."

"I wish," Finn muttered, looking at Olivia and the rumpled bed through his grandmother's matchmaking eyes. Yeah, this was definitely not something he wanted her to see. Not after her comments of this morning. "Olivia, go lock yourself in the bathroom and don't make a sound." He turned to head his grandmother off in the kitchen and realized Olivia hadn't moved. "Look, unless you want Kitty to…" He frowned. Why was she looking at him like he'd just told her to lose the robe and to jump into…

"You know who I am," she said, a stricken look on her face.

He couldn't figure out what he'd said or done to give himself away and then realized he'd called her by her real name. "Okay, I know you're upset, but believe me, the last thing you want is for Grams to find us like this. I promise, we'll talk once she's gone, but right now, you have to get in the—"

He heard the creak of the floorboards. Kitty was coming their way, and Olivia still hadn't moved. And he needed her to move because his grandmother was relentless. If Kitty thought her matchmaking plans had even the slightest chance of succeeding, they wouldn't know a moment's peace. If she caught them now, she'd have the church booked.

Given that Olivia had stubbornly refused to listen to any of his earlier suggestions, he thought he'd better take matters into his own hands. Sliding across the floor in his socks, he closed the door as quietly as possible and checked for a lock. There wasn't one.

"Finn, Dana, where are you?"

Hearing Gram's voice just down the hall seemed to snap Olivia out of her state of shock, and her gaze shot to the door. "She can't find us like this. Hurry," she said. But as she bent down to scoop his clothes off the floor, she froze with her hands out.

"Seriously, they're not contaminated by the monkshood leaf." No sooner had he shoved the pile of clothes under the bed than Olivia grabbed him by the hand and dragged him inside the closet…with her.

He shook his head. "No, this isn't going to work. You still have time to make it to the bathroom if you run. Go."

He backed against the wall, hoping she'd take the hint because it would be a very bad idea if she stayed. He was doing his best to ignore the way the robe gaped in intriguing places and how great she smelled and looked. Ignoring her in the close confines of the closet would be next to impossible. Despite it being a double door closet, there wasn't enough room for the two of them. His brother apparently thought it was a good place to store not only his clothes but also his hand weights. And Ava had a crapload of shoes.

Big surprise, Olivia ignored his suggestion. Patting her thigh, she whispered, "Miller, come here, boy."

Okay, so that was a good idea. When Miller reached the closet, Finn fit his fingers under the dog's collar to stop him from ramming his way inside. "I've got him. Now go before Grams—"

Olivia motioned for him to get Miller inside. At the creak of the floorboards right outside the bedroom door, he didn't have much choice. He lifted Miller into his arms, shuffling past Olivia. She smelled like strawberries, and he could feel the press of her warm body against his back. Which may have been the reason why he tripped over a hand weight and nearly broke his ankle. The one with the pins in it. Stifling a pithy curse, he slid Ava's shoes over with the side of his left foot and put Miller down.

Olivia winced in sympathy and then closed the closet just as his grandmother knocked on the bedroom door. "Finn, Dana, are you two in here?"

Finn could have sworn he heard gleeful anticipation in her voice.

Miller whined and headbutted the closet door.

Finn made a gun with his finger and whispered, "Miller, bang."

The dog dropped on top of Ava's shoes and played dead. Finn kept his gun finger trained on Miller while trying to keep the weight off his right foot.

Olivia, obviously trying to be helpful, wrapped her arms around his waist. She went up on her toes, her warm breath caressing his ear as she whispered, "Lean on me."

The bedroom door opened. "Finn, dear, where are you?" Through the slats, he watched his grandmother look around the room. He hoped she'd just leave, but instead she walked to the bed and smoothed the rumpled navy comforter. "I must have misunderstood Sophie," she murmured to herself while fluffing the pillows.

There was an audible hitch in Olivia's breath, and her fingernails dug into his stomach. He swallowed an aggravated *ow* and frowned down at her, mouthing, *What's wrong?*

She mouthed, *My phone.*

Kitty didn't pick it up. Instead, she went to snoop in the bathroom and seconds later came out carrying Olivia's clothes. "The lantern room," she said, and trotted off.

"She took my clothes," Olivia whispered.

"They're wet anyway. You can borrow something of Ava's," he whispered back, cocking his head to audibly follow his grandmother's progress. It sounded like she was in the kitchen. "If we hurry, we can probably get out of here before she makes it back down from the lantern room. And so we're on the same page, tell her you fell in the tide pool chasing Miller, and I gave you the key to use the shower here, but I went straight home. Right away. No contact. No conversation. You might even want to tell her I was a jerk."

She looked up at him in a way that said it wouldn't be a lie and then made a gun with her fingers. "Miller, bang."

Finn bowed his head and closed his eyes. It looked like they wouldn't be leaving the lighthouse until he came clean. "I'm sorry. I shouldn't have redialed the call before Sophie's, but I was worried about you."

He went to open the closet door, but she stopped him with a hand on his arm. "Did you say anything to Stanley? Did you tell him where I was?"

"No, I asked why he was calling the number. He gave me his name, explained he was a lawyer looking for Olivia Davenport. I told him he had the wrong number." Even though Finn had recognized the name right away.

It wasn't likely he'd forget the name of the woman Lexi and his family credited with saving her life. Being a former military cop, his ex-sister-in-law had done some digging and shared what she'd learned with Finn. He'd Googled Olivia too. What could he say? He'd been bored.

But she hadn't left much of a footprint. Olivia wasn't on social media, and in the few pictures he'd found of her, she'd been wearing hats and overlarge sunglasses. Knowing what he did now, there was obviously a resemblance to the woman they knew as Dana but not enough to ring any bells. Maybe because the last time she'd been photographed in public had been years before. She was obviously a woman who didn't like attention from the media and had the financial means to ensure no one got too close.

"Did he say anything else?" Olivia asked, looking more relaxed than seconds ago.

"No, I told him the phone belonged to Dana Templeton, and that was it. He thanked me and hung up."

She hugged herself and looked away.

"Did I say something wrong?" It was bad enough he'd invaded her privacy; he didn't want to do anything that put her in jeopardy. "It's a fake name, isn't it?"

"It was a spur-of-the-moment decision the night I checked in at the manor. I hadn't intended to disappear. It's my maternal grandmother's maiden name. Stanley would have recognized it. Or he will once he has time to think about it."

"What are you running from, Olivia? Tell me and maybe I can help."

"My life, the expectations, the memories. Learning that my husband died in a plane crash and…" Her gaze flicked away from his, and she lifted a shoulder. "I had barely recovered from losing my son. I had to get away. I couldn't stay in Boston."

The muscles in his chest twisted and tightened. It felt like the closet was closing in on him. He wanted her to stop talking. It hit too close to home. She could be describing how he'd felt the day they'd buried his mother and sister. In October, it would be eight years since the accident. Sometimes it felt like yesterday. Sometimes it felt like a lifetime ago.

"I didn't plan to stay in Harmony Harbor either." A faint smile touched her lips. "But Colleen and Kitty were hard to resist. They made me feel like part of the family, and I couldn't bring myself to leave."

It was as if Olivia's mention of Kitty reminded Miller that Grams was still around and he barked—loudly. "Miller, bang," Finn and Olivia said at almost the same time with pretty much the same amount of panic in their voices.

Miller barked at them. Even louder this time. Probably to make his point that he hadn't been paid the going rate for his acting. He usually got a treat for doing his dead-dog routine.

"No way Grams didn't hear him. You get dressed and tell her you never saw me today, and Miller was wandering around on his own."

Finn put his hand out to open the closet, which proved unnecessary because Miller decided he'd waited long enough and leaped against the doors like Superdog. One of the closet doors fell off the hinges and crashed to the floor, right at the feet of his frowning grandmother.

Colleen Gallagher had always known Olivia's secrets would come to light. Too many people were privy to them. But she was the only one who knew about Olivia's deepest, darkest secret. And just like everyone else's in town, Colleen had written them in her book, *The Secret Keeper of Harmony Harbor*.

Late yesterday afternoon, Olivia had informed everyone of her true identity, but Dana, as they knew her then, had been a guest at the manor for a little more than ten days when Colleen saw signs that caused her concern. Despite the short time Olivia had been staying with them, Colleen had grown fond of the young woman. Not only had she sensed that Olivia, like her, knew the pain of loss, but they'd also discovered they shared a passion for flowers and books, and the manor too. When Olivia had heard about Kitty's plan to auction off Mistletoe Cottage, she'd offered to decorate it for the brochure. It was at the cottage that Olivia confided what had happened one May night two years past.

The family didn't realize the sacrifice Olivia had made by contacting her old friend to take on Lexi's case. It pretty much guaranteed that her past would come back to haunt her. But Colleen knew Olivia well enough to know she'd consider the sacrifice worthwhile. Lexi was doing well, and that would be all that mattered to Olivia. She was a good friend to the Gallaghers.

Now it was Olivia who needed their support. It was two years ago today that she'd buried her son. But whether Olivia would admit that she needed their comfort, or take it if it was offered, was a different story. The girl was private and stoic. Traits Colleen had once admired but had come to believe that, like anything, could be harmful when taken too far.

Colleen walked through the guest bedroom door on the second floor of the manor and spotted Olivia standing at the green marble sink in the bathroom. Colleen was surprised to see her wearing a rose pink knitted skirt and jacket with a pair of nude high heels. She obviously intended to work the Mother's Day brunch after learning they were short-staffed. If Colleen were here, she'd put a stop to it.

Well, she was here, just not here, here. She'd been dead—or undead as the case may be—close to seven months now. Perhaps "passing" would be a more accurate term because she seemed to be betwixt and between. She'd seen the light all right, only she'd been lollygagging, worrying about the ones she was leaving behind, and therefore missed the magic carpet ride to heaven.

Over the past several months, she'd come to believe it was for the best that she had. The good Lord still had plans for her it seemed. Plus, she had a few of her own. She'd gotten the ball rolling in her will. She'd left the five-thousand-acre estate to her great-grandchildren. In order to bring them closer together, the estate would be held in trust until they unanimously agreed to keep it or sell it.

To date, only three of her great-grandsons had signed on to the Save Greystone Team. It wouldn't be easy, but then nothing worthwhile ever was. Colleen was determined to protect the Gallaghers' legacy and see all her great-grandchildren happily married and living in Harmony Harbor where they belonged.

So far, she'd married off two great-grandsons to their true loves. She was canny like that. She had a gift, she did. Now it was time to move on to her next couple. Olivia didn't know it yet, but she was one half of that couple. Finn was the other.

They were the perfect match. Colleen had seen signs, even as late as yesterday afternoon when they returned from the lighthouse with Kitty, that the couple might disagree with her. She supposed she could understand why. In some ways, they were complete opposites. And both held long-standing prejudices that might initially cause them problems.

But Colleen saw beyond their bumpy beginning to the wonderful union it could be. Olivia would be as good for

Finn as he would be for her. She'd steady him, ground and support him, force him to confront his grief. In turn, Finn would force Olivia to face hers. He'd validate the choices she'd made and help her to find happiness and live again. They'd bring out the best in each other.

"I wish he was here for you now, girlie. You could use his support. He'd help you to deal with your grief instead of hiding from it in a medicated fog," Colleen said to Olivia, who was twisting the cap off a prescription bottle.

Of course, she couldn't hear her. Still, looking at Olivia's red eyes and blotchy face, she felt bad for her remark. The girl was suffering.

"I wish you could hear me, Olivia. It might bring you some comfort to know that the light and love they talk about seeing and feeling is truly there. Life doesn't end, of that I'm now certain. One day you'll see Cooper again."

Olivia took an antianxiety pill, the glass of water shaking as she brought it to her lips. Colleen cursed Stanley Morton and Olivia's late husband, Nathan Sutherland. Before Stanley had started calling her last week, Olivia had been doing well. But no matter what, today would be difficult for her young friend.

"Take care of yourself for a change. They can handle the brunch without you." She was worried about Olivia working today. She wasn't herself. Colleen followed her to the bed and sat on the mattress beside her.

Olivia pulled out the nightstand drawer. From beneath the papers, she withdrew a gold-framed photograph, cradling it lovingly in her hands.

The day Olivia had shared her secrets with Colleen,

she'd brought her here to show her this very photograph. Cooper had died days after the photo had been taken. In it, he wore a Boston Red Sox ball cap pulled low on his bald head. Olivia had managed to get her little boy's favorite player to visit the hospital that afternoon. It was the last photo she had of her son.

"I miss you, my sweet boy. I miss you with all my heart," Olivia said, clutching the photo to her chest.

Colleen placed a hand on the girl's shoulder, hoping that somehow Olivia sensed she wasn't alone. Colleen understood her grief better than most. Sometimes living to a hundred and four had seemed as much a curse as a blessing. She'd buried her husband, children, her granddaughter-in-law Mary, and her great-granddaughter Riley, so many friends and enemies too.

Olivia set her son's photograph on the nightstand. Now that everyone knew who she was, Olivia wouldn't feel she had to hide his existence anymore. Colleen imagined that at least would bring her some comfort. She hoped that would be enough to get Olivia through the next few hours. The thought had barely crossed her mind when Olivia's cell phone rang. Colleen felt her stiffen beside her.

Olivia took a deep breath, squared her shoulders, and then answered the phone. "Hello, Stanley. I understand you've been trying to reach me." She paused, briefly closing her eyes. "I can't believe it's been two years either. I know. Thank you. Stanley, I don't mean to be rude, but I'm rather busy at the moment, so if you could tell me what you need from…Yes, I'm well aware Nathan had a wife and a daughter, but I don't know what that has to do with me." She listened to the man on the other end. "I'm very sorry to hear Nathan's wife is missing. If you like, I can reach out to the foundation's community partners in Kenya…Sorry, I must have misunderstood." Whatever he said had Olivia rising to her feet while frantically shaking her head. "No. No, I can't. I don't care what Nathan wanted, Stanley. It's cruel of you to even ask."

"Oh, but I wish I could put my hands through the phone, Stanley Morton. You must hear the pain you're causing her, but still you don't let up."

Olivia sat back down on the bed as Stanley droned on. Colleen could hear his muffled voice but not what he said. Whatever it was, Olivia looked like she was in shock. She hung up a few moments later, and then, as though in a daze, she walked to the bathroom.

Colleen followed her. Olivia picked up the prescription bottle, her gaze unfocused.

"No! You already took one. Put that down right now. You don't know what you're doing," Colleen cried as she tried to wrestle the pill bottle from Olivia's hand. It was no use.

Chapter Five

♥

Colleen paced in front of the French doors in the manor's dining room. They opened to the patio where family and guests were currently enjoying the Mother's Day brunch. May had been unseasonably warm, and people were taking advantage of the weather. Colleen would like nothing more than to enjoy the scent of lilacs and the animated conversations that were floating in on a gentle spring breeze; instead she was fretting about Olivia.

Just as Colleen had been unable to stop her from taking the pills, she'd be unable to keep her from working the brunch. Apparently, her family was oblivious to the fact that Olivia was high. Then again, she'd been in the conference room for the past hour working on flowerpots with the children who weren't staying at the manor but had come with their families for brunch.

Colleen couldn't imagine it was easy for Olivia to be

around the little ones today, but it kept her from trying to help serve the tables. The waitstaff was overrun at the moment, and knowing Olivia, she'd jump right in to help. Colleen supposed she should go and check on her again but had hoped to get her once-right-hand man and confidant's attention.

Not that Jasper could hear or see her; he merely sensed her presence. Though her ability to make her presence known was inconsistent at best. She believed Jasper knew she was around because of Simon.

Or as Jasper referred to him, her partner in crime. Simon was the only one who could both see and hear her. And right now, she was glad of it. Jasper was busy ordering about the staff in his brisk, no-nonsense manner, and as Colleen had learned from previous experience, she couldn't step foot outside of Greystone. For some reason, she was tied to the manor. She needed someone who wasn't.

"Simon, come here," she called to him, frowning when he slinked to her side and looked both left and right. Usually he acted like lord of the manor, but today he seemed almost fearful to be caught in the dining room.

"Did Jasper catch you in the kitchen again?" she asked him. He gave an exaggerated shake like he'd gotten wet. Colleen wasn't sure if that was a no or a display of how frightened he'd been. "Don't mind Jasper. His bark is worse than his bite. Just stay out of his way. Now, here's what I need you to do for me, Simon. Tug on Finn's pant leg to get his attention. Once you have it, make him follow you to the conference room. He'll know what to do once he gets there."

She'd heard him talking to Sophie out on the patio

yesterday, so she knew he already had his own concerns about Olivia. Besides, it played into her matchmaking plans. Olivia needed a broad shoulder to cry on, strong arms to offer her comfort.

Simon didn't move.

"What is wrong with you?" she asked, glancing at the table where her great-grandsons Liam and Finn sat. She blinked. Finn sat in a wheelchair with his wounded leg extended in front of him, same as it had been back in March. His arms were crossed, and there was a scowl on his handsome face.

She could see how being back in the wheelchair would bother him. The lad had been the most active of Colin and Mary's four boys. There wasn't a sport he hadn't been involved in or excelled at. A daredevil at heart, he wouldn't like to be confined.

"All right, get Sophie instead," Colleen said, eyeing the other family members at the table. "Once she sees the state Olivia is in, she'll probably get Finn anyway." Simon took off like a shot…in the opposite direction.

Frustrated, Colleen looked back at the table. Sophie was making her rounds, speaking to the guests at other tables. Surely the fact that Sophie wasn't at the family's table wasn't enough to throw Simon off.

But an exchange between Liam and Finn distracted Colleen from her thoughts about Simon, and she stepped to the edge of the door.

"Don't look now, but trouble's coming your way, bro," Liam said to Finn.

Liam was watching his grandmother, who was making her way toward their table. She wore an elegant sapphire pantsuit, and Colleen wasn't surprised to see several of the older gentlemen following Kitty's progress across the patio. She was a fine-looking woman with her white-blond hair and blue eyes.

"Do me a favor and head Grams off at the pass," Finn said. "I seriously can't have another debate with her about why I won't take over for Doc Bishop without losing it."

"You've been away for a while, so I'll reeducate you on her subtleties. I've seen that devious little smile and calculating little twinkle before. It's Gram's matchmaking look, not her headhunting one, and it appears to be directed squarely at you and Olivia." Liam grinned. "Grams already had a soft spot for her. Imagine what she thinks of her now that she's found out Dana's Olivia, the gazillionaire who saved Lexi."

At least her daughter-in-law had a plan to keep Finn in town. It was nice to know they were on the same page this time around. Both Kitty and Jasper had unwittingly undermined Colleen's matchmaking schemes with Ava and Griffin. But in the end, true love and Colleen prevailed.

Though she wondered how Kitty's attention could be focused on Finn and Olivia when the girl was in the conference room. Colleen glanced over her shoulder to see the woman in question walking across the dining room like she was on a ship in the midst of a hurricane.

Mia, Sophie and Liam's eight-year-old daughter—the apple of Colleen's eye—ran down the stairs into the dining room waving a flowerpot. "Olivia, you forgot your present." The small pot had been painted purple to match the hyacinth inside.

It was obvious that receiving a gift on Mother's Day was

testing Olivia's mettle. As soon as she'd hugged and thanked Mia, the little girl skipped off to join the family. And Olivia waved down a waitress carrying a tray of mimosas.

"Thank you, Ivy," she slurred, taking a champagne flute off the tray. She tossed it back, returning the empty glass to take another. She gave the waitress a half-smile. "It's one of those days, you know."

"I'm sorry you're having a bad day," the waitress said kindly, only to roll her eyes when she walked away to re-fill her tray.

Colleen looked around for help but Jasper and Simon were nowhere in sight.

"Olivia dear, come join us," Kitty called from the patio.

That was not the help Colleen was hoping for. Finn confronting Olivia in the conference room was one thing; out on the patio was a whole other kettle of fish. She heard Finn groan and Liam laugh.

Olivia must have heard Finn, too, because she muttered to herself as she walked toward the French doors. "Does he actually believe I'm any happier about Kitty trying to get us together than he is? Of course he thinks it's my fault she caught us half dressed in the closet. I'm so tired of men blaming everything on me. I really am. They're all so judgy."

Olivia seemed to believe that, like her walking, she was talking normally. She wasn't. She was slurring her words in an overloud voice.

Everyone had turned to stare at her, including Finn. Olivia didn't seem to notice.

"You're back in your wheelchair!" she cried, tripping out of the French doors and rushing to Finn's side. "It's all my fault. I'm so, so, so sorry." She grabbed the push handles. "Don't worry, I'll take you to the hospital. I promise, I'll make this up to you, Finn. I'll get you the help you—"

"Uh, in case you've forgotten, I am a doctor, Olivia. Trust me, my leg's"—he looked up at her—"not that bad. The only reason I'm in a wheelchair is because Grams and my dad—"

"No, don't try and argue with me. It's common knowledge that doctors make the worst patients. They're so busy saving the world, they don't take proper care of themselves or their families," she said fiercely, her face flushed as she shoved at the chair, moving it back and forth. "What is wrong with this thing?"

"Olivia, stop…" Finn's eyes widened when the violent jerking motion started knocking over things on the table.

Beside him, Liam covered his laugh with a cough. "The brake's on, Olivia. Just—"

"Are you insane? Don't tell her how to take off the brake," Finn said to Liam, but Olivia had already figured it out.

Finn looked back at Olivia while trying to put the brake back on. "Stop, I'm not going to the hospital."

"You don't have to be so cross. I'm just trying to help you," she said as she pushed him along the outer edge of the patio.

Jasper, wearing what Colleen thought of as his black butler suit, came to stand beside her. Clasping his hands behind his back, he watched the drama unfolding with a furrowed brow. "I'm not sure I'd trust Miss Olivia to steer Master Finn clear of that tree."

Colleen wasn't sure how it happened—maybe it was because Finn was trying to escape from his wheelchair and Olivia looked like she might have tripped over something—but the wheelchair and Finn were now careening wildly toward the tree trunk.

"Master Liam, your brother…" Jasper waved, releasing a shuddered breath of relief when Olivia got hold of the push handles in the nick of time. "For a woman who appears to be inebriated and wearing high heels, Miss Olivia is surprisingly fleet of foot. Though despite saving Master Finn from a head-on collision with the tree, it appears he isn't quite ready to forgive her."

Colleen sighed. Jasper was right. It looked like getting these two together was going to take longer than she'd thought.

"Miss Kitty's yoga lessons seem to be standing her in good stead," Jasper said, a fond smile on his face as he watched Kitty hurry after Finn, who was now power wheeling to the French doors.

"Finn darling, give Olivia a chance to make it up to you. It was an accident. She didn't mean—"

"If I ever see Olivia Davenport again, it will be too soon," Finn muttered, wheeling his way into the dining room.

Colleen grimaced. Olivia, who'd just reached Kitty's side, overheard Finn's parting remark.

"Given Master Finn's apparent aversion to Miss Olivia, I think it best we set our sights elsewhere, Madame. I've always thought Lexi and Master Finn would be a fine match. What do you say?"

* * *

At the sound of car doors slamming and older women's voices outside his childhood home on Breakwater Way, Finn stopped in the middle of a leg lift to shoot an apprehensive glance at Miller. The retriever raised his regal head from his plaid bed by the fireplace and snuffled the air before giving Finn a look that seemed to say, *What's your problem?* and went back to sleep.

"My problem is you have a sixth sense and only bark if it's a stranger. Which means they've found me," he half whispered, half muttered at the dog. A fact that had been proven four days earlier at the lighthouse.

Finn had been hiding out at his dad's place for the past three days in hopes of avoiding his grandmother and the Widows Club. As an added bonus, it kept him out of Olivia's crosshairs. The less contact he had with that woman the better. He grimaced at the forcefulness behind the thought. It made him like feel like a hard-hearted jerk.

No parent should have to bury a child. In some ways, he couldn't imagine her pain. While in other ways he too easily could. In third-world and war-torn countries, losing a child was almost an everyday occurrence. Olivia deserved his sympathy more than his censure.

And he did, he really did sympathize with her. Not only did he pride himself on being an empathetic guy, but he and his family had suffered loss too. It had been traumatic and devastating and had torn them apart. Seven and a half years later, the scars were still there. Time, as he well knew, didn't always heal.

So he totally got that everyone handled loss differently. In their own way and in their own time. Turning to booze and drugs though…Yeah, that kinda tested the bounds of his sympathy and compassion. But that wasn't why he was avoiding Olivia. The reason he was staying out of her way was because he couldn't afford another Olivia-related injury. He'd just rebooked his flight to the Congo and was leaving in two weeks' time.

The chatter of old ladies' voices coming up the walkway tore him from his thoughts, spurring him into action. He carefully lowered himself to the floor to avoid being seen by the white heads bobbing by the bay window. But there was one problem with his plan. Because of his knee replacement, crawling on all fours was out. So was doing the backward crabwalk, because the plate and screws fusing the bones in his foot and ankle weren't ready for that kind of action, especially after Olivia's strawberry scent had driven him to distraction in the closet and he'd tripped over the hand weight.

Instead, he rolled onto his stomach and pulled himself across the wide-planked hardwood floor with his arms.

His dad, coming out of the kitchen eating a bacon sandwich, spotted him and lowered the sandwich from his mouth. "Son, what are you doing?"

"No time to explain. Just get down before they see you. Hurry." Finn pointed to the floor, sighing when a shadow of concern crossed his father's face. "I'm not having a flashback." He'd been lucky. He hadn't suffered from nightmares or flashbacks since he'd come home. But that didn't stop his old man from worrying. Probably because his dad had helped Liam through his flashbacks a few months back. "This is for real, and those old ladies about to knock on the door are as dangerous as any rebels. Do. Not. Answer," he warned his father when someone rang the doorbell.

"Finn, Colin, I know you're in there. Open up," his grandmother called through the door.

"Dad, if you get down and stay quiet, they'll go away, and you can enjoy your lunch in peace."

"Finn, it's my mother. I have to let her in."

"No, you don't. I'm your son, and that means I'm higher up on the familial loyalty hierarchy than Grams. So would you just—" There was a knock on the front window. Finn inched up to see Ida Fitzgerald's and Evelyn Harte's faces pressed against the glass, waving. "Yoohoo, Colin. We're here."

Finn slowly turned his head, eyes narrowed at his father. "Yoo-hoo, Colin, we're here?"

His father made a face like he'd been caught and set his half-eaten sandwich on the dining room table. Walking to the couch, he extended a hand to Finn, who'd been struggling to come to his feet. "You're not ready to go back, son. You're champing at the bit because you have nothing to do and you're bored. Just hear them out. It'd be good for you and the town."

Finn wouldn't hurt his dad's feelings by telling him his need to leave Harmony Harbor didn't stem from only boredom or because his family drove him nuts on occasion, which they did. He knew he'd won the lottery in the family department. He loved them. He just didn't feel like he fit in anymore. Everything seemed different. His years with Doctors Without Borders had changed his perception of things. So did losing his mom and sister.

His father walked to the front door, adding, "You know, Finn, your brothers had no intention of moving home and look how well it worked out for them."

Finn considered his chance of escaping. Obviously, the front door was out. He didn't trust one of the older women not to tackle him. Sneaking out a bedroom window like he used to as a kid was not in the cards either. The house was situated above the harbor, a steep and perilous descent to the rocky shores below. His days of playing Tarzan and Spider-Man were over.

The reminder evoked a sharp stab of pain in his chest. It wasn't easy acknowledging that his active lifestyle was limited by his injuries. Then again, no one knew better than he did how much worse it could have been.

As his dad opened the door, Finn lowered himself onto the couch and picked up his cell phone. He texted Griffin and Liam. *Get your asses to Dad's. I need backup. STAT.*

Both his brothers had the day off, and unlike their father, they'd have his back and not Grams's. Though he was beginning to think his dad had an agenda, too, and it conformed with Finn's grandmother's. Good thing he could count on his brothers. Just because things had worked out well for Liam and Griff didn't mean they'd expect him to stick around. They understood his passion for working with DWB, his need to make a difference. They got that he was addicted to the rush and the adventure and thrived on the challenge, cherishing his independence and freedom.

But when his brothers walked through the front door, Finn had a feeling he'd misjudged their loyalty. The first sign he was in trouble was the triumphant look his grandmother shared with two of her fellow club members when Liam arrived with eight-year-old Mia in tow and Griffin with two-month-old baby Gabe. Grams was obviously counting on Finn's niece and nephew to win him over.

But more than that, she was probably hoping the kids would curb his surly attitude. Finn didn't like to be backed in a corner and they'd been doing their best to put him in one. So far, he'd managed to escape their emotional manipulations.

Looking down at Mia, who wriggled her jean-clad butt in beside him on the couch, he figured that wasn't going to last much longer. She smiled up at him, and he sighed. It was hard not to see Riley in Mia's pretty, heart-shaped face. His little sister hadn't been much older than Mia when she died.

They shared the same bright blue eyes and long, wavy chestnut brown hair. Finn imagined that Liam hoped Mia had inherited Riley's talent for wrapping the Gallagher brothers around her baby finger. Whatever Riley had wanted, she'd gotten.

If he had any doubt that was the plan, Mia cleared it up when she glanced at his dad and then lifted her forlorn gaze to Finn. "I don't want you to go back to the place where you got shot."

He sent his family a you've-got-to-be-kidding-me look before trying to reassure his niece. "They wouldn't let us go back if it wasn't safe, sweetheart. I'll be fine. Who's going to help all those little kids if I don't go back?"

"Who's going to look after the little kids in Harmony Harbor if you don't stay? My mommy's having a baby, you know. And me, Daddy, and Granddad are really worried about that. Maybe you could just stay until the baby comes? It's only a few months away."

It was May. The baby wasn't due until early October. "Your mommy and the baby are doing great. And Doc Bishop isn't going anywhere until someone replaces him. Even if he did, the hospital's not far—"

She cut him off with a crooked finger. When he leaned in, she whispered in his ear, "Granddad and Great-Grandma Kitty are getting old."

He didn't want to admit it, but she got to him big-time with that one. His dad and Grams *weren't* getting any younger. The loss of his great-grandmother Colleen late last year had reminded him how quickly time went by. He'd been shocked to realize he hadn't seen her in more than two years, hadn't seen any of them. He wasn't even able to make it home for GG's funeral. Whether his family believed him or not, it wasn't easy being away from home and missing out on so much. Only there were two sides to that coin. Sometimes it was just as hard to be here.

The reminder helped him hold strong against his adorable niece, who was now happily smiling up at him while covertly giving her dad a thumbs-up. Finn, behind Mia's back, gave his brother the thumbs-down.

His father, catching the exchange, gave his head a re-signed shake. "Come on, Mia mine, let's take Miller for a quick walk before Granddad has to get back to work. You're welcome to join us, ladies."

Finn waited for his grandmother and the Widows Club to take the hint and leave. They didn't. But Griff, who up until now had stayed quiet, took care of that. "Hey, Grams, would you and the ladies mind changing Gabe for me? I haven't quite gotten the hang of it. There's a bottle in the bag. I think he might be hungry," he said, passing the diaper bag to Mrs. Fitzgerald and buzzing the baby's cheek before he handed him to Kitty.

Enamored as they all were with Gabe, the women didn't protest and headed up the short flight of stairs to the second level. Without his grandmother and the Widows Club to harass him, Finn might have relaxed if he didn't know his brother as well as he did. Griff got rid of the women for a reason.

Finn was about to open his mouth to tell his brother not to waste his breath when Griff quietly said, "If you could stay until September, I'd appreciate it. For Lexi's sake. I know I can call you anytime, but having you here while she goes through the rest of her treatment gives me peace of mind. I need you here, little brother, and so does she."

And that was how Finn found himself, two days later, at the clinic on Primrose Lane, wondering what the hell he'd gotten himself into.

In the seven and half hours he'd been there, he'd seen forty-five patients. Only five of whom actually had something physically wrong with them. All five were female and under the age of sixteen. As far as he could tell, not one of them was interested in marrying him.

The other forty had nothing wrong with them. And, as far as he could tell, were very interested in marrying him. If they weren't, their grandmothers and mothers were. Interested in him marrying their daughters and granddaughters, that is.

At the beginning of the day, it was kind of amusing,

even a little flattering. But by ten forty-five it had gotten old and annoying. It didn't help that he kept thinking of the patients he saw while working with DWB. Those people needed him, desperately. They weren't fake coughing or complaining about phantom chest pains. They were sick and hungry, wounded and scared. They weren't spoiled and whiny and ungrateful.

He winced at his unflattering characterizations and intolerance. While there was some truth to his observations, the throbbing ache in his leg was making him grumpy. Knowing his father had been right and Finn wasn't ready to go back to the Congo wasn't doing much to improve his mood.

Sherry, Doc Bishop's nurse and a woman Finn had dated in high school, opened the door to the closet-sized office. She was pretty in a fresh-scrubbed kind of way with rosy cheeks, dark eyes, and long, dark hair held back in a low ponytail. More importantly, she showed signs of being an excellent nurse. There was just one problem. She wasn't married and wanted to be. "Pain hasn't let up, has it?" she asked with a compassionate smile.

"I'm good. Just had to return a couple of phone calls." He set down the cold cup of coffee he hadn't had a chance to drink, removed the ice pack from his knee, and surreptitiously hid it behind the welcome-to-the-clinic plant from the staff, which Finn now mentally referred to as the matchmaking clinic from hell. He pushed to his feet with a closed-mouth smile that hopefully hid his clenched teeth from Sherry's observant gaze.

"Really? I rescheduled Molly, Sally, and Karen's physicals to tomorrow, but if you're okay to see—"

"No, tomorrow's good. On second thought, why don't you schedule them with Doc Bishop? They've been going to him for twenty years. I'm sure they'd be more comfortable—"

"They would be or you would?" she said with a laugh, and then proceeded to share way too much information about all three women before adding, "Dr. Bishop won't be in tomorrow. Mrs. Fitzgerald invited him to make up a foursome, remember?"

Finn rubbed his jaw. "I'm not sure that's something you should share—"

She made a ha-snort sound and then cuffed him on the shoulder. "Not that kind of foursome, silly. They're playing golf." She ha-snorted again. "It's no wonder that's where your mind went after the offers you've had today. Kerry will get a good laugh over that one."

If Sherry had her master's in gossip, Kerry, the receptionist, had her PhD. Finn figured he'd provided them with enough to talk about for a month at least. He lifted his chin in the direction of the examination rooms. There were five. "Who's next?"

"I cleared out the waiting room of all but legit complaints, so you only have four. Patient number one won't take long. She just needs her script renewed." She handed him a file.

He looked at the name and handed it back. "Might be better if Doc Bishop sees Ms. Templeton."

"He left early. Mrs. DiRossi invited him for dinner, and I think he wanted to get spiffed up." Sherry frowned and looked from Finn to examination room number one. "Is there a reason you don't want to see Dana?"

Chapter Six

♥

Olivia moved from the chair to the examination table. Smoothing her white linen skirt over her thighs, she carried on a pleasant conversation with Dr. Bishop in her head. It became less pleasant when she went from talking about the weather to the reason she was there.

She'd taken the last of her antianxiety medication three days before. Talking to Stanley on Mother's Day had broken the dam that held back a tidal wave of hurtful emotions and painful memories. Now she was drowning in them. She needed something to help her shut down the crippling panic. An anguished sob broke in her throat at the thought of what Stanley expected from her. She pressed a fist to her mouth to keep the sound from escaping.

In for four, hold for seven, out for eight, she told herself. It took a few moments of controlled breathing for her pulse to slow. Once it did, she felt a little light-headed and weak and stretched out on the examination table.

She held up her phone to check the time, wondering what was keeping Dr. Bishop. It was just a simple prescription renewal. An anxious knot tightened in her chest. What if he wanted to know why she needed the pills? What if she had to tell him about the whole sordid affair? She'd be a babbling basket case if she told him what was actually going on.

Surely he would just give her the prescription with no questions asked. He was a lovely man, kind and warm. He wouldn't embarrass or shame her or make her feel weak. It wasn't as if she had a problem. It wasn't like she visited the clinic every few weeks asking for more. The only time Dr. Bishop had renewed her prescriptions for temazepam and lorazepam was her first week in Harmony Harbor, so of course he wouldn't question her. She was getting herself worked up for nothing.

She looked up at the buzzing fluorescent light, closing her eyes against the brightness. The sterile, white room reminded her of the hospital, and she began redecorating it in her mind. But as she lay there daydreaming of a calming color scheme—imagining the ceiling painted powder blue and decorated with marshmallow clouds—her breathing slowed, her sleep-deprived body growing heavy and relaxed. The colors melded together, and the buzzing faded to a peaceful hum. She uttered a silent hallelujah just before falling asleep.

"Olivia."

No, no, no, she inwardly cried at the deep voice intruding on her sleep. "Go away," she said aloud, her thick tongue garbling the words. She turned on her side.

"Olivia, wake up. You're at the clinic."

She blinked open her eyes and stared at the white wall. That voice sounded disturbingly familiar. She glanced over her shoulder and uttered a mortified groan. Finn Gallagher stood behind her wearing a powder-blue button-down shirt that did amazing things to his eyes and was just as flattering to his broad chest. At the sight of the stethoscope around his neck, her absolute worst fears were confirmed, and she quickly flipped onto her back to get up…and slid on the paper and off the table. She would have landed on the floor if Finn hadn't reached out to grab her. His handsome face contorted with a pained grimace as he bore the burden of her weight.

Her cheeks warmed. "I'm so sorry. I'll just…" She couldn't believe she'd hurt him again. Obviously, she couldn't be in the same room with the man. And that was completely fine with her, because the last person she wanted to ask to renew her prescription was Dr. Judgy himself. An image of her spinning his wheelchair on the patio came to mind. She had a lot of nerve criticizing him.

Half hanging on the table and half in his arms, she hurriedly slid her feet to solid ground and stood. Only she hadn't factored in how close they were standing, and the movement sent him back on his heels.

"Oh no." She grabbed his stethoscope to keep him from falling backward. It's possible she was a little overzealous in her effort to save him because the drum came off in her hand. "Sorry, I didn't mean to break…" She winced as the tubing snapped free and sprang up to slap him in the face.

Finn stared at her and then gave his head a slow shake as if unable to believe what had just happened.

"I know, crazy, right?" Olivia said with a little laugh, trying to make light of it as she handed him the drum.

He didn't laugh.

Her smile fell. "Can you not move?" She went to grab the wheeled stool for him.

"Stop. Please don't try and do me any favors, okay? Stay right where you are." Keeping an eye on her, he moved slowly backward and then reached behind him for the stool. She winced as he carefully lowered himself onto it. He pointed to the chair against the wall. "It might be less dangerous if you sat closer to the floor."

"Thank you, but I'm here to see Dr. Bishop. So I can wait in the—"

"You'll be waiting awhile. He's left for the day." Finn took a pair of black-framed glasses out of his breast pocket. He put them on while swiveling to the open laptop on the counter beside the small hand sink. After he'd typed something on the keyboard, he glanced at her with his eyebrows raised. "Sherry said you were looking to have a script renewed."

It was a little disconcerting to see Finn wearing glasses. Of course he looked just as gorgeous, but he looked older and more serious too. Because she was distracted, it took a moment for her to register the hint of censure in his smooth voice. Once she did, she picked up her red purse from the chair. "It's all right. I'll come back when Dr. Bishop's in."

Finn stretched out his legs, crossed an arm over his chest, and tapped his thumb against his full bottom lip while keeping his probing gaze on her.

She should have left before he opened his mouth. All

she had to do was look at his arrogant pose to know what would come out of it.

"It won't do you any good, Olivia. I'm going to recommend that Dr. Bishop not renew or write you any further scripts for opioids, sleeping pills, or antianxiety meds."

She stared at him, stunned. That was far worse than what she expected him to say. "You're making me sound like a drug addict. I've never been prescribed opioids."

He turned the computer screen. "Dr. Bishop prescribed Percocet, an opioid, for you last December."

"I know what an opioid is. And Dr. Bishop prescribed Percocet for me because I broke my wrist when the carriage house burned down. I'm sure that's on there as well as the only two other prescriptions he wrote for me. Last September. Months ago. Hardly the pattern of an addict, wouldn't you agree?"

"I would, if I hadn't seen what I did on Mother's Day. You were dangerously high. Your behavior was erratic."

Panic seized the muscles in her chest, and not just because everything he said was true. She was afraid he'd follow through on his threat. She couldn't keep going on little to no sleep. She had to tell him something to make him understand. "I was upset."

"We all get upset, Olivia. But we don't all turn to drugs and booze when we do. That type of behavior indicates there's a problem, don't you think?"

"Yes, of course it does. But this isn't an everyday occurrence, and it certainly wasn't an everyday stressor. I'm an event planner. I deal with problems all the time, and I don't need to take a pill or have a drink. I don't," she said defensively when he raised an eyebrow.

"You don't know me. You have no idea what I'm dealing with."

The chiseled angles of his face softened. "I do. I know you lost your son and your husband within a year of each other. I'm sorry, Olivia. I truly am sorry for your loss. But that alone doesn't mean I'll turn a blind eye to your problem."

"I don't have a problem!" She briefly closed her eyes, embarrassed that she'd lost her temper. "I just need something to help me get through the next couple of weeks. I'm not sleeping and—"

"No, I'm sorry. I can't. But I'm here and so is Doc Bishop whenever you need to talk. And when you're ready, I have a list of support groups, and there's a couple of facilities I can recommend. But, Olivia, you won't be getting any prescription drugs here or at any other clinic or pharmacy in the area."

"You're going to flag me?"

He typed on the keyboard. "No, I'm not going to. I already have."

"How could you do that to me? Do you know how embarrassing that will be for me to walk into the drugstore knowing that Mr. Carlson thinks I'm an addict?" She sniffed back angry tears and shot to her feet. "I don't know why I bothered to ask. Why I expected any compassion or kindness from you. You made up your mind about me the first day you met me. You're a judgmental and sanctimonious ass, Finn Gallagher. And if I never see you again, it will be too soon," she said, repeating his hurtful words from the brunch back at him as she strode from the room. It took everything she had not to slam the door behind her. She hurried down the hall.

"Olivia," he called after her, sounding almost conciliatory.

She didn't often lose her temper and couldn't remember the last time she'd been rude to someone. But if that's what it took for Finn Gallagher to see reason, she'd consider using the tactic more often. She swiped a finger under her eyelashes before turning to face him. "What is it?" She kept enough snap in her voice to let him know she wasn't a pushover.

"Give me your keys," he said, walking toward her with his hand extended.

The nurse, who'd just come out of the examination room at the end of the hall, glanced their way.

"I'm not giving you my keys," Olivia hissed.

"Yeah, you are. It's obvious you haven't slept in days, Olivia. You look like hell, and you shouldn't be driving."

"How dare you! I'm going to talk to Dr. Bishop about this, you, you…"

"Go ahead," he said, looking almost bored.

He was now close enough that she had to tip her head back to look up at him. He was over six two, and she'd worn flats today. She wished she could look him right in the eye, go toe to toe and nose to nose with him. "I'm going to talk to your grandmother, and your brothers, and…and your father."

"You do that. Because, Olivia, if you don't get a handle on your problem, I'm going to be talking to them about *you*. Now give me your keys."

She stared at him and then stretched up on her toes,

to get as close to nose to nose as she could. The action didn't have the desired effect. He didn't look the least bit repentant or intimidated, which was maddening. "The only problem I have is you, you and my husband, who…who…" Her eyes filled with tears, a choking sensation rising up in her throat as she was reminded of why she was here.

She had to leave before she made a complete fool of herself. Finn had already done his level best to besmirch her reputation. She hurriedly unzipped her purse, dug inside to grab her keys, and shoved them at him. "Here." She spun on her sandals, about to sprint down the hall before the tears started to fall when strong fingers gently closed around her bicep.

"Olivia, if you give me half an hour, I'll drive you to the manor. Liam or Griff can bring me—"

"No, I can't stay. I can't…" She shook her head, unable to go on. Pulling her arm from his hold, she hurried down the hall.

The nurse and receptionist looked up from where they'd been talking at the front desk. Her stomach sank at what appeared to be the disapproving looks they sent her way. Finn's deep voice had obviously carried. If the press…She couldn't think about that now. The press was the least of her worries.

She bowed her head and walked quickly through the empty waiting room. She wished someone had warned her that Finn was working at the clinic. She only had herself to blame. After Stanley's phone call, she'd been trying to stay out of everyone's way. Knowing that she had last-minute details to firm up on next week's wedding, a prom party, and bridal shower, no one had questioned her absence.

Given how she was feeling, it was almost a surprise when she walked out of the white Cape Cod clinic to find the weather was just as sunny and warm as when she arrived. If the weather were to mirror her emotions, rain would be slashing down from angry black clouds, forks of jagged lightning spearing the sunbaked ground, thunder so violent it would rock the peaceful coastal community of Harmony Harbor on its moorings.

As she tried to get a grip on those raging emotions, her gaze went to her black Lexus parked under a shade tree. Maybe the exercise and fresh air would do her good. At least she'd worn sensible shoes. She'd walk until she dropped from exhaustion, and hopefully then she'd sleep through the night.

She thought about the upcoming events at the manor and considered cutting her walk short and returning to Greystone to work. But as angry as she was with Finn, she wasn't enamored with the idea of running into his grandmother. And there was nothing that said she couldn't work while she walked. She hefted her purse onto her shoulder and pulled her phone out of the side pocket.

Thankfully, she was the list maker of all list makers and had stored several on her phone. Though there was nothing that made her happier than finding a beautiful planner or notebook and filling them too. It calmed her to have a plan, to have her days, weeks, and months mapped out. If her days were full, she wouldn't have time to re-member. Maybe one day she'd get back to filling her

planners with her hopes and dreams for the future. She'd
learned the hard way that dreams don't always come true,
but she found having a plan gave her a feeling of control.

So that's what she'd do. She'd feel better once she'd
listed all the reasons why Stanley's plan would fall
through. Her stomach plunged to her feet at the thought
that she should make a list of what she'd do if he success-
fully completed his mission. She didn't need a list. She
already knew she couldn't do what he expected her to.

Which she'd told him when he'd called her from the
airport. He'd been on his way to Kenya. It was above
and beyond what most lawyers would do for a client and
friend, especially a deceased one. But Stanley had been
more than just Nathan's friend; he'd taken on the role of
his big brother. Olivia still hadn't found a way to forgive
Stanley for keeping her in the dark about her husband's
secret life.

"Ma'am!" someone called out at the same time a car
door opened in front of her and clipped her on the hip.
Olivia sucked in a pained gasp but forced a smile and
waved off the man's apologies. It wasn't his fault she was
distracted. And obviously working on her phone while
walking along the twisty, narrow streets wasn't ideal either.

She considered heading for Main Street, but she knew
too many of the shop owners and wasn't up for friendly
chitchat, so she decided it would be safer to walk along
the harbor. It was close to the dinner hour on a weekday;
she wouldn't have to battle any crowds on the waterfront
because the brightly painted fishermen's shacks that
housed local artisans didn't open until mid-June, when
tourist season was well under way.

She walked on the sidewalk down the hill, passing by Colonials, Cape Cods, and Victorians that had once belonged to merchants and sea captains. Harmony Harbor had been founded in the early seventeenth century by William Gallagher and was steeped in maritime history. Plaques commemorating the history of the homes and their prominent owners were displayed on stone and wrought-iron fences partially hidden by bridal wreath spirea with their tiny white blossoms and arching branches. Rhododendrons showed off their lush clumps of shocking pink blossoms.

Olivia loved the picturesque town with its family-owned boutiques, art galleries, and gift shops. The relaxed and friendly atmosphere and the strong sense of community had been missing from her world in Boston. Somehow she fit here. She felt safe and protected. But Finn with his threats and accusations had managed to color her perception of the small town she loved.

Maybe she was being unfair laying the blame solely at his feet. So much had happened in such a short time that it was no wonder she felt unhinged. Revealing her true identity was difficult enough, but then for Stanley to reveal Nathan's last request…

A horn beeped, alerting her to the fact that she'd veered into the street. She lifted a hand in apology and got back on the sidewalk. As she got closer to the harbor, she heard the low bleat of the fishing boats' horns announcing their return.

She was used to the briny smell of the ocean by now, but it was sharper here by the docks. Walking along the paved path past the marine blue, citrus yellow, and fire-engine-red fisherman shacks, she spotted an empty wooden bench on the dock and headed toward it.

She noticed an older man fishing, a dark-haired man in a gray hoodie leaning against the rail as she took a seat on the bench. The man's gaze briefly landed on her and then moved on as he appeared to scan the area. He straightened when two men approached. They glanced in her direction, and she bowed her head. She may have led a sheltered life but it was obvious to her what was going on. The man in the hoodie was selling drugs.

There wasn't a huge issue with drugs in Harmony Harbor, but there had been problems in nearby Bridgeport. No matter how desperate she was for sleep and to get her nerves under control, Olivia would never stoop so low as to buy street drugs. Or so she'd thought until moments later when her phone pinged with an incoming text from Stanley.

Chapter Seven

♥

His father, sometimes referred to as the silver fox by the women in town because of his supposed resemblance to Paul Newman, had his face buried in the *Harmony Harbor Gazette*. He cast a surprised glance over his shoulder when Finn walked in the front door of the brick two-story on Breakwater Way. "I thought you were going to call me for a ride. Don't tell me you walked home."

Finn tossed the keys for Olivia's Lexus on the hall table, debating whether to tell his father the truth. Despite what Olivia thought, he wasn't trying to shame her or ruin her reputation. He hadn't flagged her in the system.

Because of her cash and contacts, he'd told her that he had, in hopes she wouldn't immediately go elsewhere, that the thought he'd flagged her would make her think about what she was doing and realize she needed help—and not the help that came from escaping in a drug-induced haze. "I didn't want to bother you. Olivia lent me her car. I could use a ride to the manor though. I need to return—"

His father rattled the newspaper and waggled his eyebrows at Finn. "Olivia, eh? I told your brothers you were interested in her. Your old man's still got it. I saw right through your act."

"Sorry to disappoint you, but that was no act. The woman is a walking disaster. I've never been around anyone so clumsy in my life."

"Olivia? She's one of the most graceful and elegant women I know."

"Okay, are we talking about the same Olivia? Because the one I'm talking about took me out more than once last week." He was going to list off the incidents at the tide pool, in the closet at the lighthouse, and his almost-encounter with the tree at the brunch, but his dad had only borne witness to the event on Mother's Day, and he didn't want to have to explain the other two. Hopefully his dad had missed the *more than once* part of his remark.

"So what? It was Mother's Day. A hard day for a woman who lost her child. You should give her a second chance, son. She's a sweet woman."

He knew his old man well enough to change the subject. "I'll just ice my leg and then we can head to the manor."

"Sure, no problem." His father frowned. "What happened? Your limp is more pronounced."

Your sweet and graceful Olivia struck again, Finn thought. Good thing the mark from the stethoscope tube hitting him in the face had disappeared. That would be harder to explain away. "First day back at work. It'll take some time to adjust."

"Maybe you should give it another couple of weeks. I'll talk to Doc Bishop and—"

"No, I'm good, Dad." Finn didn't want to stay home. The last thing he needed was more time to think. He didn't just like to keep busy; he had to. Miller came over and dropped a ball at his feet. "Later, buddy," he said, giving the retriever a quick rubdown before heading to the refrigerator.

As he pulled out the bag of ice from the freezer drawer, the sound of the fishing boats' horns came through the open window. He smiled. There were things he didn't miss about home, but there were plenty he did. He walked to the window. This was one of them, the sights, sounds, and smell of the harbor. If ever he settled down, he'd live by the sea.

His gaze traveled over the rocks he'd clambered up and down as a kid, the trees he used to climb and swing from, the dock he used to…He frowned at the woman sitting on the bench in a familiar white skirt and sleeveless top, wearing a pair of shiny red flat sandals that matched her expensive red bag. It was Olivia. If he hadn't recognized the outfit, he would have recognized her honey-blond hair. Her clothes were nothing special, but she had beautiful hair, he thought as the sun painted the strands gold.

She was bent over her phone, and then her head came up sharply. From his vantage point, he couldn't see the expression on her face, but her body reacted as though she'd taken a hit. She seemed to be looking at something on the dock. He followed the direction of her gaze. Three men were talking just down from her. A guy in a hoodie reached into his pocket, pulled out a small bag, and handed it to one of the other men.

Finn couldn't believe what was happening right before his eyes. That wasn't completely true. Whether you lived in a small town, big city, or in the country, drugs were readily available. But here and now in front of a woman who was desperate to get her hands on what that guy was apparently offering? It was like the universe was conspiring against all of Finn's good intentions, against Olivia too. Maybe he was wrong and she was looking at the schooners or the old man fishing. God, he hoped she wasn't stupid enough to buy street drugs.

She stood up, grabbed her purse, and then glanced in the men's direction, hesitating for a minute as though politely waiting for the transaction to be completed. Disappointment and anger twisted his gut. He couldn't believe she was going to do it. Something about the way the taller guy reached in the back pocket of his jeans drew Finn's attention.

He focused on the guy's profile. He knew him. He was sure of it. And if it was who he thought it was, he had to stop Olivia. He had to stop her anyway, but unless she wanted to end up behind bars, he had to do it before she got any closer to the men and made her intentions known. But there was no way he'd make it down there in time.

Wrenching open the screen, he yelled, "Olivia!" As he suspected, his voice didn't carry above the boats' motors or the seagulls.

"Son, why are you yelling for Olivia?" His dad's confused yet hopeful question came from the living room.

It was a good question. Why should it bother him that the woman was going to wind up in jail? She wasn't family or a friend. In fact, it'd be easier if he didn't have anything to do with Olivia Davenport. Because sometimes when he looked at her, the sorrow in her eyes grabbed him by the throat. Her loss reminded him too much of his own.

"Better get your ears checked, Dad. I hit my knee on the fridge and yelled *O Lordie*." He rolled his eyes at his pathetic excuse and then went back to tracking Olivia, praying she'd come to her senses on her own.

She took a step toward the three men.

He should have known better, he thought, scanning the room. His gaze landed on his best shot. "Come here, boy."

Miller galloped to his side. Finn grabbed the tennis ball from the dog's mouth. But as soon as he drew back his arm, Finn realized throwing it through the window would limit the amount of power he could get behind it.

Cursing Olivia under his breath, he grabbed a chair and climbed out the window. "When I get a hold of you, Olivia Davenport, you're goin' wish—" His knee hit the window frame, and he broke off on a loud curse.

"Finn, what's going on—"

"Just having a game of catch with Miller, and he nipped me." The dog barked enthusiastically at Finn's announcement, bouncing from one side of the kitchen to the other. "Yeah, yeah, as soon as I save Olivia from herself," Finn grumbled, lowering himself to the ground.

Turning to scramble carefully over the rocks, he quickly searched out his best vantage point. She was walking toward the men, who just then had turned to look in her direction. He imagined her giving them her wide, innocent smile and drew back his arm and fired the ball.

"You were about to buy drugs in front of an undercover cop. What did you want me to do?" Finn asked Olivia, who sat in the passenger seat of the Lexus holding an ice pack to the side of her face.

"How many times do I have to tell you? I wasn't buying drugs."

"Give me some credit. You were at the clinic not thirty minutes earlier practically begging me to give you drugs."

"You make it sound so lurid and sleazy. I wanted my prescription renewed, that's all." She moved the ice pack to her temple and winced. "Did you ever think of calling out to me or calling my cell phone instead of beaning me in the head with a ball?"

"I tried shouting at you, and I would have called your cell phone if I had your number, but I don't. You wouldn't have answered anyway. Instead of yelling at me and giving me grief, you might give some thought to thanking me."

"I never yelled at you."

"Yeah, you did. Just ask my dad and anyone else who was down on the dock."

Olivia drew in a deep breath and then slowly released it before glancing at him. "All right, thank you for trying to *help* me"—she made one air quote because her other hand was occupied—"even if it was misguided and unnecessary and you gave me a concussion. And I appreciate you keeping those same misguided accusations to yourself and telling your dad you were trying to see if Miller would jump out of the window and go after the ball. Though, if you ask me, you should have come up with something more believable."

"My dad believed me. He should, seeing as I did the same thing to Max, our first golden, when I was twelve."

"Yes, but that's my point. You were *twelve*. You hadn't been shot and recovering from your injuries when you climbed out of the window then. It wasn't very smart, you know. You could have fallen out the window or, worse, tumbled down the rocks."

"I fully understood the consequences of my actions and was willing to take the risk to protect you, Olivia. So in my book, that means you owe me."

"I'm afraid I don't have any cash on me. Will a check do?"

He wasn't sure if she was being sarcastic or serious. Either way, he wasn't impressed. "That's the thing about you rich girls—you think you can buy your way out of anything."

"If only that were true," she said quietly, and he realized she was probably referring to her husband and son.

He didn't want to think about that now or he'd be tempted to give her a pass. Instead, he planned to use this to his advantage. So he pretended he didn't hear her. "Well not this time, Princess. I—"

"Princess?" She gave him an irritated look. "You obviously have a problem with people, or more precisely, women, who have money. I don't know what she did to you…Honestly, I don't care. But I'm not her. You don't have a clue about who I am. If you did, you'd know I have never, not once in my life, acted like a princess."

Since Amber had done a number on him, she hit a little

too close to the mark. "Defensive much? It's just a nick-name. Who said it had anything to do with the size of your investment portfolio or how you live? You're the one who jumped to that conclusion." He glanced at her. She looked out the window, moving the ice pack back to her red and puffy cheek. "Okay, Sweet Cheeks, here's the deal."

She slowly turned her head, a flicker of amusement crossing what he could see of her face. It was replaced with more than a flicker of annoyance when he continued. "You go into treatment. Ideally, I'd like to see you in in-patient care for six weeks, but I'll settle for you seeing an addiction therapist three times a week."

"You'll settle…You want…" Her jaw was clamped so tight that he didn't know how she managed to squeeze out the words. "You are the most maddening man I've ever met. How many times do I have to tell you I'm not ad-dicted to prescription drugs? I do not have a problem. I take that back. I have problems, several of them, one of which is you."

"Denial. Classic. That's you, Sweet Cheeks. The clas-sic picture of an addict in denial," he said as he drove past the open wrought-iron gates and under the stone arch leading into the Gallagher estate. "And you're apparently suffering from blackouts too because, not more than two hours ago, you were about to buy a bag of opioids from a dealer on the dock." He waited for a reaction, prepared to catch a flying ice pack if she completely lost control. Though he got the impression that she rarely lost her tem-per, especially to that degree. So he probably shouldn't have been surprised when she went completely silent and stared straight ahead. But this felt different, off.

He turned into the parking space at the far end of the lot that faced the side of the manor. He assumed the spot was Olivia's because he'd seen her car parked there before. Unlike its owner, the Lexus wasn't the type of vehicle that faded into the background.

He turned off the engine, shifting in the seat to face her. At some point, she'd lowered the ice pack to her lap. Her face, other than her cheek, was completely devoid of color. He winced. "I'm sorry, Olivia. I went too far. In my defense, I'm worried about you." She didn't move. It was like the other day at the lighthouse. He wondered if the CT scan had missed something.

He gently cupped her cheek and turned her to face him. Her eyes were wide, her pupils dilated, a whimper coming from deep in her throat.

Afraid she was going into shock, he drew her into his arms and rubbed her back. "I need you to talk to me, Olivia, okay? Tell me what's going on. Tell me what you're feeling."

"She's here. He brought her here," she whispered against his neck.

"Who's here? Who brought who here?" He looked around. There was an older couple walking down the path to the parking lot, a guy with binoculars coming up from the beach, and a stocky man with salt-and-pepper hair and a goatee unloading luggage from a silver Audi with a little dark-haired girl standing at his side.

"Stanley brought her. Stanley brought Nathan's daughter here." She pulled away, looking trapped and panicked. "I can't do it. Nathan named me her guardian, but I can't do it. It's not fair that he would ask me to take in the child he had with another woman while he was married to me. It's not."

Between the way her voice was breaking and how the words were running into each other, Finn was sure he'd misunderstood. There's no way she could have said what he thought she did. He put his hands on her shoulders. "Liv, you have to calm down and talk to me. Maybe I can help if I understand what's going on, okay?"

She cast a covert glance over her shoulder. "Do you think he saw me?"

He thought about what she said and guessed. "The stocky guy getting luggage out of the silver Audi?" She gave him a jerky nod. "No, he's crouched down talking to the little girl. Is that Stanley?"

"Yes, he's my late husband's attorney. He and Nathan were very close. He knew all about his affair. Every sordid detail." She looked down at her hands and then raised her gaze. "My husband was a bigamist. He married a woman, another doctor, when he was still married to me. They had a daughter together. She'll be six in November. Her name's Georgina."

"My God, I'm sorry, Liv. That's unbelievable. What an asshole. And you're saying he named you as his daughter's guardian?"

"Yes, her mother has been missing for six weeks and is presumed dead. She was working in a village in Kenya. That's where she and Nathan met. They were with the International Red Cross. Stanley flew to Kenya. And given that he's here, that means Nathan's wife didn't leave a will or have friends or family who would take Georgina. Stan...Stanley said if that turned out to be the case, it's only right that I…that I should honor Nathan's request."

"Yeah? Well Stanley sounds like an asshole too. Doesn't Nathan have any family who can take the little girl?"

"His parents are older. They were devastated when they lost him and, Stanley tells me, deeply ashamed when they learned he had another wife and child. Stanley says he tried talking to them about Georgina's situation, but they shut him down. The only interest Nathan's younger brother showed was asking how much was in it for him. He's single and in a band. Not the life for a child. Stanley believes that Nathan had his reasons for choosing me."

"And what do you believe?"

"That any minute now, I'll wake up. None of it makes sense. I don't know why or how Nathan could do this to me. It's like he's reaching out from the grave to punish me one more time. Like he didn't do enough to hurt me."

"So this is why you haven't been sleeping and the reason for the panic attacks and self-medicating?" At her reluctant nod, he said, "You should have told me. You should have told someone. This isn't a situation you had to deal with on you own, Liv. You have friends here. People who care about you."

"I know. But if I didn't talk about it, I could sometimes convince myself it never happened. I didn't want to be that woman. I didn't want my life to have been a lie."

"Sunday, today for that matter, could have turned out differently. You could have wound up in serious trouble because you didn't open up to your friends. From now on, I want you to promise that you'll talk to Soph, Ava, or Lexi if you start feeling like you're in over your head. Okay?"

"I'm in over my head, Finn. I can't do this," she whispered, her eyes swimming in tears.

As he gave her hand a sympathetic squeeze, he got a sense someone was looking at them and glanced over his shoulder. The lawyer must have recognized Liv's car. He was walking their way with the little girl's hand in his.

The kid was adorable with a tumble of short, curly dark hair. She wore a Red Sox T-shirt and jeans and a pair of light-up red sneakers. As though she sensed him looking at her, she met his gaze straight on. Her big, bright blue eyes were awash with hurt and fear, but there was a proud jut to her small, pointed chin. His heart ached both for the little girl and the woman beside him. Neither deserved to be put in the position they were in.

He turned back to Olivia. "In your place, I don't know what I'd do. You have every right to be angry and hurt. What your husband did to you, the position he's put you in, is indefensible. But that little girl doesn't deserve to be punished because her dad was a loser and an asshole. She's lost both her parents within the space of a year and was taken away from her home by a man she probably doesn't even know. She needs someone to make her feel safe and loved."

"I don't think I can do it."

"I think you can." But as he spoke the words aloud, he felt a flicker of doubt, a sense of unease. What if she couldn't? What if this was the thing that finally broke her?

Chapter Eight

♥

It felt like Olivia was in a made-for-TV movie with the family lawyer preparing to hand off his late client's child in the shadow of a nineteenth-century castle. A Gothic, haunting soundtrack played in her mind as she forced herself to greet Stanley and look at her husband's daughter for the first time.

The music screeched to a halt in her head, and her knees buckled. It was like looking at a five-year-old version of Cooper, only Georgina's skin was sun-kissed and glowed with good health. Her little body was sturdy and strong and…Oh, God, she had on one of Cooper's T-shirts. What was Stanley thinking? Olivia opened her mouth to ask him how he could be so cruel but the words were blocked in her throat by a thick ball of paralyzing rage.

"Just breathe. I'll help you get through this, I promise," Finn murmured as he reached her side. He put an arm around her shoulders before extending a hand to Stanley. "Hi. Finn Gallagher. You'll have to give Liv a minute. She had a run-in with a tennis ball, and it's taking her a little longer to recover than I expected."

"Should she see a doctor?" Stanley asked, looking from Finn to Olivia, his brow furrowed.

"She has seen one, me. She's had a CT scan too." He angled his head to look at her. "You up for this?"

Less than ten minutes ago, she'd been as furious at Finn as she was at herself and tempted to throw the ice pack at him. Now he was the handsome white knight riding to her rescue. Or at the very least, the man who'd saved her from breaking down in front of a parentless child who had been taken from the only home she'd ever known.

"Yes, I'm good. Thank you." She hoped he could tell just how grateful she was from her smile because right now she had to say something to the little girl who was the spitting image of the child she adored and the man she'd come to despise.

Finn must have decided she wasn't quite as good as she claimed to be, because instead of letting her speak, he smiled at the little girl. "*Jambo*, Georgina."

Nathan's daughter's narrow shoulders dropped from where they'd been attached to her ears, and a look of relief came over her face. "*Shikamo.*"

"I'm not that old." Finn laughed at her use of the respectful form of hello in Swahili that was used to address the elderly and then glanced from Stanley to Olivia. "Why don't I take Georgina down to the beach and show her around while you two talk?"

"I don't know, Finn. That's a lot of stress to put on your leg." She forced a smile for the little girl. "Besides, Georgina and I haven't had a chance to get to—"

The little girl cut Olivia off with an irritated look that was markedly similar to the one Finn also gave her, and then she raised her small chin. "My name's George," she said in a husky voice, and then looked up at Finn. *"Nenda ufukwen. Tafadhali."*

"Kidogo tu. I only speak a little Swahili, George. I understand *tafadhali*, please, so I take it you want to go to the beach?"

"Tafadhali." She nodded, giving Finn a winsome smile. She was missing her two bottom teeth.

He held out his hand and smiled when the little girl took it and then raised an eyebrow at Olivia as though asking if she was okay. Despite wishing she was the one holding his hand and heading to the beach, she smiled and nodded.

"You didn't mention you had someone in your life, Livy. I'm happy for you. Fortuitous that he speaks Swahili and Georgina seems to like him. It should help with—"

She drew her gaze from Finn and Nathan's daughter as they took the path to the beach. "Finn and I aren't dating, Stanley. He's my…friend." She'd been about to say doctor, but thought *friend* would avoid unwanted questions. And going out of his way like Finn had done made it feel like he might just be one. "Finn's with DWB. He's been in the Congo for the past few years." Which explained his knowledge of Swahili, although French was the primary language spoken there.

"Ah, I see." Despite his neutral tone of voice, he undoubtedly was surprised by her friendship with Finn because of Olivia's rather well-documented criticism of doctors who left their families to work abroad. Over the years, Nathan had shared her letters, texts, and e-mails with Stanley. Something else she hadn't known until everything came out that rainy night last September.

Stanley had used them to defend Nathan. In Stanley's opinion, they were evidence as to why her husband had strayed. He'd found comfort in the arms of a woman who understood and appreciated him. A woman who shared his passion.

Both men felt Olivia had been unsupportive of Nathan. She'd been too demanding, expecting him to fly home any time Cooper's blood counts were low or their son was having another experimental treatment or Olivia was scared or just plain lonely.

In her husband's eyes, she'd been the nagging shrew while he was the unappreciated heroic husband off saving the unfortunates of the world. He didn't have time for Olivia and Cooper. She was wealthy. Whatever they needed, she could buy. But Nathan was wrong because all the money in the world couldn't save their son.

And now, after everything Nathan had done, after every humiliating and demoralizing accusation Stanley had made, Olivia was supposed to do as she was told without complaint or question.

"I'm glad you see, Stanley. I wish I did. I wish I understood why a man who hated me and thought I was a horrible mother left me his child." Stanley's face blurred as tears filled her eyes, and she poked him in the chest.

"How dare you dress her in my son's T-shirt. That's beyond cruel, even for you."

"Livy, I swear to you, I didn't do it to hurt you. I tried to get her to change, but it's like her security blanket. When I arrived at the village, she had on a Sox T-shirt and a ball cap. You know how much Nathan loved the Sox. He must have—"

"Passed that on to her like he did his son? Yes, I'm sure he did. Unlike his son, he probably played ball with her. Remember how Cooper would beg for Nathan to play catch with him, Stanley?"

"Livy, don't, don't do this. Cooper wasn't strong enough. Nate was just overprotective. He didn't want him to get hurt. It killed him to see the kid suffering. You know that. You've gotta believe that."

"If Nathan truly cared about his son's feelings, he would have stayed home. He would have accepted the offer from Massachusetts General. He knew Cooper didn't have much time left and still he got on that plane. It makes sense now. We'd been replaced a long time ago. By the little girl he's left in my care. Tell me, Stanley, does that not strike you as odd?"

"You're so bitter, Livy. I thought by now…Sorry." He held up his hand. "That was insensitive. I know what I'm asking of you. What Nathan is asking of you. But she's a sweet kid, smart and funny, and she's lost so much. If I could take her, I would. But she needs a mother. She needs you, Livy. And maybe you need her?"

He didn't understand what he was asking of her, not really. No one did. She crossed her arms and looked away. Was it even fair to Georgina to take her? Would she ever be able to look at the little girl without seeing Nathan and Cooper?

"I think that's why he named you as her guardian, Livy. I think he'd come to regret what he did to you and Cooper. Maybe he saw her as your second chance. His way of trying to make up for all you've lost."

"You can't replace one child with another. Cooper's irreplaceable. And it's certainly not a burden you place on a child. Georgina is not a pawn or a peace offering or a bribe. I wonder what her mother would have thought. But none of this makes sense unless you're telling me Nathan developed a latent psychic ability and foretold his own death."

"No, but he began to talk about his own mortality. After Cooper died, Nathan developed breathing problems. It worried him. Isabella diagnosed it as a panic disorder, but he thought it was his heart."

"But why me? You out of anyone knows how he felt about me, Stanley." She gave a brittle laugh. "Better than I did, it seems."

"He loved you, Livy. No, don't roll your eyes; you know he did. Everything changed when Cooper got sick. He couldn't handle it. You saw it yourself. At the hospital. Something like that either brings a couple closer or tears them apart.

"Do you remember when he came home that last time? It was about three months before he died, I think. In June. He stayed for a couple of weeks. He talked a lot about that visit. About you. He had a lot of regrets. He…he was going to leave Isabella and come home to you, Livy. I don't know, but I've always suspected he'd left her and was on his way back that afternoon in September. In some ways

I think I blamed you for his death. I didn't handle it well. The way I broke the news to you wasn't right. I'm sorry. You didn't deserve that, especially not that night."

"No, I didn't," she whispered, turning to wipe her eyes. She caught sight of Finn and Georgina coming up from the beach and turned back to Stanley. He had a hankie out, dabbing at his eyes. "I'm going to take Georgina, Stanley. Not because you think I owe it to Nathan to honor his request or because you think she's my second chance. I'm doing it for Cooper. My son would want me to look after his little sister, so that's what I'll do."

She quickly scrubbed the tears from her face as Finn's and Georgina's voices came closer. Olivia turned with a smile. "Did you guys have a good time?" she asked, making sure she sounded warm and welcoming.

"Yeah, yeah, we did," Finn said, his smile more of a grimace.

When he began rubbing his hand over his stubbled jaw, Olivia nervously asked, "What's the matter?"

"It's not that big a deal, is it, George?"

Stanley glanced from Finn to Olivia. "Why don't I just go get her luggage?"

"Uh, Stan my man, might be better if you hold off on that."

"No, it's okay, Finn. Everything's good. Georgina's going to stay with me. You're going to live in a castle, sweetheart. Isn't that exciting?" she said to the little girl in that same warm and welcoming voice.

"My name's George, and I have bugs," she said in her husky little voice. It sounded like she was introducing herself at an AA meeting.

"Bugs? You mean bug bites?" Olivia looked to Finn for confirmation.

"No, head lice. Like I said, no big deal." He grinned at Stanley, who'd started scratching his head. "I'll go pick up a couple of nit combs and some almond oil."

"What about the suitcases and my car?"

"I'll take George's clothes to the Laundromat. As for your car, you can either leave it in the lot for two days or vacuum wherever George sat. I'll put the suitcases and booster seat in garbage bags and stick them in my dad's freezer."

"You don't have to worry about a booster seat. I don't have one. What?" Stanley said defensively when both she and Finn looked at him. "How was I supposed to know?"

"I'll pick up a booster seat, and you better call the airport and let them know, Stan."

"Finn, you don't have to run around doing this for us. I'll pick up what I need later."

"Relax, I've got it covered." He glanced at the path leading to the manor. It sounded like a stampede was headed their way. "Hey, George, remember the little girl I was telling you about, Mia?"

George nodded, her shoes lighting up as she shifted from one foot to the other.

"Don't be nervous. Everyone's excited to meet you." He lifted his chin. "Here they come now."

The little girl sidled up to Finn. He smiled and rubbed her shoulder. "I promise, you're goin' to love it here, kiddo."

Finn's family came over to introduce themselves. While everyone got acquainted, Stanley excused himself to take care of his car. It wasn't long before Mia coaxed a giggle out of George and the two little girls skipped after the rest of the family for the promised welcome-to-the-manor tea.

"Liam," Finn called to his brother, who was bringing up the rear. Liam looked over his shoulder, and Finn scratched his head.

Liam chuckled, his hand going to his head. "Thanks for the reminder."

"Is it just me or was that weird?" Olivia asked as she and Finn were left alone. "No one pulled me aside to ask who George was or where she came—"

Finn cut her off, looking uncomfortable. "Yeah, about that, I texted Griff and laid out the situation for him. I told him to tell the rest of the family."

"How much of the situation did you lay out?"

"Everything you told me. Look, I know you're a private person, and the last thing you want is word of this getting out. I Googled you, so I know it hasn't. But you know as well as I do that you can trust each and every one of them. They'll have your back. And from where I'm standing, you haven't had someone in your corner for a while. Besides, it saves you from laying it out for them later. You want to tell them more, that's up to you."

"You're right, and it does make it easier. Thank you, Finn. I don't know what I would have done without you."

"You would have been fine."

"Hardly. I wouldn't have noticed that George had head lice before it was too late. You saved the manor from an infestation." She shuddered at the thought. "You were great with her, by the way."

"She's a sweet kid. A bit of an old soul." He paused for

a minute before saying, "It's not going to be easy, Liv. For either of you. Did you know she's never been outside of the village in Kenya? Between that and losing her mom so soon after losing her dad…She's going to need a lot of TLC."

"You don't think I'm up for it, do you?" That made two of them.

"I never said that. I just don't want you to get discouraged. Give it time. And don't be afraid to ask for help. The family will be happy to lend a hand."

He was probably trying to make her feel better but he seemed as concerned about her ability to do this as she was. She thought of something that would help her combat the fear. That something was tall, dark, and ridiculously handsome. Which made her think she was being ridiculous for even considering the idea, but…

She smiled and nodded while saying, "You know, George really took a shine to you. So I was thinking, you should move into the manor." She'd read somewhere that if you nodded during a conversation or negotiation the person would automatically agree with you. In Finn's case, it didn't have the desired effect.

He emphatically shook his head. "No. No way."

"You don't have to be so cross."

He ducked to look her in the eyes. "Seriously? How old are you? You sound like you're sixty-five when you say that."

She gasped, offended. "I can't believe you just said that to me."

"I can't believe I'm the only one who ever has. Some friends you've got."

"I have very good friends, thank you very much. And maybe they don't say anything because, first, it's unbelievably rude, and second, you are probably the only person I've said it to because you are the only person who ever gets cross…ticked at me."

"Really? That surprises me. Because, Sweet Cheeks, you can be annoying." He grinned, tapped her nose, and then headed for Stanley's Audi.

Her cheeks heated, but as she watched him walk away, she got a little panicked about facing George without him by her side. "Finn, if I promise not to annoy you, would you please stay at the manor?"

"Nuh-uh. No way."

"What if I pay you?"

He turned and walked backward. "How about that? You just proved my earlier point. Rich girls really do think they can buy everything. Sorry to disappoint you, Sweet Cheeks, but I'm not for sale."

Chapter Nine

♥

Colleen sat in the window seat of the study, anxiously waiting for the meeting to start. There was big news in the making for the manor, but from the woebegone expressions on Sophie's, Ava's, and Lexi's faces, it wasn't of the positive kind. "Go on, get on with it. If it's like the past three days, Olivia will be another hour—"

The door swung open. "Where is she? Have you seen her?"

The women stared at Olivia. The only reason Colleen could be sure it was Olivia was because of her voice and the color of her hair. Her eyes and nose were peeking through the electrified strands. It looked like she'd stuck her finger in a light socket.

Colleen wondered if that was what the god-awful shriek she'd heard earlier had been about. Ever since the wild child had arrived, the racket started up like clockwork at the butt crack of dawn.

Who needed a rooster or an alarm clock when they had the wild child? As Colleen understood it, George didn't like to get the nits picked out of her hair. Colleen supposed it was a kindness Lexi had done for the guests when she'd insisted Olivia and the wild child move into Colleen's suite of rooms in the tower. At least the bone-chilling screams were muffled.

"Olivia, come and sit down. You look like you're about to collapse. I'll go find the demon spawn," Lexi said, and got up from her chair. She lifted a shoulder at Ava's and Sophie's horrified looks. "What can I say? I got cancer and lost my filter."

"You never had a filter, hardass. But she's a little girl who lost her mama and papa. Show some compassion," Ava said.

"No, don't. It makes me feel better knowing it's not just me," Olivia said, limping to the wingback chair near the window. She had one pink high heel on, the other off. Though she supposed the one dangling from Olivia's fingertip no longer qualified as a high heel because it was missing its heel. The way her sundress was slipping down her shoulder, it appeared to be missing something too. Maybe a button. The usually put-together Olivia was a hot mess.

"Here, let me get you a coffee," Ava said, half standing to reach the tray Jasper always prepared for their meetings. "Cream and one sugar?"

"Make it four sugars, thanks, and if there's whiskey anywhere in this room, add a shot or two." She pushed her hair from her face. It stood up like a rooster's tail. "Make it three."

"Umm, Olivia, you're not serious about the whiskey, are you? Because Finn—" Ava broke off as she glanced at Olivia and did a double take. "You have a black cross on your forehead."

"A black cross on my forehead." Olivia nodded and kept nodding. "I don't know why I'm surprised. She must have done it while I was sleeping. Around the same time she put this goop in my hair and sawed into my heel just deep enough that it didn't break off until I started walking and fell and nearly broke my neck. She's diabolically devious. I think she's possessed."

"What did I tell you? Total demon spawn. And no judgment on my part—she'd drive me to drink too—but just how drunk were you that you slept through her pranks?" Lexi asked, standing by the door.

Olivia covered her face. "Oh God, I wish it was because I was drunk. I can't…"

Lexi cleared her throat and coughed. It was an odd cough. It almost sounded like she was saying Olivia's… Colleen cast a glance in Lexi's direction and grimaced. This wasn't good. Where was Simon when she needed him? From where she sat in the window seat behind Olivia, Colleen tried to tap the back of her head with her foot to get her attention. It went through it.

Olivia kept digging her hole deeper. "…tell you how much I wanted a drink. A lovely glass of wine or two or three…"

Ava and Sophie fake-laughed. "Olivia, you're so funny. Ha! Ha! You, the responsible one. You would never drink when you—" Ava sighed when Olivia talked right over her.

"I'm like that woman from the Christmas Jammies

family video. Did you see the one they made for Thanks-giving last year?" she asked, and then started singing something about wanting a Chard-a-nay-nay.

"Hey, wino, you got a visitor." Lexi shook her head, obviously not impressed that Olivia hadn't clued in at their attempts to warn her they had company.

Colleen's great-grandson looked about as unhappy with Olivia as Lexi was.

Finn leaned against the door frame with his arms crossed, an eyebrow raised at Olivia.

She straightened, glanced his way, and rolled her eyes. "It's not what you think, so take a chill pill."

"Great, now instead of talking like a sixty-five-year-old, you're talking like you're twelve." He pushed off the door frame and walked across the room to take the coffee from Ava.

"Eight," Sophie said. "It's Mia's new favorite expression."

"I wouldn't want a drink if George was like Mia. Mia's an angel. I wish a little of Mia would rub off on George."

Finn sniffed the coffee and handed it to Olivia. He angled his head. "Nice do. The cross is a good look on you too. So, where is Picasso?"

"I don't know. Probably up in a tree eating her nits."

Lexi guffawed, and Ava showered the desk with a mouthful of coffee.

Finn tried to keep a straight face, but Colleen caught the glint of amusement in his eyes. "That's not nice."

Olivia's face fell, and her bottom lip quivered. "I know. I'm a horrible person. But I'm trying so hard and she hates me and says mean things and does even meaner things to me." She lifted her gaze to Finn. "And it's hard because I'll turn around, and for one minute, I think it's Cooper and I forget he's gone and it hurts so bad when I realize it's George that I can't breathe. And then she'll give me a look like Nathan used to or she'll use one of his expressions and I…" Her shoulders slumped. "I don't know why I thought I could do this."

Colleen reached over to pat Olivia's shoulder. "Don't be so hard on yourself now. Your grief was so big and all-consuming it terrified you, girlie. So bit by bit, piece by piece, you buried it. But until you've faced it head-on, you can't heal, you can't become whole and move on. You'll not say out loud what you're feeling in your heart, and I can't say I blame you." In Olivia's shoes, Colleen would have felt much the same. The child was as difficult as the situation.

"But as much as the child doesn't like you, you don't like her. She senses how you feel, you know. Once you're honest with yourself, you'll come to terms with your hurt and anger. Until you do, no good will come from keeping it buried. And mark my words, there is good to come from it. For the both of you. And for the man crouched at your side right now."

Colleen turned a fond eye on Finn. "Oh yes, laddie, you judge Olivia for not dealing with her grief when you've done the same. Just like your brothers."

Colleen watched as the girls joined Finn in comforting Olivia and lifting her spirits. That's what life was all about, friends and family looking out for…

A streak of movement at the corner of her eye caught her attention. She turned to look out the window. If her heart were still beating, it would have stopped. "For the love of all that's holy, you little hoyden, get out of the gardens!" she yelled at George. She flapped her arms in hopes of drawing Finn's or the girls' attention before the wild child picked every flower from the garden. Olivia had spent the better part of yesterday planting the beds with pink and white tulips for the weekend's wedding.

Lexi rubbed her arms. "Anyone else feel a draft?"

"Maybe the window's…" Sophie's jaw dropped, and she started making choking sounds while stabbing her finger at the glass.

"Soph, what's…Oh, hell. Don't worry, I'll take care of it." Finn sprinted for the door. "Just keep Liv away from the Chard-a-nay-nay."

Olivia felt reasonably human again when she returned to the study three hours later. A thorough scrub in a hot shower had taken care of the goop in her hair and the black marker on her face. George hadn't had enough time to damage Olivia's entire collection of shoes or wardrobe, so she was now attired in a bubble-gum-pink sleeveless dress and heels. She probably should have chosen another dress. It was the exact color of half the tulips George had beheaded. Tulips that Olivia had sweated and toiled over when she planted them in their perfect patterns the day before.

She wasn't buying George's excuse, which Finn had relayed to Olivia with a flicker of amusement in his warm, blue eyes, that the flowers were too pretty to be sitting in the dirt. But nor was she about to call out a five-year-old for lying, especially after the horrible things Olivia had said earlier.

Sophie looked up from where she sat behind her desk in the study and pushed her glasses on top of her head. "You look better, but how are you really feeling?"

"If you mean have I recovered from my meltdown, the answer is yes. I'm good, thanks. I'm just sorry you guys had to witness it."

"Olivia, come on. We're your friends. We know how tough this has been on you. The last thing you need is to be worrying…Sorry," Sophie apologized when her cell phone rang and she picked it up.

Olivia had a fairly good idea what her friend had been about to say. But it didn't change the fact that Olivia had lost control, and she simply did not lose control in public. Ever. Well, apparently, this was the new version of herself because she'd publicly lost control several times in the past ten days. Though the public part of it was mostly limited to an audience of one—Finn.

She could only imagine what he thought of her ode to Chardonnay. It seemed she couldn't be within six feet of the man without making a complete and utter fool of herself. Which led to the question: Why did she ask him…? All right, so she had pleaded with him—again—to move into the manor. She knew why, of course. George actually liked and listened to Finn. Come to think of it, George liked and listened to quite a few people. She was the only one the little girl couldn't stand. The only human, that is. Olivia had noticed she wasn't overly fond of Simon either.

She glanced to where the black cat lay curled on the window seat soaking up the sun and walked over to check on the garden. Finn, with the help of his brothers and father, saved what flowers they could and planted the flats of tulips that In Bloom, the local floral shop and nursery, had delivered two hours before. George, according to Finn, had supervised. It was also his opinion that George hadn't maliciously murdered the flowers; she was bored and should be in school.

Maybe he was right. Her late father's favorite quote had been "An idle mind is the devil's playground." Olivia thought the devil had had quite enough fun in George's mind today. There she was doing it again, thinking the worst of the child. It was as if she did it on purpose. Focusing on all the reasons the little girl was unlovable so George didn't find a way into Olivia's heart.

Olivia pushed the thought aside to lean across the window seat and check out the newly planted tulips, shivering when a cold sensation crawled up her spine, goose bumps rising on her arms and neck. She rubbed her arms. It was like the sunshine didn't penetrate the glass on this side of the window, leaving it surprisingly cold.

"That was Liam," Sophie said as she hung up the phone. "He wanted you to know everything's fine and that George seems to be enjoying herself. She's caught four fish. With her bare hands."

Olivia laughed, positive Liam was teasing. "Your husband's a godsend. George actually stopped snarling at me when I told her Liam was taking her fishing."

Sophie grinned. "Then you'll be happy to know he plans on taking her fishing twice a week. He's signing her up as his partner for the fishing competition in June."

"Wow, she must have gotten the crazy out of her system with me and the garden. I'm so glad she's behaving for him. There must be something about the Gallagher men. She's well behaved for Finn too."

Lexi, who must have caught the last part of the conversation as she walked in, said, "Doesn't matter if they're young or old, all females are putty in the experienced hands of the Gallagher men."

The look Lexi gave Olivia seemed to say, *You know what I'm talking about, girlfriend.* She needed to correct the impression. Fast. She knew only too well what happened when the women of Harmony Harbor went into matchmaking mode. Heck, she'd done the same. That group mentality kind of took hold, and you didn't know when to stop. "Not all of us," Olivia said firmly.

"Of course you're not affected, Sweet Cheeks." Lexi laughed and took a seat. She looked around. "Where's Ava and Kitty?"

"Ava got a call from Griffin to meet him at the lighthouse. She should be back any minute. And Kitty has a lunch date at the Yacht Club."

Ava walked in, groaning at the news. "Do not tell me she's going out with Dr. Bishop?"

Sophie wrinkled her nose and nodded. "Just pray that it's quiet at the club this afternoon and Nonna doesn't get wind of what's going on."

"Why? Does Rosa like Dr. Bishop too?" Olivia asked.

"Every woman over a certain age likes Dr. Bishop. And now that Finn's working at the clinic and he has more time on his hands, the good doctor has decided dating is his new hobby. Auntie Rosa and Kitty's feud has the potential to spread," Ava said.

"Great. As if we don't have enough going on." Sophie

sighed and glanced at Lexi. "You wanna do the honors and tell Olivia what Byron told you?"

"Yes, do share your pillow talk with Byron." Ava chuckled into her coffee cup.

"Pillow talk? You and Byron? How did I not know this? No one tells me—" Olivia began, even though she knew that if she'd missed anything over the past ten days, it was her own fault.

"Mouse is just trying to be funny. Which she isn't. I'm not dating Bryon. We went out for coffee a couple of times. That's—"

Ava grinned and started moving her shoulders. "She really, really likes him. She thinks he's sexy. She thinks—"

Lexi narrowed her eyes at Ava. "You and Griff watched *Miss Congeniality* without me, didn't you?"

"Yes, after you put us off for the third time because you were pillow talking with Byron and getting the inside scoop on the Marquis's upcoming plans."

Sophie did a face-plant on her desk. "Yeah, their plans to put us out of business," she said, her voice muffled in the stack of papers.

"Sophie, your baby hormones are making you pessimistic. It'll be fine. The Marquis can't compete with our location, and what bride-to-be doesn't want to have their wedding at a castle?" Ava asked.

"A bride who wants the ultimate spa package," Sophie said.

"The Marquis is putting in a spa?" It was an excellent idea. There wasn't a bride who hadn't asked Olivia about spa services. Plus it's something all their guests would enjoy.

"Yep." Lexi pulled out her phone and turned it to Olivia. "It's all hush-hush, but they're planning on opening in the fall."

"Wow. It looks"—Olivia glanced at Sophie—"nice?"

"Admit it, it's state-of-the-art. They even have flotation devices. I want to go," Sophie grumbled, rubbing her baby bump.

"There's no reason we can't put in a spa. And it'll be just as wonderful as theirs. Maybe not so modern and sleek though." The more Olivia thought about it, the more excited she got. This is exactly what she needed. She had to keep busy. She felt better already. "I'll start sourcing products from around here. Maybe we can even have our own line of—"

"Hold up." Sophie waved her hands. "We can't afford it. Even if we could, where would—"

"It wouldn't cost as much as you think. The family rarely uses the cottages, and you only rent them out during the summer. So why not turn one of them into a spa? We can bring your mom on as a consultant, Sophie. She's quite knowledgeable about this sort of thing, and that'll keep her busy and out of your hair. I'll come up with a preliminary budget for you by Monday, and we'll go from there." She looked at the three women staring at her like she was possessed. "I need a project like this right now, okay? I have everything organized for the upcoming events, so this won't take time away from anything."

"Umm, what about George?" Sophie asked.

"Right, George," Olivia said, sounding a little disappointed even to her own ears. And that was the thing—she was failing miserably as a stepmother, but she knew how to make a project like this succeed. "Wait. She starts school on Monday, so it's fine." She felt like cheering.

"I don't think you realize how tight our budget is, Olivia. And with the Marquis set to start advertising the spa for fall bookings, I have to adjust my income projections for the last quarter."

"Look, you know who I am, so obviously you know I have money."

Lexi snorted. "Money? You were listed in the top ten of Boston's wealthiest women last year."

"Yes, along with two of my cousins. And we didn't have much to do with it. Our grandfather and fathers deserve the credit. But the one thing my grandfather and father taught me was to follow my instincts. I truly believe a spa would be good for business and the financial outlay will be minimal. Let me do this for the manor, for all of you. If it wasn't for Colleen and Kitty, I don't know how I would have survived those first few months. If it makes you feel better, instead of just financing the spa, I'll be the majority shareholder."

Sophie tapped her pen against the files on her desk. "But it's part of the estate. If we can't get the rest of the Gallagher great-grandchildren to agree to keep it in the family, you'll lose your investment."

"It's a risk I'm willing to take," Olivia said.

"Why don't you just buy the rest of the great-grandchildren out? That'll at least be something we don't have to worry—"

Sophie's eyes went wide, and she cut off Lexi. "We can't ask Olivia to do that."

"Why not? She's rich, and she loves the manor. It seems like a perfectly reasonable solution to me."

Olivia smiled at Sophie and Ava, who were sharing I-can't-believe-she-just-said-that looks. "I do have money, Lexi. But a lot of it's tied up in investments and the foundation. And like my grandfather and father, I'm careful with my money. That's not to say I don't think Greystone is a good investment, I do. But Colleen knew who I was, and she never broached the subject of me buying the manor. I don't think her plan was only about keeping Greystone and the estate in the family. It's just my opinion, but I believe this has as much to do with bringing the Gallagher family together again and bringing them home to Harmony Harbor. It's working so far. Liam and Griffin wouldn't be here without Colleen and her will."

"Hmm, you might be right. Oh well, it was worth a shot. So looks like we have to marry Finn off." Lexi looked at Olivia. "Any thoughts on who would be his perfect match?"

Before Olivia could disabuse Lexi of the idea that she was his match, Sophie said, "If Jasper has his way, that would be you, Lex."

Olivia blinked, looking from Sophie to Lexi, who waved her hand and laughed. "Get out of here. There's no way—"

Olivia didn't know why she was relieved to hear Lexi's response, but there was no denying that it was relief that erased the uncomfortable tension that had tightened her chest.

"I can't believe you haven't noticed how Jasper goes on about Finn when you're around." Ava mimicked the older man's stiff upper-crust voice. "Did you notice how wonderful Master Finn is with baby Gabriel, miss? He's a fine doctor. One of the best. It would be good to have a doctor around, not just for you but for the wee one, too, don't you think?"

Lexi made a face and rubbed her forehead as though she couldn't believe she'd missed it. Or maybe she was reacting to Ava's creepy older man's voice.

Ava continued. "He's always been very popular with the ladies. I wouldn't wait if I were you, miss."

Lexi scowled at Ava. "Jasper did not say that."

Ava laughed. "No, that was me. But it's true. There's been standing room only at the clinic since he started."

Their conversation shouldn't bother her. Olivia wasn't interested in Finn or any other man. Relationships and marriage were the last thing on her mind. Once was enough, thank you very much. Obviously, she needed to build a stronger case because the uncomfortable weight in her chest had returned. She had the answer. Finn was too young for her. Better yet, he was a doctor. She had that T-shirt too.

But when neither objection produced the desired result, she brought in the big guns. The man had flagged her as a drug addict, and no doubt thought she ranked right up there with Lady Tremaine—the evil stepmother in *Cinderella*. Even that didn't seem to help, she thought with a disheartened sigh. It was probably because of his pretty-boy looks.

No, she reluctantly admitted to herself. It had nothing to do with his looks and everything to do with how kind and supportive he'd been the day George arrived. All right, fine, he was ridiculously handsome too. She had to change the subject. "So, about the spa, are we all agreed? I'll do some research this weekend and get back to you with the preliminary numbers on Monday?"

She glanced at Ava, who was looking at her while nodding. Olivia frowned. "What is it?"

"You paid for the ballroom renovation, didn't you?" Ava wagged her finger at Olivia. "No, don't try and deny it. I bet you're my fairy godmother too."

"I'm not sure what you mean by your fairy godmother, but I did pay for the ballroom reno, and it brought me a great deal of pleasure to see it restored to its former beauty. So don't even think of giving me grief."

"Giving you grief? We should have a parade in your honor. Look what you've done for all of us."

"Sophie's right. Without you stepping in for me, Olivia, who knows where I'd be. And knowing I'm the reason Stanley was able to track you down…It means a lot to me." Lexi leaned over and hugged her. Sophie's and Ava's eyes filled with tears, as did Olivia's. And not just because Lexi wasn't known for public displays of affection. It was because Olivia was grateful for them too.

Feeling a little emotional herself, Colleen got up from the window seat. Since Olivia had arrived at Greystone, all she'd done was make life better for everyone at the manor and in Harmony Harbor. And none of them had known just how much or how deeply she'd been hurting at the time. They still didn't. Olivia hadn't told them everything.

Sophie sniffed and furtively swiped at her cheek. "So, what did you mean by Olivia acting as your fairy godmother, Ava?"

"That's why Griffin called. Someone left a wedding card at the lighthouse for us while we were away. Inside was a gift card for ten thousand dollars to cover the renovations that Chase Halloran is doing, and it was signed *your fairy godmother*."

"It wasn't from me," Olivia said.

Lexi snorted. "Don't look at me, Mouse. I love you guys but I don't have that kind of coin."

Colleen smiled and left them to their guessing game. She knew exactly who Ava's fairy godmother was. They'd all find out soon enough.

Colleen walked toward the door, stopping to give a fond pat to Olivia's cheek. "If it's the last thing I do, you'll find your happy here, my girl. I promise you that."

Walking through the door, she shuddered at the odd sensation that traveled up her spine. The only time that happened was when she walked through someone. Sure enough, a woman with silver-streaked dark hair stood with her ear pressed to the study door. "Now, what would you be about?" Colleen murmured.

It was the recent hire. Ivy, she thought her name was. When the fortysomething woman wasn't helping out at events, she worked in housekeeping. Colleen looked around for a service cart. There was none to be found.

The woman straightened, her dark eyes narrowed. She headed down the hall, glancing over her shoulder before she slipped into the library. Colleen followed her inside.

The woman stuck her head out in the hall to take another quick look before closing the door with her hip. She removed a cell phone and folded piece of paper from the pocket of her black uniform. Smoothing the paper on a bookshelf, she punched a number into her phone, impatiently tapping her black work shoe against the hardwood floor while waiting for someone to pick up.

As soon as a voice came over the line, she launched right in. "You said you had a plan in play to force the Gallaghers to sell before the end of the year. Tell me it wasn't the spa at the Marquis." The woman ran the tip of her tongue over her teeth while the other person spoke.

There was something familiar about this Ivy, but Colleen couldn't quite place her.

"Yeah, well, I'm telling you it ain't going to work, Ms. Townsend. They're building one of their own, and the woman who is bankrolling it is probably richer than your boss. So tell me how you're going to get me my money now?" While the person on the other end of the line spoke, the woman once again ran her tongue over her front teeth. She made a sucking sound that caused Colleen's hair to stand on end. She knew the woman. She was sure of it.

Ivy shook her head. Not at Colleen but at Paige Townsend, the local Realtor who represented the corporation trying to buy the estate and manor out from under them. They wanted to tear down Greystone and build high-end condos.

Ivy rolled her dark, blue-shadowed eyes. "Yeah, I don't think so. Here's the new deal. I'm on the inside, and I'm going to make Ms. Richy Rich Davenport go away.

And you're gonna up your game to get them all on board to sell because, in case you've forgotten, you can't sell Old Lady O'Hurley's place for me till you do. It's only a matter of time before her kids come snooping around wanting a piece of what's mine."

Colleen gasped. Now she knew why the woman seemed familiar. She'd worked as a paid companion for Colleen's old friend Patty O'Hurley. The Gallaghers and O'Hurleys went way back. The family had lived a couple of miles up the road for as long as Colleen could remember. Their Victorian was built on a half acre of Gallagher land just up from the cottages.

There was a story there, a reason why the O'Hurleys had been leased the land; Colleen just couldn't remember it at the moment. Her memory wasn't what it used to be. She had an uncomfortable feeling there was much more she had to remember. Something about Patty's last visit to the manor.

Feeling in need of an ally, Colleen called to the only one who could hear her. "Simon!" she yelled, and then scowled. "A lot of good that'll do you. He can't walk through doors," she told herself. The threat against Olivia had obviously rattled her.

"Don't worry about it. I have a plan," Ivy was saying into the phone. "And since it's my plan, and I'll be doing all the work, I'd say that makes us equal partners, wouldn't you, Paige? Fifty-fifty seems fair. You do that," she said, and disconnected.

At the sound of scratching on the door, the woman smoothed her uniform and pasted a genial smile on her face before opening it. When she saw that it was Simon, she dropped the act, pushing him away with her foot. "Stay away from me, flea bag."

"Mind her and do as she says, Simon. There's something not quite right about that one. Come on, we have to find Jasper. We're going to need his help to protect Olivia. She's in trouble, Simon. Serious, serious trouble."

Chapter Ten

♥

A shower of pink and white rose petals cascaded like confetti over Finn, Liam, and Griffin as they sidestepped the wedding guests. Back in the day, Finn and his three brothers had a band. They'd been fairly popular on the local circuit. Something that, unbeknownst to him, his sister-in-law Sophie had been exploiting—promoting them as the "harmony" in Harmony Harbor.

At eight this morning, he'd found out that he and his brothers were part of the wedding package. It had been their job to sing Train's "Marry Me" as the bride walked down the garden path to the recently erected, flower-draped gazebo that overlooked Kismet Cove. Now they were singing "7 Years" by Lukas Graham as the newly-weds took the recessional walk. Only, the newly married couple took a slight detour to compliment Finn and his brothers, hence the rose petal shower.

"Don't worry. This time Olivia actually wanted flower petals to be tossed," Liam said with a grin as he brushed a pink one off the shoulder of Finn's black tux.

"Thanks. I kinda got that seeing as how they're in those paper cones and not attached to a stem." Finn glanced to where he'd last seen Liv.

She had a manicured hand raised while talking into a headset, trying, it appeared, to get the photographer's attention. She was like a general orchestrating her army. There was nothing the woman missed. Even a detail as small as one of the bridesmaid's bra straps peeking out from under her pink cap sleeve. The photographer acknowledged Liz's directive with a nod and then went to the bridesmaid, tucking the strap out of sight. Liv smiled her thanks.

This version of Liv, calm and completely in control, was the one Finn was most familiar with since he'd been home. Her air of cool competence had irritated him. He remembered a time last month when he would have taken one look at her in her tailored black jacket and skirt, her hair straight and sleek, her makeup perfectly applied, and would have rolled his eyes. He wasn't proud of it. But that didn't mean he was any happier about how he felt right now.

She impressed him, fascinated him even. He told himself it was the striking dichotomy between this woman and the one in the study the other day singing about her Chard-a-nay-nay.

It could also be because he'd never met a rule he didn't want to challenge or break, and he could almost guarantee she'd abide by each and every one. He didn't care about making a good impression, she did. His room was as messy as his office; hers was probably color coded and…

Where the hell was he going with this? And why was he still staring at her? If he wasn't careful, his grandmother or Liv might catch him and misinterpret his fascin…curiosity, for—

He cut off the thought with a tug on his bow tie. "I'm out of here. You two enjoy the rest of your day. I'd suggest you stay out of…Hey," he said when Griff grabbed him by the arm and put a stop to his forward motion.

"Good try, little brother, but we have to stay and so do you."

Finn pulled his arm away. "Ah, no, I don't. You're forgetting, unlike you two saps, I'm not a member of the Save Greystone Team. So while you two take one for your team, I'm going home and getting out of the monkey suit, and then I'm gonna grab a beer and watch a game."

"Change of plans. There was a mix-up with the DJ and Olivia's scrambling," Griff said.

Finn glanced over his shoulder. She was directing the waitstaff, who were serving flutes of pink champagne to the guests. "She doesn't look like she's scrambling to me."

Liam snorted a laugh. "Believe me, Miss Cool and Collected isn't so collected. She's just really good at faking it."

Finn frowned. "What are you talking about?"

"If you hadn't arrived two minutes ahead of the bride, you'd know," Liam said.

"I told you. Miller escaped, and I couldn't get him back in the house."

Griff tucked his hands in his pants pockets and looked around. "But you did get him in the house, right?"

"No, I brought him with me." His brothers shared a tell-me-he-didn't-just-say-that look. "Okay, what part of *I can't run* do you not get? It doesn't matter anyway. Miller will be fine. George is looking after him for me."

"Does Olivia know? Because last I heard, George was banished to her room and was getting bread and water for a week."

Liam had to be joking. George seemed happy enough to Finn, and she wasn't in her room. One of the waitstaff was feeding her milk and cookies on the front step. He figured Liv had paid Ivy to watch George for the day. "Don't tell me Liv is still mad about the tulips?"

"George has gotten even more creative in her how-to-drive-Olivia-batshit-crazy strategy," Griff informed him.

"That kid could have taught us a thing or two, and that's saying something. Gotta give Olivia credit though. She didn't lose her shit when she found a mountain of those empty little cake boxes in George's bed last night. They were wedding favors for today's guests," Liam explained to him. Because, obviously, he looked like he needed an explanation.

His brother continued. "Olivia made an emergency call to Truly Scrumptious at midnight last night, and Mackenzie took care of it. Well, she took care of the cakes. Olivia was running a box assembly line in the dining room until right before the ceremony."

"You're right, bro. She handled that pretty well," Griff agreed, and then grinned at Finn. "But she might have had a nip or two of Chard-a-nay-nay."

"Har har, you're a laugh a minute." He looked from Griff to Liam. "She wasn't really drinking, was she?"

"Not last night, but I'm pretty sure she was looking for a bottle at six this morning when she came down to discover George had liberated the butterflies," Liam said.

It's like they were talking in code. "Where and why were the butterflies trapped?"

"It's a wedding thing." Liam must have gotten from Finn's second blank look within minutes that he didn't have a clue what he was talking about. "Instead of a cone of rose petals, the guests were to be given envelopes that contained live butterflies that they open and release. I guess George thought they were going to die, so she let them go. All of them. I hear it was quite the sight."

Griff chuckled. "Olivia having a meltdown or George standing in a mini-tornado of monarch butterflies?"

Finn didn't find his brother or the situation amusing, and as soon as he got a minute, he was going to have a talk with George. He'd tried to explain a few things to her the day she'd arrived, and again when they were replanting tulips, but just then he realized how overwhelming it must all be for her. Especially at the manor with all the different events and people.

It was probably too much stimulation, too much to deal with all at once. If he thought he was having a difficult time readjusting, he could only imagine what it was like for her. Poor kid. He felt sorry for Liv too. "Okay, so back up to the beginning. Obviously George had nothing to do with the DJ mix-up…She didn't, did she?"

"Not that we know of. But someone at the manor told him the wedding was canceled so he left, and he won't come back until Olivia agrees to triple his fee. And you may not know this about Sweet Cheeks"—Liam smirked like he knew Finn's dirty little secret—"the woman might be a gazillionaire, but she's cheap and a tough negotiator. Now that I think about it, it's no wonder she's a gazillionaire. Anyway, we're singing first dance, father and daughter, et cetera, et cetera. Hopefully either Olivia or the DJ breaks—my money's on him—and he gets here in time for the reception because I don't know if we have enough songs in our—" Liam broke off with a frown. "What's that noise?"

"I don't hear…" He did now. It was a loud hissing sound, a cacophony of hissing…and a barking dog, and, oh hell, a little girl's husky voice.

Griff cocked his head. "Swans, Miller, and flipping George."

"Swans? Since when do we have swans?" Finn asked while trying to keep up with his brothers, who were giving Liv an it's-okay-we've-got-this wave as they headed for the pond. Fortunately, the white tent where both the dinner and reception were being held blocked the view of the pond.

"We didn't have swans until this morning. Olivia special ordered them for the wedding," Liam yelled over his shoulder as he and Griff broke into a sprint at the sound of a loud splash and George yelling for Miller.

Seconds later, he heard both his brothers calling for the dog. Their voices were drowned out by splashing, hissing, barking, and cursing. The cursing was coming from Finn. It burned his ass that he couldn't keep up with them.

Keep up with them? In his dreams. He was barely

managing his skip-hop, and he could tell by the stabbing pain each time he landed heavily on his foot that he wouldn't get much sleep tonight. But this was on him. If something happened to either Miller or George…

He heard the sound of someone coming up behind him and glanced over his shoulder. It was Liv. She was talking into her headset as she ran his way. Her heel sank in the grass, throwing her off balance. He slowed to a stop, but she managed to stay upright while continuing to talk. "I don't care what the mother says; the child is five. She can't have champagne. Fine, tint some ginger ale with pink food coloring." She shot him a panicked glance while pulling her heel out of the grass. He was a little surprised by the fear in her eyes. He hadn't heard even a hint of worry when she was speaking into her headset. Maybe Liam was right and she was good at hiding how she really felt.

"I heard George. She didn't fall into the pond, did she?" Liv asked as she slipped off her heels.

"Not that I know—" And she was gone, running like the hounds of hell were nipping at her heels. Maybe he should have been more definite. "I'm sure she's fine, Liv," he called after her.

He was drowned out as well as contradicted by Griff yelling, "George, keep your clothes on! Miller is—" There was a loud splash, followed by his brother shouting his favorite curse word, and then another splash. Some hissing and flapping too. Correction, lots of hissing and flapping.

Finn saw why as soon as he rounded the corner of the tent. Two angry and aggressive swans stretched up to fan their wings over the water while their feathered friends practically ran across the surface of the pond chasing after Miller to beat on him with their wings. Miller might be a big dog and outweigh the birds three to one, but he didn't have an aggressive bone in his body.

The little girl with the head of curly dark hair swimming across the pond to his rescue did. "Shoo, shoo! *Nenda zako*! Go away!" she repeated in English, sounding like an irate, five-year-old schoolteacher.

His brother ducked out of the way of the two posturing swans to head for George, power walking through the water to where she was now splashing the birds beating on Miller. Apparently, Griff forgot there was a drop-off in the middle of the pond and disappeared into the murky, dark depths. Finn wasn't worried about his brother—he was a Navy SEAL, after all—but the swan's wingspan was easily seven feet and could take George out and push her under the water.

Finn toed off his shoes, stripping off his jacket as he skip-hopped toward the pond. With George's rescuer now underwater, Liv took action. Shrugging off her jacket and throwing it down on the grass along with her headset, she charged into the water seconds before Finn.

Liam slid down the small hill on the opposite side of the pond to get closer to Miller and George. He waved them over, shouting, "Miller, come here, boy. You, too, George, get over here!"

The noise had drawn an audience. Waitstaff and wedding guests went from shouting advice to crying out in alarm when a ball of slimy-looking weeds popped out of the water inches from George. She gave a startled yelp, and then her determined little chin jutted in the air, and she hauled off and whacked the ball. Two large hands came out of the water. Griff pushed the weeds off his head, grabbed George, and set her on his broad shoulders, rising like Poseidon from the water.

Finn rolled his eyes at the feminine *oohs* and *aahs* coming from the crowd gathered outside the tent. Liv was staring after his brother and George, her hands pressed to her chest. No doubt starry-eyed over his brother's heroics. "It's not that big of a deal. They're not killer swans, you know." He drew in an irritated breath. He was jealous. Jealous that his brother got to play hero. Ticked off that his own days of playing one were over.

He was a doctor, so that wasn't entirely true, but right now that didn't make him feel any better. He'd come to terms with his limitations eventually. But for some reason, it hit him harder today than he expected. Maybe because George and Liv were involved. The thought bothered him because it meant there was a part of him that wanted to impress and protect them. Nah, he'd be the same with anyone who'd been through what they had. Except he wasn't really buying that. He glanced at Liv. She was staring at George with her hands pressed to her throat. Her throat? What was that…

"What are you two still doing in there? You can see that we've got Miller and George, can't you?" Liam asked.

Finn was about to make a smartass comeback when Griff shouted, "Finn, on your six!"

Their audience yelled, "Run!"

He glanced over his shoulder. Sure enough, two swans were doing their running-on-water routine and coming toward him with their wings spread wide. "Liv, get out of here!" he yelled, turning to splash the big white birds in order to distract them so she could get to shore. It didn't feel very manly or heroic, but he couldn't exactly scoop Liv up and run from the pond with her in his arms. His leg wouldn't make it. But it's the thought that counted. Or so he was telling himself when he heard the sound of a warrior's cry. If his brothers raced into the pond to rescue him, he was going to kill them.

Somebody brushed past him, knocking him off balance. It was Liv. Brandishing her shoes like weapons, she made a beeline for the birds. The swan on the right dipped forward and grabbed the shoe...and Liv's hand. Finn launched himself at Liv, wrapping an arm around her waist and dragging her away from the posturing birds.

A piece of bread hit Finn on the side of the head. The swan dropped Liv's shoe and joined his three pals to glide gracefully to where the guests were now throwing bread into the pond. Too bad someone hadn't thought of that earlier.

"If I never see a swan again, it'll be too soon," he muttered, half dragging Liv out of the pond after him. It wasn't until they'd climbed out that he realized she hadn't said a word. He slowly turned. She was pale and shaking. "What is it?"

She looked at him, stared at him really, as if she expected him to understand what was going on. And there was definitely something going on, and it had nothing to do with a lost shoe. It hit him then. It had to do with a loss of another kind, a gut-wrenching, soul-crushing, heartbreaking loss that no one should ever have to bear.

He put his hands on her shoulders and ducked to look

in her glassy eyes. "She's fine, Liv. She was never in any real danger. We were here."

"What if we hadn't been?" she whispered, looking to where his brothers were drying George and Miller with towels. "She wanders off all the time and won't come when I call. She hides from me, climbs rocks and trees, runs into the woods and the ocean at high tide." A tear rolled down her cheek. She wiped her face and looked away. "If something happened to her..." She slowly shook her head. "I can't do this, Finn."

In a way, he could commiserate. After losing his mom and sister, he vowed never to marry, never to have kids. He wouldn't, couldn't, take the risk. It was like having your heart ripped out of your chest and then shoved back inside. Damaged and broken, the docs sent you home, told you to rest and eventually you'd be whole again. You weren't. Nothing ever felt the same. "I get it, okay?"

She raised her tear-stained face to hold his gaze.

"I get that you're scared, that life feels pretty unfair right now, but what if instead of being the worst thing that happened to you, she turns out to be the best?" He glanced at his brothers, who were standing by the tent. Liam took George by the hand and started walking their way. Finn gave his head an almost imperceptible shake. His brother glanced at Liv and seemed to get that now wasn't a good time and nodded. Liam said something to George. The little girl glanced at them before walking in the opposite direction with Liam.

Finn saw a flicker of emotion cross George's face before she turned away but wasn't sure what it was. It bothered him though. He felt for both George and Liv...Well hell, this wasn't good. Not just for them, but for him. He realized then just how much he'd been thinking about them, worrying about them over the past few days. This was exactly the type of situation he'd vowed to avoid. They were a ready-made family, and he was a man who didn't want one.

Finn looked down at Liv, a part of him telling him to walk away and not look back. They'd figure it out for themselves. But when she looked up at him with those big, haunted whiskey-colored eyes, he couldn't do it.

He lifted his hand to catch the tear rolling down her cheek. "It's only been a few days, Liv." He hadn't noticed that she had flecks of yellow in her eyes. They were unique, mesmerizing. "I'll talk to George. I can bring her to my dad's. Hang out with her more often."

He felt the tension in her shoulders release, and she gave him a soft, grateful smile. "Thank you, you don't know how much I appreciate you sharing custody with me. George really likes you. She feels comfortable—"

"Just…just hold on a sec." He heard the panic in his voice and cleared his throat. He didn't know why. He should have left the panic right where it belonged and maybe it would have stopped the stupid from coming out of his mouth. "What do you mean sharing custody with you? I never said anything about sharing or custody. I said…"

She blinked. "I'm sorry. I didn't mean to put words in your mouth. I guess I just heard what I wanted to. What I hoped to. What I needed to."

She looked so damn vulnerable and defeated that she got to him and he gave in and that's when the stupid came out of his mouth. "Fine. You win. I'll move into the manor."

Her face lit up. "Really? You're serious?"

"Yeah, I'm—"

She threw herself into his arms and hugged him.

His leg buckled and went out from under him.

Colleen headed toward the dining room. She'd been trying to keep an eye on Ivy but it was difficult to do because Colleen was tethered to the manor. If she could just find a way to communicate her worries to Jasper, she'd feel better.

She spotted him standing by the French doors leading onto the patio, talking to Liam and Sophie. It appeared that Liam was passing off George to his wife. Colleen wondered what the wild child had been up to. And it was obvious she'd been up to something. She was a wet, bedraggled mess.

Sophie took George's hand, and they walked through the dining room. All of a sudden, the child froze. She looked at Colleen, really looked at her, and screamed, "Bad *juju*! Bad *juju*." Then her small chin tipped up, and she hissed and made a cross with her fingers, holding them out in front of her. "*Nenda zako*! Go away!"

Sophie tried to calm the little girl down, but the child was having none of it. Colleen walked through the wall beside her into the back hall, trying to figure out what had set George off. Then Colleen realized she'd never been in the same room with the little girl before. When it sounded like all was clear, she walked back through the wall and into the dining room.

Jasper looked down at Simon and glanced to where Colleen was standing. His lips twitched. "It would appear Miss George can see you and believes you're an evil spirit, Madame."

"And you're having a right fine chuckle over it, aren't you? Well, you won't be chuckling when you discover we have an actual evil spirt among us, and she's in corporeal form. Not much frightens me anymore, laddie, but that one does. I'm afraid for Olivia. I truly am."

And Colleen's fear was caused by something more than what she'd overheard the other day in the library. Just as she was trying to remember what it was, an image came to her. She'd been writing in her book after Patty had joined her for tea at the manor last October.

Ivy had been with her, of course. Back then it seemed Patty didn't go anywhere without her paid companion. Colleen remembered thinking that the girl reacted oddly to any mention of Patty's children. She'd made cutting remarks, said things that Colleen knew to be outright lies. Patty didn't correct her, but her old friend hadn't been herself. And it was more than just the forgetfulness that comes with old age.

Colleen had made note of other things that bothered her too. She couldn't remember what they were right now, but there was something there, something that had worried Colleen enough that she'd called Patty's eldest son and then she'd called the Harmony Harbor Police Department and spoken to the chief. Only it had been too late. Patty had died that night in her sleep.

The memories gave Colleen a bad case of gooseflesh, like someone was walking over her grave. She had to find

Jasper. He'd discovered her memoirs back in February and kept the book locked in his safe. He was an honorable man, loyal to a fault. Since the book had come into his possession, he'd only read the page that contained Ava's secret. Now Colleen needed him to read about Ivy.

And he needed to do it now before it was too late.

Chapter Eleven

♥

Does red mean go and green mean stop?" a husky little girl's voice asked from the backseat of the Lexus.

"The opposite, red means stop and green means go. There's a yellow light too. That's a warning light. You have to be cautious and slow down or—" Olivia was babbling. She couldn't help it. George had woken up with a rash and a bruise on her back. The reminder of why she was racing to the clinic caused Olivia's heart to drop to her feet. She pressed on the gas.

George interrupted her. "Do you not know which is which?"

"Of course I do. Do you?" she asked, thinking it was an odd question for a five-year-old to ask, but then again, a lot of what George said and did surprised Olivia. Just yesterday…

"I do, but my mama can't see different colors. She wouldn't drive through a red light though."

There was so much wrong with everything George had just said, Olivia didn't know where to begin. She wouldn't say anything about the little girl referring to her mother in the present tense. So far Olivia had avoided any mention of Nathan and Isabella. And then there was the implication that Olivia had driven through a red light. Something George believed Olivia would do, but not her mother.

It's possible Olivia was being overly sensitive, but that was what George's tone of voice seemed to imply. At least that was something Olivia could address. She smiled at George in the rearview mirror. "I wouldn't drive through a red light, sweetheart. I'm a law-abiding citizen. I've never gotten a ticket or been in trouble with the law before. So you don't have to worry—"

"You went through two red lights, and the policeman's right behind you. His siren sounds angry. Maybe he's going to put you in jail."

Olivia narrowed her eyes at George in the rearview mirror. She sounded practically gleeful at the prospect of Olivia behind bars. She moved her gaze from George's smirk to the car behind her. Despite what George seemed to think, Olivia had seen the policeman pull in behind her. But she'd been positive the lights and siren were for the car behind him. His mouth flat beneath his mustache, the officer gestured for her to pull over.

Fig Newton, George was right. Olivia waved and nodded, pointing to Primrose Lane, though she second-guessed her decision to get off Main Street when she found a spot just up from the clinic. Chief Gallagher was dropping Finn off at work. They both turned to look her way when the officer got out of his vehicle to approach the driver-side window.

"Don't worry, everything will be just fine," Olivia reassured George, concerned the little girl might be distressed at the sight of the big, burly policeman with the handcuffs hanging ominously at his side and the gun in his holster. Olivia opened the glove box and took out the red folder with all car-related documents before lowering the window with a smile.

The officer didn't return her smile. Instead, tipping up the shiny black brim of his hat with his finger, he said, "License and registration, ma'am." Then he glanced to his left, offering a chin lift and smile to Finn and his father, who approached the car. "Chief, Doc."

"Morning, Mitch." Finn's father ducked to look in at her. "Morning, Olivia, George. What seems to be the problem, Mitch?"

Finn raised his eyebrows in a what-did-you-do-now? kind of way, but a hint of a smile touched his mouth, so she couldn't be too annoyed with him. And really, now that he'd promised to move into the manor, she couldn't work up any emotion other than gratitude when she thought about Finn Gallagher, even when he teased her.

"Clocked her going fifty-five on Main Street, and she blew two lights. She missed taking out Old Lady Bennet by a nose."

"Excuse me? I didn't almost take out anyone, and I wasn't speeding," she objected heatedly, while dying inside. The last thing she'd ever want to do was hurt someone because she broke the law. Chief Gallagher looked surprised. Finn looked disappointed and a little concerned. He probably thought she was high.

Apparently, he wasn't the only one. "Ma'am, step out of the vehicle, please."

Before she had a chance to comply with his request, the back door flew open and George got out of the car. For a brief moment, Olivia thought she might come to her defense. She should have known better.

George walked straight to Finn. "Can I live with you when they put Livy in jail?"

"Liv isn't going to jail, George. If she was speeding and running stoplights, she'll have to pay a fine." Olivia saw the censure in his eyes when they met hers.

She didn't know why it bothered her. Maybe because this somehow validated his opinion of her as a spoiled princess who'd spent her life buying her way out of trouble. Which might have been why she blurted in her defense, "I was worried…" She looked at George and trailed off. She couldn't relay her fears in front of the little girl. Couldn't say that the bruises and rash on George's back were identical to her big brother Cooper's when he was diagnosed with leukemia. "…Worried George would miss gym class and wanted to get her in to see you first thing. She has two bruises on her back and a rash." Tears prickled the backs of her eyes, and her throat tightened. As hard as it was to relay George's symptoms, it was almost a relief to share them with Finn. He'd know what she was afraid of, wouldn't he?

His expression changed, his features softening. He slid the brown leather messenger bag off his shoulder. Handing it to George, he ruffled her hair. "We can't have you late for your second day of school, now, can we?" He turned to his father. "Dad, can you do me a favor and tell Sherry to put George in exam room number one?"

His father nodded, gave Olivia an understanding smile, and took George by the hand. "I've got a few minutes. George and I will get better acquainted while we wait for you."

"Mitch, can I talk to you a minute?" Finn asked. The officer glanced from Olivia to Finn and then nodded. They walked a little farther up the cul-de-sac. The way they glanced at Olivia indicated the conversation was undoubtedly about her.

A few moments later, she heard the officer say, "You owe me," to Finn, and then he walked toward her. "Next time you're upset, you have someone drive you, ma'am." He tapped the brim of his hat. "Have a good day now. I hope everything works out for you and your daughter."

"She isn't...Thank you, Officer. I will." *Daughter*. George didn't feel like hers. She didn't know if she ever would. Olivia had hoped to have more children, but she and Nathan had quit trying when Cooper was diagnosed. She'd wanted to try again when Cooper had been in remission. She'd wanted to give them something else to think about, to celebrate, to look forward to. Cooper had wanted a brother or sister. Actually, he'd wanted three. Nathan refused to be swayed. He said he was happy with just the one. It appeared he'd been lying about that too.

She looked up when Finn approached. "Thank you."

"I think you owe me more than a thank you. This is the second time in two weeks that I've saved you from being tossed in the slammer, Liv. And don't forget I saved you from a shoe-murdering swan this past weekend."

She gave him a look. "You weren't very helpful with the…crab."

He laughed and placed his hand at the small of her back. "This is true. But all I'll say is me and a tree—"

"Well, there was Kitty and the closet…It's June. How about we start with a clean slate?"

"All right, even though I think I'm losing out, it's a deal." He bunched the fabric of her black sleeveless dress in his hand, stopping her from walking in front of a car, and then slid his arm around her waist, rocking her against him. "Liv, trust me. I understand you going to the worst-case scenario, but I'm sure there's a simple explanation for the bruising and rash."

"When I go in to check on her at night, her hair is damp. Cooper had night—" Her voice broke, and she couldn't go on.

Instead of taking the walkway, he drew her down a lane between the clinic and the house next door. It was bordered with clumps of primroses in various shades of pink, purple, and yellow. They smelled like springtime and sunshine.

Finn stopped walking and turned her to face him.

"I can't do this again, Finn. I just can't—"

"I'm almost a hundred percent sure you won't have to, Liv. You're getting yourself worked up over nothing." He tipped her face up with his knuckle, smiled, and smoothed her hair from her face. "It's going to be okay. You're going to be okay, and so is George."

She sagged against him, and his arms closed around

her. She breathed in the scent of sandalwood and bergamot. "I almost believe you." And that's because she didn't feel so alone when she was with Finn. Which was odd. Sophie, Ava, and Lexi were there for her. She could go to them any minute of any day for support. But for some reason, it didn't feel the same.

Maybe because she'd been forced to be honest with Finn from the beginning, or maybe it was because he'd been with her the day George arrived, or maybe it was because it felt so good to be held in his arms, and my God, the man smelled amazing. "You smell really good," she told him, and then lifted her head from his chest. "I didn't mean to tell you that."

Noting the stunned expression that came over his face, she mentally kicked herself for blurting it out. "I'm not hitting on you if that's what you're worried about."

He rubbed his jaw. "I didn't think you—"

"I'm not interested in you. Well, not you specifically. I'm not interested in any man. Even if I was, I wouldn't be interested in you. You're younger than me for one, and you—"

A window slid open, and Sherry stuck her head out. "Dr. Gallagher, Dr. Bishop wanted me to let you know that you're late, and the waiting room is filling up."

"I thought he was retiring. Isn't that why I'm here?" Finn asked in a ticked-off tone of voice. Olivia wasn't sure his irritation was entirely directed at Dr. Bishop or the nurse.

"Retiring? Dr. Bishop isn't retiring. He just wanted to be able to cut down his hours and enjoy life a bit more. I'm surprised you didn't know. It was your grandmother's idea, after all. Oh, and the little girl in exam room one broke the lift on the table. Your dad's trying to fix it now."

At the news, Olivia did a face-plant on Finn's chest. Given their conversation of only moments before, it was the last place her face should be. But honestly, she didn't know how much…Her thoughts trailed off when she spotted Kitty Gallagher sneaking around the back of the clinic.

The older woman startled when she saw Finn and Olivia, and then she grinned and gave them a finger wave.

"We'll just pretend I wasn't here. Go back to what you were doing, you two lovebirds."

Finn rubbed the bridge of his nose before facing the woman and child sitting on the table in exam room number one. He was losing his patience. Not with the child, but with her guardian. The one woman who wasn't interested in him because he was too young for her. If Sherry hadn't chosen that moment to open the window, Finn would have informed Liv he wasn't interested in her either.

Yeah, because that's how he was feeling right now, ticked off and immature. Mainly because his grandmother had manipulated him, and he'd lay dollars to dimes that his father and brothers were in on it too. And then of course Grams had to witness him in a clutch with his *lovebird*. He made air quotes in his head.

So that may be the reason why there wasn't a whole lot of sympathy and compassion in his response to Liv. "For the tenth time, I'm positive. She has poison ivy. If you'd like to get a second opinion from Doc Bishop, be my guest."

"Yes, please. I think that would be a good idea."

"Are you freaking kidding me?"

"No, I…You're the one who suggested I get another opinion, so I don't understand why you're getting cross…" She moved her left shoulder up and down and then reached behind her to scratch her back.

George looked at her. "Are you sure you don't have to go to jail?"

"I'm sorry to disappoint you, George, but no, I'm not going to jail."

"Oh." She looked at Finn. "Are you moving into the manor today?"

"You told her I was moving in?" Oh hell, now how was he supposed to get out of it? After what Grams had just witnessed in the lane, there was no way he was moving into the manor.

"Why? Wasn't I supposed to?" Liv's mouth fell open. "You're reneging on your promise?"

Finn got up and opened the door. "Sherry, can you come…Oh hi, Mrs. DiRossi, how are you?"

Sophie's grandmother was a beautiful older woman. She reminded Finn a little of Sophia Loren, so he got why Doc Bishop was interested. And he looked very interested at the moment with red lipstick smeared across his cheek. But given that Finn's grandmother was sneaking out of the back of the clinic thirty minutes earlier…Yeah, Finn wasn't exactly happy with the old guy. Granted, he wasn't happy with his grandmother either.

"I'm good. Very good," Rosa said, her thick accent making the words roll off her tongue in such a way that Doc Bishop was practically panting. Finn hoped to God the old guy wasn't acting like this with Grams or he'd deck him.

"Yes, she is. She's very, very good," Doc Bishop said in a way that Finn figured he meant to come across as smooth and charming. Sadly, it came off as smarmy. Finn decided he was going to let Liam and Sophie's brother Marco know what the good doctor was up to. They might want to have a word with him about Rosa.

The older woman said something to the doc in Italian, patted his cheek, and smiled at Finn. "Where's the bambina?" She held up a Tupperware container. "I have some of my nonnie cookies."

"Great. Can you stay with her in the waiting room for about ten minutes? I have to talk to Liv."

Rosa narrowed her eyes at him. "Why? What are you talking to her about? My Marco, he's going to ask her out, you know. No funny business, *sì*?"

"Tell him not to waste his time. She's not into younger men." He was happy that he didn't come off sounding as ticked off or as possessive as he felt. His somewhat over-the-top reaction could easily be explained away. Marco was a total player. And Liv was vulnerable. She needed to be protected right now.

When Finn returned to the room from passing off George to Rosa and telling Sherry he needed ten more minutes, Liv was lying on the exam table. The paper crackled as she energetically rubbed her back. A couple of pointed questions later and he knew the problem.

"I promise if you just let me take a look, I'll give you something that will make you feel better." He helped her sit up.

"The only thing that will make me feel better is if you tell me you're moving into the manor. Please, Finn."

"We'll see, but I can't this week. My, ah, my dad needs me." He took her by the shoulders and turned her so he could see her back. "Undo your dress for me."

"Excuse me?"

"Liv, I have to be sure it's poison ivy and not something else."

"Like what?" she said, reaching back to undo her zipper. "You'll have to do it the rest of the way."

"Shingles, for one. You've been under a lot of stress," he said as he slowly lowered her zipper to expose her back, which was a red, blistered mess.

"Only old people get..." Her eyes narrowed at him. "That's not funny."

"I wasn't trying to be. You have poison ivy, by the way." He walked to the cupboard and pulled out a corticosteroid cream and a sample box of antihistamines. Drawing a small paper cup from the dispenser, he filled it with water and brought it to her. "Here you go."

Resting his hip against the table, he squeezed the cream onto the pads of his fingers. "It'll be a little cold, but it should relieve the itch fairly quick."

He smoothed the cream onto her back. She shivered at first but was practically moaning within seconds. Okay, this was not good. How could he be looking at a back covered in a rash and be turned on? He knew exactly how. And it wasn't only those sexy sounds she was making in her throat, it was the strap of the lacy black bra that made his mind go to where it shouldn't. One flick and...He pulled his gaze from the bra strap to watch her dress slide off her shoulder, leaving it bare. The way her silky, blond hair spread over her skin made him think…

He cleared his throat. "Okay, you're good—"

"Can you put some here?" She reached around to pat her bra strap. "It's really itchy under there, and I won't be able to reach it."

It was well past six before Finn saw his last patient. He would have thought by now the novelty of a single doctor in town would have worn off. Given that the waiting room today had been packed with single women with fake complaints, it hadn't. The one exception being the single woman with a legitimate complaint who wasn't the least bit interested in him.

As he slowly lowered himself onto the chair behind his desk, Finn wondered if Liv writing him off as a potential love interest was why he couldn't seem to get her off his mind. Maybe that and his slightly obsessive interest in her long, slender back and her sexy black bra.

It was more than that, and he knew it. He just didn't know what to do about the situation. He was worried about Liv. George too. Because the one thing that had come across loud and clear today was that, as much as Liv didn't want to mother George, the little girl didn't want Liv as a surrogate mother. The arrangement wasn't working for either of them. Nathan hadn't given any thought to Liv and her feelings. Not really a surprise given what the guy had pulled.

Liv at least was being honest. She'd told Finn repeatedly that she couldn't do it. In his own way, had he been pressuring her too? Sure, it might be the right and moral thing to do, and Finn knew she would if she had to. But at what cost?

Technically, Liv was his patient. As much as he had to look out for George, he had to look out for Liv too. When he saw something wrong, his first reaction was to fix it. Screw the rules and red tape; as long as you got the job done and saved a life, what did it matter? It was too much to expect Liv to raise George. Liv wasn't a bad person; she just had too much baggage. As someone who had baggage himself, he commiserated with her. He'd been manipulated into a situation he didn't want to be in either.

But Liv was an adult. She could and would look after herself. George had to be his priority, his first concern. And from what he saw today, the best he could do for George was find someone who wasn't only willing to take her in, but also who genuinely wanted to. Someone who wouldn't see their dead son or dead husband every time they looked at the little girl.

He powered up his computer. With a little help from Google, he discovered Nathan's parents were alive and well and living in Boston. He did another search and found their home phone number. According to Liv, Stanley said Nathan's parents wanted nothing to do with George. Finn found that hard to believe. Then again, he was thinking how his grandmother and father would react in the same situation.

He tapped his fingers on the desk waiting for someone to pick up. An older woman's voice came over the line.

"Hello, is this Mrs. Celeste Sutherland?"

"Yes, and to whom am I speaking?"

"Finn Gallagher, ma'am. I'm a family physician here

in Harmony Harbor, about an hour northeast of Boston. Your granddaughter Georgina is one of my patients, and I was wondering if you could spare a few—"

"I'm sorry, you must be mistaken. The child lives in Kenya with her mother."

So it looked like Stan the man hadn't told Liv the truth. "Actually, Mrs. Sutherland, your granddaughter arrived in Harmony Harbor two weeks ago. She's living with your daughter-in-law, Olivia." He told her what he knew about George's mother, Isabella, the stipulation in Nathan's will, and the problems that both Liv and George were having adjusting to the arrangement.

"No, that won't do at all. Olivia isn't even a blood relative, and she's unstable. Unfit to mother any child."

"Mrs. Sutherland, I'm sorry if anything I've said led you to believe that Liv is unstable or unfit. It couldn't be further from the truth. I'm more concerned for Liv's well-being than I am for George's. Kids are resilient, and I have no doubt Liv would provide a good, stable life for George. But you have to understand how difficult this is for her. I don't mean any offense, but your son cheated on her, he had a secret life and family, and he expected Liv to raise his child with another woman. I'm sorry, but in my—"

"That's quite enough, thank you. We'll handle the situation from here."

She disconnected. Finn stared at the phone. He had a bad feeling that while he might have gone into this with the best of intentions, he should have left well enough alone. And now he had to tell Liv what he'd done.

Chapter Twelve

♥

Finn sat in the passenger side of Liam's Jeep. He'd made the mistake of calling his baby brother and asking for a ride to the manor. Now he was trapped while Liam lectured him. Finn hoped he wasn't getting a preview of how Liv would react to the news that he'd called her in-laws.

"I'm telling you, Finn. This is going to end badly. You pulled a GG. Remember Grandpa Ronan telling us how bad she was? His father threatened to divorce her if she didn't stop putting her nose in everyone's business."

"I'm not married, so I don't have to worry about anyone divorcing me. Besides, what GG did was meddling. I was fulfilling my duty to George and Liv as their primary health care provider. It was my job to—"

"Doesn't the Hippocratic oath you took say something about doing no harm? How do you think Olivia's going to feel about you basically telling her ex-in-laws she can't handle a five-year-old? It's guaranteed they're going to draw some pretty unflattering conclusions from that, bro."

"They're not her *ex*-in-laws. Her husband died. He didn't divorce her." Finn rubbed the bridge of his nose between his fingers, surprised to find he still wore his glasses. It spoke to his panic to get to Liv before she received a call from Stanley, he supposed. He took them off and tucked them into the breast pocket of his white button-down. "I didn't tell her mother-in-law she couldn't handle George. I explained that Liv had been put in an untenable situation no one should ever be put in and that the arrangement wasn't a healthy one for either her or George."

"I hear ya. Soph and I were talking about it the other night. But I feel bad for the kid. She's just settling in at school, making new friends, and now, because of you, she's going to be ripped away from the only—"

"Seriously? I can't believe you're saying crap like that to me." He gave his head an irritated shake. "There are reasons I did what I did, Liam. Concerns I can't share with you. So back off. This wasn't an easy decision to make."

"Sorry, I guess I was just thinking how Mia would feel in George's shoes. She'll be sad to see George leave. She liked having another kid around."

Finn glanced out the window, gauging how badly he'd be hurt if he opened the door and jumped. He decided not to risk it. The manor was just up the road, and given the crap his brother was giving him, he might have to make a quick getaway after telling Liv.

"It's not as if Liv will cut George out of her life. She's not like that. I'm sure she'll take George for weekends once she settles into a routine with her grandparents. Hell, if they'll let me, I'll bring her back for a visit. You signed her up for the striped bass tournament in two weeks, didn't you?"

"I was *going to* sign her up, but then I discovered she's total catch and release. We caught a great-looking black sea bass, and she got it unhooked and back in the water before I even got the camera out." Liam frowned, lowering his window when Griff slowed his black truck alongside them. "What's up?"

"Heading to Dad's place to pick up the camping gear. George says she saw an evil spirit in her bedroom and refuses to sleep in the manor."

"Soph said she freaked out the other day in the dining room. Said something about seeing a ghost then too. Always did think the place was haunted," Liam mused. "Why do you need the camping gear? George can stay at our place. It might be a good idea seeing as the good doctor here has something to tell Olivia that might have her two-fisting some Chard-a-nay-nay."

"Sometimes, I wonder why I missed you," Finn muttered, and then responded to his oldest brother's what's-going-on? frown. "I got in touch with George's grandparents. It looks like they want her to live with them." He waited for Griff to give him hell. To tell him he was as bad as GG.

Instead his brother lifted a shoulder. "Might be for the best. Olivia lost it on the kid. I think that's the real reason George wants to sleep outside. She told Ava she used to sleep under the stars with her mom and dad. Sounds like she's homesick."

"Come on, Liv wouldn't lose it on George just because the kid said she saw a ghost," Finn said, troubled by the news even if it did work in his favor.

"Probably not, but the ghost moved from George's room into Olivia's. George was trying to scare it off by throwing stuff at it. She threw a framed photo of Olivia's boy. It shattered, and the cup of coffee George threw next damaged the picture beyond repair. It was taken not long before Olivia's son died."

The silence that fell over the three of them was heavy. Every picture they had of Riley and their mom was precious. But as tough as losing the photo of her son would be on Liv, Finn knew she would be most bothered that she lost it on George. "Thanks for the—"

The fire engine ringtone they'd programmed in their phones for their dad blasted out of his and his brothers' cell phones. "Looks like Dad figured out how to send a group text," Finn said, pulling his phone from the front pocket of his chinos. He scanned the text. The three of them whistled at almost the same time.

"It's gotta be bad for Aidan to quit the DEA. He loved his job," Liam said.

Finn was thinking it had to be really bad if Aidan was moving back to Harmony Harbor. Because if his dad's text was to believed, that's exactly what their brother planned to do. But Finn figured he'd best keep that thought to himself instead of voicing it and ticking off his brothers.

"This latest job didn't help his case. If he didn't quit, Harper would have his balls to the wall, and he'd never get to see Ella Rose," Griff said, looking like he had a foul taste in his mouth.

"Harper might end up regretting backing Aidan in a corner. I wouldn't put it past him to turn the tables on her and go after full custody." Finn might not see his brother often, but he knew his MO. You don't mess with Aidan or his family. And his brother adored his six-year-old daughter.

"First thing he should do is hire a new lawyer. Might be a good idea for Aidan to talk to Mike about what he needs to do to increase his chances of beating Harper at her own game," Liam said.

Their cousin Mike was a former ADA with Suffolk County. He'd left to go into law enforcement and was a couple months away from becoming a special agent with the FBI.

"It's no game, bro. Ella Rose will pay the price if Harper and Aidan end up in a battle for custody. The best thing they can do is go into mediation and settle this before it gets contentious," Finn said.

"You weren't here for GG's funeral, Finn. It's already past contentious. There's no way Aidan will be able to deal reasonably with Harper. The woman's a nutjob, and she's out for revenge," Liam said as a car came up behind Griff.

Their brother lifted his hand to let the other driver know he was on his way. "We'll talk when I get back with the camping gear. Good luck with Olivia and George, Finn."

He gave his brother a weak smile. Talking about Ella Rose and Harper made him think about his conversation with Celeste Sutherland. Harper came from money and had that same self-important vibe Finn had picked up from George's grandmother. He scrubbed his hands over his face as Liam pulled into the parking lot at the manor. What if he'd made a mistake? What if Stanley had a valid reason for not informing the Sutherlands that their grand-daughter needed a place to live?

"Hey, bro, looks like Stanley got to Olivia first." Finn shifted in the Jeep to see her talking to Stanley beside the silver Audi. He cursed under his breath, and Liam patted his shoulder. "Olivia's good people. She'll understand that you meant well. She's not the type of woman who will sue you for breach of patient–doctor confidentiality. Maybe if she needed the money she would, but we both know that's not the case. It's all good."

Finn groaned and leaned against the headrest. Closing his eyes, he went over his conversation with Olivia's mother-in-law in his head. Was he in breach? He didn't think so, but because he'd been trying to relay the depth of his concern for Liv and George, maybe he'd said too much.

"Okay, prepare yourself, here she comes."

He opened one eye to look at his brother. "How ticked is she?"

"Can't tell. But I suggest you get out of the Jeep. I don't want blood all over my seats."

"You're seriously not funny, baby brother."

"I wasn't joking."

Finn bowed his head and reached for the door handle. Before he had a chance to open the door, it was flung open, nearly ripping his arm from the socket.

Face flushed, eyes shining, Liv stared at him with her hands pressed to her chest. "You wonderful, amazing, ridiculously gorgeous man, I don't know how I'll ever be able to repay you. Thank you, thank you, thank you," she said, and grabbed his face.

She kissed him enthusiastically, like a sexy, bouncy cheerleader on her first date. And then the kiss slowed and became warm and languid. Her lips moving softly over his, gently exploring as she wound her arms around his neck, those tantalizing curves he'd become aware of in the tide pool pressed against the side of his body.

At the sound of someone clearing their throat, he drew back, his breathing ragged. "You got into the Chard-a-nay-nay, didn't you?"

Olivia glanced at George in the rearview mirror. She hadn't said more than two words since they'd left the manor this morning. Somehow, Olivia had to make it up to the little girl for how she'd behaved last night before she dropped her off at Celeste's and Walter's. Olivia hadn't meant to shout at her or let all the pain and anger of the past two weeks come out of her mouth.

It was no excuse, but seeing the very last photo of Cooper destroyed by the little girl who had stolen Nathan from her son had been too much to bear. Until that moment, Olivia hadn't realized how much bitterness and anger she'd locked inside. Nor had she realized how much she blamed George and her mother for destroying her family, her life. She was being unfair. George was innocent.

She smiled at the little girl, who'd stubbornly refused to wear anything other than a pair of jeans and her Red Sox T-shirt and light-up sneakers today. "Are you excited to meet your grandparents?"

George's shoulders rose in response and remained up around her ears. Olivia tried to ignore the guilty twinge in her chest. This was for the best. They couldn't continue like this. It wasn't healthy for either of them. Finn, who Olivia believed knew her better than anyone in Harmony Harbor, agreed with her. If he didn't, he wouldn't have made the call to Mother Sutherland. He'd taken the decision out of Olivia's hands, and for that she'd be forever grateful. As she'd proved yesterday. In front of witnesses. Lovely.

"Your grandparents have a beautiful town house on Beacon Hill. It's right near the Charles River. Your grandma Celeste loves plants and flowers. She opens her garden to tours every year. It's very—" Olivia stifled a groan. Why on earth had she brought up the gardens given George's propensity for digging up flowers? Celeste would have heart failure if someone even breathed on her prized roses. "Actually, George, it might be best if you stayed away from your grandmother's garden. There's a lovely park across the road."

"Is there kids?" she asked in that husky little voice.

Olivia made a note to ask Finn about that. She should have asked him to check George's vocal cords before, but with everything…It really wasn't her concern now, was it? It would be up to Celeste and Walter to make sure George didn't get sick. And they'd be much better at that than Olivia.

George had asked her a question. What was…"Oh yes, I'm sure there are. Lots and lots of children for you to play with." She couldn't be sure though. "But if there's not, you'll have lots of friends at school." Snooty little friends, because no doubt Celeste would insist that George attend the same private school that Nathan had. "You'll most likely go to the same school your daddy did. Won't that be fun?"

George stared at her, a pucker forming between her big blue eyes, and then the tiniest of smiles curved her bow-shaped lips. It was the first time Olivia had mentioned Nathan and the first time George had smiled at her. "Did my brother go there?"

Olivia picked up on the hesitation in George's voice. Probably because of Olivia's meltdown last night. But George's curiosity obviously outweighed her fear that Olivia would have another breakdown at the mere mention of Cooper.

"No, your brother went to a public school not far from where we lived." Her fingers tightened around the wheel. "George, I'm sorry for how I acted yesterday. I know it was an accident. It's just that…" She trailed off, afraid anything she said would make everything worse.

"You miss him?"

"Yes, very, very much."

She nodded. "I miss my mama and daddy too."

Olivia strangled the wheel, biting her bottom lip to keep the tears welling in her eyes from falling. She couldn't talk, so she nodded too. *Please, please, God,* she prayed, *don't let me cry.* It took her a few moments to get herself together. "I'm sorry that I didn't talk to you about your mommy and daddy, George. I thought it would make things worse for you. I should have known it would help. No one would let me talk about Cooper when he died, and I guess I just fell into the same pattern with you."

"That's okay."

"No, George, it's not. We didn't get off to the best start, but I hope you'll let me make it up to you. If you'd like, during the summer holidays, maybe your grandparents will let you come visit me in Harmony Harbor."

"Can we go see the house where my daddy and brother lived too?"

"Yes, yes, we can. I'll show you your daddy and Cooper's Red Sox collection."

"Let's go now."

"Your grandparents are expecting us. We don't want to be late." Celeste would never let Olivia live that down. "You know, your daddy grew up in your grandparents' house, so you'll be able to see some of his keepsakes."

"Pictures too?"

"Yes, pictures too."

But Olivia soon discovered that there were no pictures or keepsakes. Celeste had packed away any sign of Nathan and Cooper.

Olivia smiled at George, who had whispered the question seconds ago, only to receive a sharp rebuke from her grandmother. "Don't worry, I have lots of pictures and mementoes at my house. I'll come into town next week, and we'll go have a look," Olivia said, offering George a reassuring smile.

The meeting between George and her grandparents had been strained at best. They didn't approve of her chosen name or the way she dressed. Since Olivia had felt the same, she didn't feel she should judge.

Her reunion with the Sutherlands hadn't gone much better. Though of course they approved of her white linen pantsuit, designer shoes, and bag. She wasn't surprised. Celeste and Walter were all about image.

Celeste glanced at Walter and lifted her chin. The older woman played the part of the little woman, always deferring to her husband. It was so far from the truth it was laughable. Celeste wore the pants in the family.

Walter cleared his throat, his wattle wobbling. "Perhaps it would be best to hold off on any future visits until the child settles in," he said, unable to meet Olivia's eyes.

George looked up at Olivia from under her dark, curly lashes. There was no evidence of distress on her face, but Olivia sensed it in the way she pressed against her. "Why don't we leave that up to George?"

"That always was your problem, Olivia. You never set proper boundaries for Cooper. You gave in to his every whim. His—" Celeste began.

Olivia raised a finger to cut off her mother-in-law and call for Anna, the housekeeper who'd been with the Sutherlands for as long as Olivia could remember. She smiled when the older woman bustled into the room. Anna was her favorite member of the Sutherland household and had seven grandchildren of her own. She'd adored Cooper. Knowing she'd be here for George made it easier for Olivia to assuage the concerns that had begun to crop up the moment Celeste had greeted them with her nose in the air. "Anna, would you mind taking George up to see Nathan's room and the bedroom where she'll be staying?"

"It would be my pleasure." Anna smiled, giving Olivia an almost imperceptible wink. She held out her hand to George. "Oh, look at you with your daddy's and brother's big blue eyes. Such a pretty little thing. I have a grand-daughter about your age. Would you like me to bring her to play one day?" Anna asked as she led George from the room. The little girl glanced at Olivia over her shoulder, and she gave her an encouraging nod.

Celeste narrowed her eyes at Olivia. "It's no longer your place to order around the help. You aren't a member of this family. Now I think it's best you leave."

"Anna is hardly the help. But I thought it best that George didn't hear what I have to say," Olivia said, coming to her feet. "Don't try and keep me out of that little girl's life because I failed to meet your standards of grieving mother and wife."

"You failed to show up at your own husband's funeral. Do you know the questions I had to field, the gossip that started? You embarrassed us. Embarrassed this family. Sullied our good name and your husband's with your behavior."

"Your son was a bigamist, Celeste. And the only way your *good* name would have been sullied is if I hadn't paid a small fortune to bury the story. I didn't do that for you, or for me. I did that in memory of my son. A child *your* son abandoned. Perhaps if *you* had set better boundaries for Nathan, we wouldn't be here today. As for George, your son named me her *legal* guardian. So I *will* be here next week to pick her up for the day. I'll also be calling to speak with her every night before bed."

Her face tight with fury, Celeste opened her mouth. Walter covered his wife's fisted hand with his. "That will be fine, Olivia."

"Good, I'm glad we've reached an understanding. I'll just say goodbye to George."

Twenty minutes later, Olivia hurried down the steps of her in-law's town house, waiting for the sense of relief and gratitude to wash over her. There was nothing other than a horrible heaviness in her chest. Something made her glance over her shoulder, and her breath caught in her throat. George stood alone in the front window. Maybe because of the dark, masculine furniture in the background, she looked smaller than Olivia remembered, paler too.

Olivia raised her hand, forcing a smile because her throat ached from keeping the emotions at bay. Not happy ones, not the ones that she'd expected to feel. She mouthed that she'd see her soon. George lifted her stubborn little chin. It was an action Olivia had seen many times over the past couple of weeks…whenever the little girl felt vulnerable and scared.

"Damn you, Nathan Davenport, damn you to hell," Olivia muttered under her breath, and turned around to walk back up the steps and press the bell.

Chapter Thirteen

♥

Olivia may not have felt either the relief or gratitude that she'd expected to feel when she walked out the Sutherlands' front door and left George behind. But thirty minutes later, the elusive emotions washed over her as she sat on the end of Cooper's bed looking through his baseball card collection with his sister.

Olivia hadn't been back home since she'd left last September. Nothing had changed. Cooper's bedroom was exactly the way it had been the day they left for the hospital that last time more than two years before. Nathan, his parents, even Olivia's cousins had told her it wasn't healthy. She needed to box everything away. But she'd felt close to him here. It was the same today. And even nicer that she had someone to share it with.

The little girl spotted Cooper's collection of signed baseballs and bats and ran across the room. Olivia joined her on the blue-carpeted floor and told her the story behind each souvenir. In turn, George shared the stories her father had told her. The same ones he'd told his son. But unlike last week or the week before that, George's stories no longer made Olivia want to cry. They made her smile. It felt like she and George shared a history, a love for Cooper.

Because the more George opened up, the more Olivia realized that Nathan hadn't forgotten his son after all. He'd built Cooper up in the stories he told George. He created a life for the little boy he would have been, had he been healthy.

After more than an hour of sitting on the floor playing with Cooper's toys and looking through albums, Olivia said, "We should probably head back to Harmony Harbor before traffic gets bad, George."

She looked disappointed but nodded. "Can we come back another day?"

"We can come back anytime you'd like." She started picking up the toys and noticed the way George petted them as though needing to touch them one last time. Olivia smiled. "You know, your brother would have wanted you to have his toys and baseball collection, George."

Her eyes went wide. "He would?"

She nodded. "Yes, he would. So why don't we get a box and you can fill it with whatever you want?"

They'd ended up filling four boxes and two suitcases. Olivia had also snuck in two family photo albums that she'd go through before she gave them to George. She'd pick out some photos of just Nathan and Cooper for the little girl.

George gave Olivia a gap-toothed smile from under Cooper's Red Sox baseball cap while sitting in her booster seat eating a chocolate fudge ice cream cone. Nathan would have had a conniption. Petty as it may be, that gave Olivia a great deal of pleasure. Though that wasn't the reason she'd parked the Lexus and taken Nathan's black Range Rover or bought George an ice cream cone. The SUV was more practical for carting around a little girl and all her treasures.

In George's eyes, it seemed the afternoon they'd spent together had more than made up for Olivia even thinking of leaving her with Nathan's parents, but just in case, she'd thrown the ice cream cone in for good measure. Celeste and Walter weren't horrible people. In some ways, Olivia felt sorry for them. The loss of both Cooper and Nathan had affected them profoundly. But they had always been judgmental and strict disciplinarians, and that didn't seem to have changed.

They'd been the same with Cooper, but they had genuinely loved him, and of course Olivia had been there to mediate and offset any hurts that might arise. But George wouldn't have had her there, and she didn't think the little girl would have fared as well with them as her son had. She imagined Nathan had thought the same or he would have named his parents as George's guardians. Or maybe Stanley was right and George was a gift to make up for all the pain Nathan had caused.

She was beginning to think Stanley was right about something else. She hadn't thought much about it until she'd opened the garage at the town house and spotted the Range Rover. Nathan had purchased the SUV when he was home last June. He'd driven it once—taking it off-roading with a couple of friends. It gave credence to Stanley's belief that Nathan had planned to come home after all. She couldn't help but wonder if he would have abandoned the little girl in the backseat as easily as he'd abandoned his son. She'd liked to think that he wouldn't have.

She glanced at the sign announcing ten miles to Harmony Harbor, and the reality of what she'd done set in. For better or for worse, that smiling little girl in the backseat with chocolate all over face was now hers. No one had forced Olivia to do this. She'd made the decision all on her own.

No matter how terrified she was of letting this child into her heart, she had to. From now on, George would know she was wanted, loved. There'd be no half measures. This time, Olivia was all in. Her pulse raced at the thought and instead of heading for the manor, she headed straight for Primrose Lane. George had her Red Sox T-shirt, and apparently Olivia had Finn. "Why don't we stop by the clinic on our way to the manor and say hello to Finn? Good idea?"

George gave her a smile and a thumbs-up.

Ten minutes and ten cleansing wipes later, they walked into a packed waiting room. The busty blond receptionist sighed when Olivia approached the desk. "Unless it's an emergency, I don't have any openings today."

Olivia glanced around the waiting room. She'd guarantee half the women with appointments to see Finn had nothing wrong with them. "It's an emergency."

"And the nature of the emergency is?"

"I'd rather not say. It's personal." The blonde gave her a look. "I have poison ivy. It's spread to places it shouldn't spread."

Sherry, who'd been pulling a file from the jam-packed shelves behind the desk, pursed her lips at Olivia before saying, "Poison ivy doesn't spread. Maybe you have an STD."

Olivia stared at the woman. She couldn't believe she'd actually said that to her. It more or less confirmed her suspicion that Finn's nurse didn't like her.

Maybe because she didn't respond, Sherry said slowly and loudly as if Olivia were deaf, "What I said is that you may have a sexually transmitted disease."

"I understood you the first time. I was just surprised you'd be so rude and unprofessional as to say it out loud in front of witnesses."

George tugged on her sleeve and asked in her husky voice, which was almost as loud as Sherry's, "Do you have HIV, Livy?" The only difference was that, while Sherry was trying to embarrass Olivia, George was genuinely worried about her. As the daughter of physicians based in Kenya, the little girl had no doubt overheard her parents talking about STDs.

"No, George, I'm fine. Sherry thought she was being funny."

Realizing she'd perhaps taken the joke too far, Sherry pointed at the computer screen and the receptionist said, "Dr. Gallagher can see you, but you'll have at least an hour wait."

From the looks of the waiting room, it would be longer than an hour. "All right, we'll be back then." She wasn't going to make George sit around a stuffy waiting room, at least a quarter of which may be filled with actual germs. "George." She looked around. She was gone. "George, where are you?"

"Olivia," a woman called from behind. Olivia turned. It was Brie Fitzgerald. She managed Guppies, a high-end children's clothing store on Main Street. Sitting beside Brie was her grandmother, Widows Club member Ida Fitzgerald, who'd made it clear she was actively seeking a husband for her granddaughter. Olivia was a little disappointed to realize the young, pretty blonde must be okay with her grandmother's plan to ensnare Finn. Brie smiled. "I think she went back to the examination rooms."

"Thanks, Brie," Olivia said, and took a step in that direction.

Sherry blocked her way with her arms crossed and feet spread wide. "You're not bumping ahead. So, if you sent her back there to get in faster, you're out of luck. Sit down and wait your turn. I'll get her," she said, and flounced off.

If Olivia were running the office, Sherry would be gone. The receptionist too. As would half the women sitting in the waiting room. When Nathan first started out, he and two of his friends opened a practice together. Olivia had just finished her MBA and organized their office for them. She ended up staying on because she'd enjoyed working with Nathan. She had fond memories of that time in their life together.

"Olivia," a woman called from the other end of the waiting room. It was Julia Landon, the owner of Books and Beans. She appeared to be there with the mayor, Hazel Winters. Last year, the mayor had joined forces with Paige Townsend to strong-arm the Gallaghers into selling out to the developer who wanted to buy Greystone. As of late, they hadn't heard much from the heavyset woman with the big hair.

Julia patted the empty chair beside her. "Come sit down. It looks like we're in for a wait."

"Are you not feeling well?" Olivia didn't know why—it was silly really—but she hoped Julia wasn't there because she was vying for Finn's attention like the majority of single women in Harmony Harbor. Which made her feel guilty because it was almost like wishing Julia was sick. And Olivia would never wish an illness on anyone, least of all Julia, who was one of the sweetest women she knew.

Julia turned in her chair to look at Olivia, making her violet eyes go wide in the universal sign of *I don't want to be here.* Olivia nudged her head at Hazel, and Julia nodded. She sat back in her chair. "Hazel, have you met Olivia Davenport?"

"Yes"—the woman nodded and gave Olivia an uneasy smile—"but I thought your name was Dana...something."

"It's a long story." Olivia smiled, leaving it at that. Even Julia didn't know everything. Olivia hadn't spent much time hanging out on Main Street these past few weeks. She used to spend quite a bit of time in the shops and went out for dinner at least twice a week. Those days were over now that she had George.

The mayor's cell phone buzzed. Hazel glanced at the screen and frowned. Then she looked at Julia and Olivia. "I'll take this outside where it's not so noisy," the sixty-something woman said, and got up. "Hold my place, dear."

Julia smiled, slumping in the chair once Hazel was out of sight. "I can't believe I let her talk me into this."

"Into what?" Olivia asked, craning her neck to look for George.

"Don't worry, she probably ran into Kitty. She's back there having a visit with Dr. Bishop." Julia smiled. It was the kind of smile that made you smile in return. There was something otherworldly about the bookstore owner. Fae, Olivia's Scottish grandmother would have said. Maybe Julia gave off the whimsical aura because she spent so much of her time immersed in fairy tales, either reading them or acting them out for the children. "I'd heard you were bringing George to your in-laws to live. Since you're both here, I take it that you had a change of heart?"

Olivia nodded. "I couldn't do it. She's been through enough."

"So have you from what I've heard. If you ever want to talk, I hope you know I'm here for you, Olivia."

"Thank you, I appreciate it. And I might take you up on that. Maybe I'll bring George in for story hour. You wouldn't happen to have a book on childhood fears, would you?"

"Of course I do. Is there anything in particular that you're looking for? I can hunt it down for you when I get back to the store."

"George calls it bad *juju*, an evil spirit. So maybe something about ghosts?" Olivia pulled a face. "I really didn't think this through. She slept outside in a tent last night. I hope Finn has some suggestions because I'm not sure I feel like spending the next few weeks roughing it."

Julia grinned. "Do you realize you light up when you say his name?"

"I do not," she said, feeling the heat rise to her cheeks. "It's not what you think. He's just been a very good friend to me through all of this. And he's wonderful with George."

Julia gave her a knowing look.

Olivia thought a subject change was in order. "Before Hazel gets back, tell me what you're doing here with her."

"Hazel is doing what half the older women in this room are doing for their daughters and granddaughters—she's trying to find me a husband. And if you haven't already guessed, your very good *friend* is on the top of their lists."

Matchmaking mothers and grandmothers converging on the clinic wasn't news to Olivia, so she didn't understand why she felt an anxious twist in her stomach. "But why is Hazel interested in finding *you* a husband? She isn't your mother or your grandmother, is she?"

A small frown pleated Julia's brow and then smoothed out. "Of course, what am I thinking, you wouldn't have known. I was engaged to Hazel's son Josh. He died six months before we were to be married. It didn't change my relationship with Hazel though. She's always treated me as her daughter-in-law, and I've always thought of her as my mother-in-law."

"I didn't know, Julia. I'm so sorry."

"Thank you." She smiled and gave Olivia's hand a gentle pat. "Let's get back to you and George and your ghost. And just tell me to butt out if I'm overstepping, but now that you're keeping George, have you thought about getting a place of your own? I mean, the manor is lovely, but wouldn't it be a nice to have some privacy?"

"To be honest, it's a little terrifying to think of just the two of us on our own. And…" She looked over to see Finn standing by the desk with George. He was looking at Olivia with an expression on his face that she couldn't read. He lifted George's hand and raised an eyebrow as if to say, *You're really doing this?* She nodded, and he gave her a smile that she felt straight to her toes. A smile that seemed to say, *You did good. I'm proud of you.* And her chest filled with a fuzzy, warm glow.

Julia looked from Finn to Olivia and smiled her sweetly mischievous smile. "Do you know, I think I've just thought of the perfect solution." She took out her phone and texted someone. She waited a few moments, then smiled and looked at Olivia. "How would you like to live right next door to the clinic?"

Olivia pressed a hand to her chest. "Are you kidding me? That would be ideal. If George wasn't feeling well, Finn would be only steps away." She caught the triumphant gleam in Julia's gaze and waved her hand. "I don't know why I said that. Probably because we're here and Finn's right there, you know. Just ignore me, sometimes I babble. What I really meant to say was that it's an ideal location because it's close to the school. And the library. And you, it's close to you too." Fig Newton, she had to stop talking. Then she thought of the pretty Cape Cods on the street with their well-tended lawns and gardens. "But I didn't see any homes for sale."

Julia smiled. "You just leave that to me."

Two weeks later, Finn walked into the examination room. "Hello, Mrs.…" He slapped a hand over his eyes and backtracked out of the room, walking into someone. Before he apologized to whomever he'd bumped into, he said to the naked woman on the examination table, "Mrs. Edwards, you're here for"—he glanced at her chart to be sure he'd read it right the first time—"a sore throat, not a"—he mentally deleted the curse word before finishing—"physical. Get dressed, and I'll be with you in a minute." Not without Sherry, he wouldn't be. He closed the door and turned to apologize to…the reason he couldn't tell his grandmother and Doc Bishop what they could do with this job.

Lexi leaned against the wall with her arms crossed and a grin on her face. "Gotta love a job where married women drop their clothes and jump on your table and half the single women in town are packed like sardines in your waiting room just to get a look at your pretty face."

"Har har, you're spending too much time with Liam." He pretended to look around while doing a quick visual search of her face to gauge how she was feeling. Lex didn't stop in just to razz him or shoot the breeze. She broke out in a cold sweat anytime she had to go to the hospital or clinic. "How did you get past Kerry without an appointment?"

Her lips flattened, and she pushed off the wall. "I have an appointment. Your brother made it."

"The guy's been a pain in the ass since he learned to talk," Finn said, gently throwing an arm over her shoulders. "Always checking up on you, making sure you're okay. Yeah, Griff's a real pain in the ass."

"Oh, shut up. I know I got lucky as far as exes go. But he hovers and gets this worried look on his face if I say I'm tired or complain about a sore arm or back." She leaned against him, her voice going low. "And then I get paranoid that maybe it really is something. Maybe it's not because Gabe weighs a shit ton or I was up with him three times in the night."

And this is why his brother wanted him home, and why, when Finn caught the tiny break in Lexi's armor, saw a touch of fear in her eyes, he knew he wasn't going anywhere anytime soon. And he realized he was good with that.

Finn leaned past her to open the exam room door. "You're fine, Lex. I'll just check you out to make my brother happy. Now go get bare-ass naked and get up on my table," he teased to distract her.

She elbowed him. "In your dreams. Besides, I wouldn't want to ruin you for the hordes of women coming after me. It's standing room only out there."

He blew out a frustrated breath. "Grams and the Widows Club are behind this, you know. I'm tempted to tell them I'm gay so they'll just leave me alone. They're taking time away from people who are actually sick." It was weeks past amusing. He'd already planned to talk to Doc Bishop about it tonight.

"Or you can just tell them the truth and say you and Olivia have a thing."

"We don't have a thing. The only thing we have is a standing appointment every second day at four o'clock because the woman is neurotic. She's going to turn George into a hypochondriac if she doesn't stop."

"But she's beautiful. Olivia, I mean."

An image came to him of the other day when he'd walked into the exam room to find Liv on her hands and knees hunting down the baseball that George had dropped on the floor. She had on a pink skirt that gave him the perfect view of her sweet cheeks. He felt his lips curving and quickly corrected that. Making sure to sound uninterested, he said, "Some people might think so, I guess."

Lex gave him a look.

"All right, yeah, she's got incredible eyes, great hair, and a nice bod. That better?"

"Why are you asking me?" She patted her chest. "This is what matters to me. I care what's in here, and Olivia has heart. I couldn't ask for a better friend. She puts herself out there for everyone. The woman is tireless, and what she's doing for George…that says everything about her. She's one in a million."

"Yeah, she is." He smiled as he remembered the day she was supposed to bring George to live with Nathan's parents. Finn had been thinking about her, about both of them, and then George had opened the exam room door—much to the chagrin of the patient having a physical—and announced that she was staying with Liv. The kid had been beaming, happier than he'd seen her since she'd landed in Harmony Harbor. And Liv, well, she'd gotten to him that day, not that he'd tell either her or Lex. Because his ex-sister-in-law was right—the most beautiful thing about Liv was her heart.

"So there's your answer," Lex said.

He blinked, afraid he'd said the last out loud. "Does everyone around here talk in code? I have no idea what you're getting at."

"Olivia can be your fake girlfriend. Everyone will buy it and back off, and you can get back to what you do best, taking care of your patients, not just the ones who want to get naked with you."

"They don't want to get naked with me…Okay, a couple might, but mostly they want a ring on their finger."

Or to feed him, he thought several hours later as he looked at the casseroles piled up on the reception desk. He'd forgotten to say that to Lex this morning. He'd tell her when he dropped by the manor later. She'd made him promise to have a talk with his brother. Which he planned to, but he'd talk to Ava first. Because if anyone could alleviate some of Griff's fears for Lexi, it was his wife.

"There's no more room in the fridge," Sherry said, gesturing at the two foil-wrapped casserole dishes on the desk. "Or the freezer," she added when he'd opened his mouth to suggest exactly that.

"All right, what about…" He turned to see what Sherry was scowling at, thinking it was another casserole-bearing patient. It was Liv. "Hey, you're early. Where's George?" he asked, even though all he could think about was his conversation with Lex earlier. He couldn't ask Liv to be his fake girlfriend, could he? No, no way. It was a bad idea.

She looked confused. "Early for what? George is in school."

"Why are you acting all innocent? You're only in here every other day. You're going to give the kid a complex if you're not careful," Sherry said.

Finn looked at his nurse and picked up the casserole dishes. "Find room for them. And I want to talk to you before you leave tonight, Sherry."

"Fine. Whatever. You want to keep seeing patients who have absolutely nothing wrong with them while patients like poor Mr. Taylor, who is dying, have to wait hours to see you, fine." She turned and headed for the back, making as much noise as she possibly could wearing rubber-soled shoes.

He might not like how she handled the situation, but Sherry was right. He had to do something.

Her cheeks bright pink, Liv said, "I'm sorry. I didn't realize how often I'm here. Sherry's right, I shouldn't be using you like our own private physician. I just get worried, that's all. I promise, I'll get a handle on it. We won't bother you anymore."

Finn looked out into the waiting room, wondering if he had a big enough audience, and then he remembered where he was. He took Liv's hand and smiled down at her. "It's okay, Princess. You come by anytime. You know how much I love playing doctor with you." He inwardly grimaced. He'd taken it a bit too far, as evidenced by the stunned and possibly horrified look on Liv's face.

"Kerry, I just need two minutes before I see the next patient," he said, tugging Liv after him.

"Uh-huh," his receptionist said, looking kinda shocked and disappointed, which was heartening. Because if he was going to make an idiot of himself, it was good to know his plan had a chance of succeeding.

"Give me a minute, and I'll explain," Finn said to Liv as he dragged her down the hall. When he was out of earshot of the waiting room, he stopped and put his hands on her shoulders. "Okay, I know that was weird, but it's about to get weirder. I have a favor to ask."

"You want to play doctor with me?"

He gave his head a slight shake to clear the image of Liv in the same position as Mrs. Edwards this morning. "No, if there's any playing, it will be of the pretend kind. So would you be up for that?"

"Are you feeling all right?"

"Sorry, I'm messing this up." Probably because a voice inside his head was yelling, *No, don't do it! You were never any good at playing let's pretend…*"I need your help, Liv. Sherry's right. I spend three-quarters of my day seeing patients who should be on Match.com, not at the clinic. What do you say? Will you do me a huge and be my fake girlfriend? But you can't tell anyone it's not real or my grandmother and the Widows Club will find out."

She rolled her eyes. "No one will believe we're dating, Finn. You're too young for me, and—"

Finn heard the squeak of Sherry's shoes coming toward them. "Trust me, they will. And I'm going to prove it to you right now," he said, lifting his hands to frame her face. "Pucker up, Princess, and make it good." His lips closed over hers, swallowing an irritated huff that was soon replaced with a tiny, far-from-fake moan. And he couldn't be sure, but he thought he may have groaned when her fingers tightened around his shoulders and she pressed against him. The reason he couldn't be sure whether he was groaning or not was because he was high from the feel of her soft, plush lips under his, the warmth and the taste of her mouth, the…

"I knew it! I knew there was something going on between you two," Sherry muttered. "You can bet I'm going to tell Dr. Bishop about this, Dr. Gallagher. Making time with your girlfriend while patients are waiting."

Finn slowly pulled back from Liv. This was when he was supposed to smugly point out to her that he was right. But he couldn't because, the way his heart was pounding and his head was spinning, he had a feeling that he should have listened to the voice in his head.

Chapter Fourteen

♥

Every time the wild child came near, Colleen made sure to disappear behind the door in the closet. She didn't want the little girl throwing Olivia's treasures at her from across the room again. It would be a long time before Colleen banished the image of Olivia desperately trying to save the photo of her son.

But watching them from where she hid in her old closet in the tower, Colleen could see their relationship was much improved. She was happy for them. They deserved...

Colleen startled at a quiet rustling beside her. Before she had a chance to investigate, a head poked out from among Olivia's dresses. "You! What in the name of all that is holy are you doing here?" Colleen said to Ivy, but it was obvious the woman didn't hear her.

No good, that'd be for darn sure, Colleen thought. She

had to alert Olivia to the danger. Simon was down in the tunnels chasing mice, so she'd get no help from him. She peeked around the door. Olivia, who moments before had been folding clothes, was down on her hands and knees with her head under the bed. She backed out and came to her feet, holding a baseball.

"Here you go." Olivia looked at the ball for a moment, turning it in her hand before carefully tossing it to George, who stood by the fireplace. "No playing in the manor though."

"Is Finn coming after work?" the little girl asked.

"Umm, I'm not sure. Maybe. But he might be busy, so don't get your hopes up, okay?"

"I wonder whose hopes you're really worried about, the child's or your own?" Colleen murmured, taking in Olivia's flushed cheeks. It appeared the rumors she'd heard this afternoon about Finn and Olivia might be true after all.

The members of the Widows Club had been all in a tizzy thanks to Evelyn Harte, owner of the *Harmony Harbor Gazette*, announcing what she'd seen and heard at the clinic. There were a lot of sour faces at the meeting, including Evelyn's. She'd hoped for a match between Finn and her granddaughter Poppy. But no sourer than Rosa's and Kitty's. Though their pussfaces were not about Finn and Olivia. They were after the same man again.

If Sophie hadn't called the meeting to discuss the spa, the two wouldn't have deigned to be in the same room together. They were acting like teenagers, fighting over Kyle Bishop the way they were.

Colleen didn't know why she was surprised. They'd

fought over Ronan too. If only she could find a way to communicate that evil had come to Greystone Manor, they'd at least have a common cause to fight for that would bring them back together again.

Colleen supposed she was lucky that Finn and Olivia had seen the light sooner rather than later and with little help from her. She was going to be busy, it seemed, with their resident evil. Peering through the wardrobe to get a look at what Ivy was up to, Colleen had a feeling she'd need more than luck to deal with this one.

Crouched amongst the dresses with a bottle of what looked like ibuprofen, Ivy emptied the pills into the palm of her hand and then shoved them into the pocket of her uniform. Reaching into another pocket, she withdrew a baggie of white tablets and carefully emptied them into the ibuprofen bottle.

Poison, that's the only explanation Colleen could come up with for Ivy replacing the original pills with the ones in the baggie. What other reason could there be? Colleen wished she could come up with one because the lengths this one would go to scared the bejaysus out of her. She wasn't dealing with the likes of Hazel and Paige now. Oh no, this one was tetched in the head.

"I'm sorry, child. I truly am, but I need your help." Colleen stepped out of the closet, holding up a placating hand while giving George her warmest, kindest smile.

"Bad *juju*! Bad *juju*!" The child ran on the spot, screaming.

"No, no, read my lips." Colleen pointed to her mouth. "I'm GG. I'm good. She's bad. Ivy's bad."

The little girl stopped screaming, and Colleen breathed

a sigh of relief, until she saw George's chin go up and her arm go back.

"No!" Colleen cried, when Olivia moved to comfort George and stepped right into the line of fire.

"George, it was an accident. I'm fine." Olivia held her stomach as she rolled onto her side on the floor in the tower room. "I'm just going to lie here for a moment." Red lights from George's sneakers bounced across her face as the little girl moved from side to side as though she had to go to the bathroom. Obviously, she wasn't going to relax until Olivia was on her feet. Unless something else was upsetting her…Olivia lifted her head and looked around. "Is the ghost still here?"

"No, in there." George pointed at the closet.

"Okay, then, we're going to get rid of that ghost once and for all." Olivia rolled to her hands and knees, holding back a moan at the sharp stab of pain.

"Olivia! Olivia, are you okay? Someone heard screaming," several voices, both male and female, called from outside the door. Despite the pain, she took a moment to appreciate that she had so many people in her life who genuinely cared about her.

George ran to the door and threw it open. "Livy was dead, but I brought her back to life."

Well, she supposed to George it might have looked like she was dead. The blow had stolen Olivia's breath and knocked her on her backside. She'd lain there stunned for several seconds before George began pounding on her chest. The little girl's retelling of the event was somewhat interesting though.

It reminded Olivia of something Nathan would do. Minimize his involvement if it showed him in a negative light and then overblow his actions to make himself out to be a hero. There was a difference though; he never took responsibility or apologized for his actions the way George had just done. Olivia took that as a good sign.

Jasper, Lexi, and Sophie rushed into the room, followed by a breathless Kitty. "Oh my, Olivia, what happened?" Kitty asked, pressing her hands to her face.

Olivia stayed quiet to see what George would say. The little girl glanced at her and then looked up at Kitty. "I threw the ball, and it hit Livy in the tummy."

Olivia reached for the bedpost to drag herself to her feet. "It was an accident." George didn't mention the ghost, so Olivia decided she'd stay quiet about it too. They'd deal with that later.

Jasper and Sophie helped her to stand. "Maybe we should take you to the clinic and let Finn look you over," Sophie suggested.

"No," Olivia said, more forcefully than was warranted, but she'd been horribly embarrassed yesterday when Sherry called her out for wasting Finn's time. In her own way, Olivia had been as bad as the women making up phantom illnesses just to bask in Finn's masculine beauty. Only *she* hadn't gone to the clinic just to look at him or flirt with him. Obviously, Sherry wouldn't believe her now that she'd caught them kissing in the hall.

And of course, Olivia had admired his Clark Kent good looks when he put on his glasses, his muscular forearm when he took notes, and how wonderful he smelled when he came close…All right, so she wasn't immune to the man but that was not why she'd gone to the clinic.

She'd made the appointments, each and every one, because she had legitimate concerns for George's well-being. Her husky voice for one. It was not unheard of for children to develop tumors on their vocal cords. Olivia had done extensive research into all her complaints. Like the way George stared off into space sometimes. It could have been a sign she had epilepsy. The same with the amount of water she'd been drinking. It could have been a sign George was diabetic, not just thirsty as Sherry had sniped.

Olivia had no intention of going to the Harmony Harbor Clinic ever again. Though she couldn't avoid Finn now that she'd agreed to be his pretend girlfriend. Pretend or not, she needed to call herself something other than his *girlfriend*. For goodness' sake, she was thirty-eight. If she hadn't felt guilty about how much of his time she'd taken up, she would have told him to find someone else.

She glanced at Jasper and Sophie, who were looking at her oddly. She wondered if she'd said any of what she'd been thinking out loud. Then she realized it was probably because she'd just said an abrupt *no*, so she added, "Thank you," and smiled.

Kitty held up her phone. "I've called Kyle. He's on his way."

Well, there wasn't much she could do about that. Dr. Bishop would be better than facing Finn anyway. Obviously, Jasper didn't think so. He gave a disapproving sniff. If Olivia wasn't mistaken, the older man was jealous of Kitty's relationship with Dr. Bishop.

"It's okay, Kitty. You can let Dr. Bishop know Finn is on his way. He dropped everything when he heard *his Liv* had been hurt. In case you guys didn't know, they're an item, a thing, she's his plus one, he's her boy toy, they're—"

"Boyfriend and girlfriend," George said, giving Olivia a little wink.

Olivia gave Lexi a you've-got-to-be-kidding-me look. She'd thrown Olivia under the bus to ensure Jasper stopped trying to fix her up with Finn. It was a good thing Olivia had taken the precaution of telling George the truth. The little girl was fond of Finn, and Olivia didn't want her disappointed when their charade inevitably ended.

Olivia ignored the voice in her head that said she was protecting herself as much as George. With George around to keep her feet firmly rooted in reality, Olivia would be less likely to get caught up in the fantasy that was Finn. Not that she wanted to get caught up in the fantasy, she assured herself. It was going to be embarrassing enough having people refer to him as her boy toy like Lexi had just done.

Kitty beamed. "I'm so pleased to have the rumor confirmed. I'll let Ida know. Poor thing will be disappointed. She was so hoping Finn and Brie would be a match. Oh well, there's always Aidan. He's moving back to town, you know. That reminds me, I have to talk to Chief Benson and see if I can get him to retire too," Kitty said, her head already bent over her phone.

Sophie and Jasper carefully guided Olivia to the side of the canopied bed. "Can I get you anything, Miss Olivia?" Jasper asked.

"Maybe just a glass of water and two aspirin, if you don't mind, Jasper. Thank you."

"Certainly, miss." Just as Jasper took a step away, a bottle of ibuprofen rolled out of the closet.

George gasped, and her eyes rounded. She tore across the room, picked up the bottle, and ran into the bathroom. The toilet flushed. Everyone looked at Olivia for an explanation. "We had a visit from Casper the not-so-friendly ghost," she whispered. "George said he, or she, lives in the closet. So I gather she thought the ibuprofen was contaminated by bad *juju.*"

They heard a husky "Uh-oh," from the bathroom, and then the sound of water splashing onto the floor.

Jasper sighed. "I'll call the plumber."

"Are you going to let me check you over now?" Finn asked once he'd gotten rid of their audience hours later. Since George was getting ready for bed, he thought the time was right. He'd have to lift Liv's shirt to examine her.

"No, I told you I'm fine. You shouldn't have rushed over and left your patients. Patients who actually have something wrong with them. I hope you told Sherry it wasn't me who asked you to come."

"Okay, I get that you're ticked. But I only said that to Lex because she scared the hell out of me. I thought you were seriously hurt, Liv."

"Just FYI, some people would consider broken ribs serious. And I can tell you from very personal experience, they're painful. But that's fine. I'll be okay. You can leave now."

"I'm not leaving until you let me check you over. Come on, how would it look if I don't take care of my girlfriend?" he teased.

"I'm pretty sure everyone thinks I should dump you after how you behaved."

"I've never seen you pout before. It's kind of cute."

Lips pressed together, she refused to look at him as she undid the bottom three buttons of her white blouse. And then, probably because she was ticked, she opened the shirt with a little too much force. The rest of the buttons popped off, leaving him with a perfect view of her lacy white bra cupping what looked to be exceptional breasts and a long length of sun-kissed skin. Except for the fist-sized bruise on her right side. "No," he said when she went to cover up. "You took a good hit, Liv. Let me have a look." He shifted on the bed and, as gently as possible, checked to see if her ribs were…

"Holy Fig Newton, don't do that…Oh," she half laughed, half gasped.

He tried to keep a straight face. "Holy Fig Newton? Now that's one I haven't heard before. I'm almost done. Are you always this ticklish?" he asked, doing his best to keep his eyes off her breasts.

"Yes, oh, ha-ha! Oh, stop, stop now."

George walked over to the bed wearing a pair of pink Hello Kitty pajamas. "Can you make it better?" she asked, her eyes glued to the bruise.

"It's not serious…" Liv glared at him, holding her shirt together. "What I meant to say is Liv's ribs are bruised, so she'll be a little sore. But nothing's broken, and I'll give her something for the pain."

"You should kiss it better," George said.

"You want me to kiss it better?" He looked at Liv's stomach. Her skin had been warm and silky beneath his fingers and definitely kissable.

George nodded.

Liv shook her head. "It's quite all right. I feel better already. Thank you, and thank you for coming. Good night."

"He can't go."

"Why not?" he asked at almost the same time as Liv.

"There's a ghost in the closet," George whispered.

"Oh, right. Okay, how about Finn gets us a vacuum, and then we'll suck the ghost up?"

George shook her head and crawled into the bed. "It walks through walls. It'll get out of the canister. But Finn can stay and protect us." She patted a spot on the mattress between her and Liv.

"I can protect us."

"No, you can't, Livy. You're sore, and I'm little. We need Finn."

"I think George is right. You need me to stay." He toed off his shoes and held out his hand. "You need help getting ready for bed?"

Liv gave him a look and then reluctantly took his hand. "No, I think I can manage." She lowered her voice so only he could hear. "You're leaving once she falls asleep."

"Finn, wake up." Someone shook him. Someone who wore satin shorts and a skimpy top and had warm, silky skin and smelled like hothouse flowers. He buried his face in her soft hair and smoothed his palm over…"Dammit, woman, what was that for?" he said when he got an elbow in the gut.

"Shush. Your hands were where they shouldn't be."

He recognized that voice. "Liv, sorry. I forgot where I was. I didn't hurt you, did I?"

She shook her head, pressed a finger to his lips, and then pointed across the room to the door. He carefully lifted up on his elbow. He saw shadows under the door and leaned down to whisper in her ear, "I don't think it's a ghost."

She curved her hand around his neck to bring his ear to her mouth. "Of course it's not a ghost, but I could have sworn I heard the door open. That's what woke me up."

He grinned at her, enjoying the intimacy of their late-night chat. Which made him realize just how comfortable he'd grown around Liv. He enjoyed being with her, and he thought that should make him more nervous than it did. "I thought I woke you up." He walked his fingers along her bare arm.

She closed her hand over his. "Don't you dare. You'll wake up George." She nudged her head at the door. "Would you mind taking a look?"

He eased off the bed so as not to wake George and padded to the door. Carefully opening it, he looked out in the hall. Simon ran between his legs and into the closet. He closed the door, put on the security lock, and returned to the bed.

"It looks like Simon stays in the closet. Could that be what George saw?"

"Going by where she was aiming the ball, I'd say her ghost is bigger than Simon. You know, she doesn't like him much either. I'll have to shoo him out of the closet before she sees him in the morning."

"How are your ribs? Do you need another pain pill?"

She glanced at him. "You're not worried I'll become addicted?"

Beneath the sarcasm, he thought he heard a hint of hurt. There was something more than bruised ribs going on with her. He wondered if it had anything to do with the favor he'd asked of her. First things first. "Liv, you know as well as I do how careful you have to be with opioids, but I'm not worried you have a drug problem or a problem with alcohol. You already know that though, so what's up with the 'tude? You were pretty prickly with me earlier."

She plucked at the sheet. "After what Sherry said to me yesterday, it hurt when you told Lexi you couldn't just drop everything for something as benign as a sore stomach."

"I didn't say that. But I'm sorry if I hurt your feelings." He slid his arm around her and gently tucked her in beside him. "You weren't the only one Sherry got to yesterday. I should have put a stop to the parade of singles. In my defense, I couldn't write them all off as marriage obsessed. And the thing was, the patients with legitimate complaints…Let's just say they're not what I'm used to. In the Congo I was dealing with life-and-death decisions every day. Not—"

"Neurotic women dragging their stepdaughters to the clinic at the first sign of the sniffles?"

He angled his head to look at her. "I don't think you ever brought her in for the sniffles."

She made a face. "In my defense, I did research her symptoms."

"Remind me to disable Google on your computer," he teased at the same time feeling a rush of tenderness for her. He knew why she overreacted and jumped to the worst-case scenarios. It was natural and no doubt incredibly stressful for her. Was it a little stressful for him too? Even a bit annoying? Sure it was. But despite his teasing, she needed to know that all she had to do was pick up the phone and call him. "Liv—"

She cut him off before he had a chance to tell her. "Don't worry. I won't bother you anymore. Julia put aside a stack of self-help books for me. I don't want to turn George into a hypochondriac." She looked up him. "You don't think I already have, do you?"

"You don't have to worry about George. The kid's resilient. But Liv, for your sake, it might be a good idea if you talked to someone. They could help you—"

"I've been to a therapist before. He wasn't helpful. He—" She gave her head a slight shake and blinked up at the canopy.

"Tell me." She was quiet for so long that he didn't think she was going to answer him.

"He thought, they all thought actually, that my fight to keep Cooper alive had turned into an obsession. That I was doing more harm than good. Nathan and his parents told me I was being selfish to put Cooper through another clinical trial. But even if there was only a small chance it could save his life, I had to take it. I couldn't have lived with myself if I just let him go without a fight. Do you think I was wrong? Do you think I was a horrible mother?"

If Nathan Sutherland wasn't already dead…"No, I think they were wrong. You loved your son. You did what you thought was best, and that's all that matters."

She nodded and then told him about the different trials Cooper had been involved with—everything she'd done to keep her son alive, all the nights she'd spent on the phone talking to doctors and researchers, searching for answers—as though she still needed to defend herself against her in-laws' and husband's accusations.

Finn took her hand. "Liv, look at me. You have nothing to feel guilty about. If Cooper was my son, I would have put him in the clinical trials too."

"Really?"

"Really. And I'm not just saying that to make you feel better. You did everything you possibly could for your son."

Chapter Fifteen

♥

Olivia stood with George in the lane watching as Julia pulled her red Chevrolet Sonic up to the front of the buttercup-yellow Cape Cod on Primrose Lane. With her inky black curls escaping from beneath a red hood that framed her heart-shaped face, Julia gave them an excited wave. George cautiously returned Julia's wave with a small pucker at the bridge of her upturned nose.

"Julia owns Books and Beans and dresses up for children's story hour. It looks like she's Little Red Riding Hood today. We'll stop by this week and buy you some books," Olivia said, while Julia practically skipped toward them with a big wicker basket on her arm.

"Good morning, George and Olivia! You have an absolutely gorgeous day for the big move. Are you excited?" she asked, looking from George to Olivia with a sweetly infectious grin.

"So excited!" Olivia said with fake enthusiasm. She didn't want to dampen Julia's obvious pleasure. She'd worked hard to make this deal happen. The older woman who'd owned the home hadn't planned on selling for another couple of years. Because of that, Olivia estimated that she'd paid twenty thousand dollars above market value. But she couldn't blame Julia for making what Olivia's father would have seen as an unwise investment.

Two weeks before, Olivia would have done whatever it took to seal the deal. Over the past few days with some deep soul searching and a plethora of self-help books, she'd come to realize Finn had turned into her drug of choice. He was her antianxiety pill, a glass of Chardonnay, and a box of chocolates all rolled into one ridiculously gorgeous package.

Just being in his presence soothed her, calmed her. It's why she would run to the clinic at any excuse. She needed him to tell her everything would be okay, and she believed him. Just like she had the night he'd told her he would have made the same choices for Cooper's treatments as she had. He had no idea how much that meant to her. Still, this wasn't healthy for any of them. It was a lot of pressure to put on Finn and, despite his reassurances, she didn't want to turn George into a hypochondriac.

So, for a woman who was doing her best to wean herself off her drug of choice, living next to the clinic was not the ideal situation. It was like a reformed chocoholic living next door to Willy Wonka's chocolate factory. Obviously, she was a glutton for punishment because she still hadn't worked up the nerve to tell him he couldn't be her fake boy toy anymore.

Even harder than that was to know that she should have zero contact with the man for this to work. It was probably a symptom of withdrawal, but the thought made her sad. Because when she wasn't using him as her security blanket, she really liked to be with him, and not only because he was pretty to look at.

"Are you okay?" Julia asked.

"Yes, of course. It's just that I didn't expect to settle in Harmony Harbor." It was true. She'd been hiding out here. She'd never given any thought to what she'd do once the truth came out.

George must have picked up on something because she said, "I like it here. I like this house best. Your other house is too big, and the ghost lives at the manor."

Olivia ruffled George's hair and smiled. "I do too. It's perfect for the two of us."

George gave her the gap-toothed smile she saw more frequently with each passing day. "Three when you and Finn get married."

Olivia waited for the conspiratorial wink. There wasn't one. Fig Newton, George had been spending time with Kitty and the Widows Club. Had she caught matchmakingitis?

"Maybe it's a good thing there's three bedrooms just in case a little Davenport-Gallagher comes along."

Olivia stared at Julia. What was wrong with the woman? She knew that Olivia and Finn were in a fake relationship. They'd been spending a lot of time together during house negotiations, and Olivia had spilled the beans. She trusted Julia. Well, she had up until now.

"I'm thinking of turning the third bedroom into an office." Noting the disappointed expressions on both

George's and Julia's faces, she said, "I'm thirty-eight. I'm too old to have a baby." In case there was room for George to take that the wrong way, she added, "Besides, I have George. I don't need any more children."

As soon as the words were out of her mouth, Olivia worried that she'd overstepped. Isabella hadn't been gone long. She didn't want George to think she was trying to take her mother's place. But she seemed fine and was soon distracted by the sounds of a disturbance on the other side of the lane.

George stepped through a bed of yellow primroses to peek through a knot in the white fence. She drew back, her blue eyes wide. "Sophie's granny and the old doctor are kissing."

Julia and Olivia exchanged a look. From the way Kitty had been talking, she and Dr. Bishop were an item. Olivia joined George at the fence and peeked through the knothole. Julia found one beside them and did the same. The older couple were kissing all right.

Julia sighed and then whispered, "I haven't been kissed like that in forever. I really need to get out more."

Not long ago, Finn had kissed Olivia like that. She should have let herself enjoy it more. There would be no kissing in her future if she followed through with her plan. She took George by the hand and together they jumped over the border of flowers.

When Julia rejoined them in the middle of the lane, George looked up at her and said in a serious little voice, "Maybe no one kisses you because you're pretending to be someone else. You don't want the big bad wolf to kiss you. I think he bites."

Out of the mouths of babes, Olivia thought, but George might have a point. "Well, I for one am glad she's pretending to be Little Red Riding Hood today because I smell something delicious in her basket."

Julia touched George's cheek. "You're a wise little girl. And Olivia has a very good nose. I have some welcome-to-your-new-home presents for you both."

"Julia, you didn't have to do that. We wouldn't have the house without you," Olivia protested as Julia lifted the red linen square from the top of the basket. "Okay, forget I said anything. You can't take your gift back. This is amazing. Isn't it amazing, George?"

George nodded, her eyes saucer-wide. The basket was filled with chocolates, fruits, cupcakes, two bottles of wine, children's books, and adult's books, with not one self-help book in sight.

Olivia raised an eyebrow at Julia. "Umm, why have we never read this at book club?" She held up a paperback. The cover was black and bronze with raised red lettering over half a man's chiseled face and sensuous lips. The book was *Warrior's Kiss* by J. L. Winters.

Julia's creamy white cheeks pinked. "It has a fantasy element, and it's, ah, spicy. I wasn't sure how the Widows Club would feel."

"You did just see how I reacted, didn't you? I think they'd love it. Looks like the perfect beach read to me. Why don't you pick it for next month?"

"I don't know. I can just imagine what Byron would say."

Byron Harte was the only male in their book club. He reported on their monthly meetings in the *Gazette*. "What do you care? It's not as if you wrote…" She looked from

Julia to the book. Julia Landon's fiancé had been Josh Winters. It couldn't be a coincidence. "J. L. Winters is you, isn't it?" She didn't have to lower her voice because George had taken an apple and was checking out the backyard.

"Yes, but please don't say anything to anyone."

"Why? This is so cool." She hugged the book to her chest. "Now I really can't wait to read—"

"Livy!" George screamed from the backyard.

"Oh God." She dropped the book and ran. As she rounded the corner of the house, she saw George standing between a mangy black and gold dog and a bunny with a bloody paw.

"He was trying to eat the bunny, Livy."

Olivia's eyes dropped to the hand George was cradling. "Did he bite you?" she asked, doing her best to keep the fear from her voice. George nodded, and Olivia's knees went weak. *No panicking,* she told herself. She was here now, and that dog wasn't getting anywhere near George again.

"Okay, you just back up real slow, sweetheart," she said quietly, although the dog had barely taken his eyes from his prey. She looked for signs he was rabid, but other than foaming around the mouth—which he wasn't—she didn't know what else to look for. He was obviously starving; his ribs were clearly visible.

The bunny moved, and the dog snarled. Behind her, Julia sucked in a harsh breath. "Julia, hand me two of the vanilla cupcakes." Once Olivia had the cupcakes in hand, she said, "George, I want you to slowly move toward Julia. Once you reach her, both of you run to the clinic."

"No, he'll hurt the bunny. I've gotta get the bunny."

"Shush, boy, good boy," Olivia said, trying to get the snarling dog's attention. She threw a piece of cupcake in the grass beside him. "I promise, I'll get the bunny. Go, go now." She relaxed a little once Julia got George safely away. Now it was just her, a possibly rabid dog, and a bunny she'd promised to save.

Finn was enjoying a nice chat with Mr. Taylor. Sherry's comment last week had made him think about how he was handling his patients, and he'd asked the older man to come in today for a follow-up. There was nothing more that Finn could do for the ninety-four-year-old. Everything that could be done to keep him comfortable was being done, but sometimes just having someone to shoot the breeze with helped. Now that word he and Liv were an item had gotten out, the daily number of patients he had to see had reached a manageable level.

"I appreciate you sorting out my pills for me, Doc. This little doodad should help," the older man said, holding up the plastic pill box dispenser with the days of the week written on each box, along with *a.m.* and *p.m.*

"Anytime, that's what I'm here for, Mr. Taylor. I think—"

He broke off at Sherry yelling, "No, you get back here right now, missy. Just because he's dating…"

"I better check—" Finn began as he heard the sound of running feet and doors opening and closing.

The exam room door banged opened. "Finn, Livy is trying to save the bunny from the dog. He's gonna eat her."

Red Riding Hood and Sherry showed up at the same time, jostling for position in the doorway. "Finn, Olivia…" Julia pushed off her hood and glared at Sherry. "Stop pushing me. Finn, Olivia is trying to rescue a bunny from being eaten by a dog with a cupcake."

He headed for the door. "Call Animal Control, Sherry. You two, show me—"

"I don't believe this. You have patients. You can't just take off whenever your girlfriend…" Sherry made a high-pitched, aggravated sound in her throat and then yelled, "If you step one foot out that door, I quit!"

Finn didn't have time to process what she'd said because, just as he reached the door, he happened to notice George protecting her hand. "Did the dog bite you?"

His grandmother walked into the clinic, carrying what smelled like oatmeal and raisin cookies, a favorite of Doc Bishop's. "Finn, darling, what's going on?"

"I can't talk now, Grams, but can you take George back to an exam room? See if you can talk Sherry into cleaning her hand. She was bitten by a dog."

"Who, Sherry?"

"No, George. If Sherry won't do it, clean George's hand with warm soapy water, and I'll be back to take care of it."

"Don't be silly. Kyle can take care of George. Come on, darling, let's go find Dr. Bishop."

Julia made a small squeak of dismay a second before George said, "He's out in the backyard kissing Sophie's granny."

"What? No, you must be mistaken. When did you—"

"Grams, not now. Where's Liv, Julia?"

"In the backyard next…"

He was out the door before she finished. George, Julia, and his grandmother chasing after him. Grams, who hadn't stopped asking questions, started yelling for Rosa and Kyle. Thankfully, both his brothers and their wives pulled up to the curb in a moving van at the same time the side gate opened and a disheveled Rosa and Doc Bishop appeared.

Any thoughts of his grandmother were wiped from his head when he reached the backyard. Liv was crouched down talking to the dog with a cupcake in her hand when the animal lunged, sending her sprawling on her back.

"He's killing my Livy! He's killing my Livy!" George cried hysterically.

Finn stood in Olivia's backyard giving her the evil eye while she tried to sweet talk Animal Control into letting her keep the dog. The dog that had tried to eat her, the rabbit, and George. "Crazy-ass woman."

"Tell me you could resist George if she looked at you with her big blue eyes and begged you not to let them put the dog down," Liam said, nodding to where George sat in the grass with the dog's head on her lap and the bandaged bunny in the box beside her. "And who says they're going to put the dog down in front of a kid any-way?"

"I'm sure the guy thought she'd be cheering since said kid had been bitten by the dog and was crying hysteri-cally not ten minutes before that the dog was going to eat her Livy. But no, she's as crazy as the woman she lives with."

Liam patted his shoulder. "You got a scare when you

saw the dog knock Olivia down and pounce on top of her, didn't you?"

Scare? He'd been terrified he wouldn't get to her in time. "Ah, yeah, wouldn't you? I thought she was crying, not laughing. And I thought he was eating her face, not licking it."

"Guess the saying *The quickest way to a man's heart is through his stomach* holds true for dogs too."

"Nice, real nice. Does someone want to tell me why I got stuck breaking up Grams and Rosa while you two stand here shooting the breeze?" Griff asked.

"You're the oldest. Besides, what would you rather have dealt with, Rosa and Grams or a rabid dog?" Finn said.

"Are you seriously even asking me that? I'd deal with ten rabid dogs over those two. I'll tell you one thing though. I sure wouldn't want to be in Doc Bishop's shoes right now." The door of the clinic slammed, and the three of them turned. "Or yours from the looks of it."

Kerry and Sherry marched down the lane and smashed papers into Finn's chest. "We quit!"

"Look, ladies, I understand it's been kind of crazy at the clinic since I started, but I'm sure we can—"

They both crossed their arms. "If you want us to stay, your girlfriend has to go," Sherry said.

Now that he was off the market, the two of them had become increasingly dissatisfied at work.

Liv glanced over her shoulder, met his eyes, and nodded. He couldn't believe it. She was seriously trying to break up with him now? He shook his head. She nodded more emphatically and mouthed *yes*. "No!" Okay, so that actually came out of his mouth.

Kerry and Sherry, presuming he was responding to them, stormed off. But not without getting in the last word. "Good luck trying to replace us!"

Liv looked at him like he was a recalcitrant schoolboy. She shook the guy from Animal Control's hand and walked over to pat the dog and hug George.

"She bribed you, didn't she?" Finn said to the twenty-something guy.

The tips of his ears pinked as he fast-walked to his truck. "I really can't talk to you about it, sir."

"How much?" Finn called after him.

"Oh, no money was exchanged." The kid turned to smile at someone behind Finn. "See you next Monday at nine, Olivia. Thanks."

Griff glanced from Liv, who was no longer smiling, to Finn's unsmiling face. "Okay, maybe we should give Olivia and Finn some time alone, go help the girls unpack the kitchen stuff," Griff said to Liam.

"You go ahead. I'd rather stay out here and watch—"

Griff grabbed Liam by the arm and dragged him to the back door, waving George into the house.

Finn crossed his arms. "Okay, let me get this straight. You were breaking up with me so you could date *him*? The guy barely looks like he's out of puberty."

"Don't be ridiculous. First, we're not really dating so I have no reason to break up with you, and second, we're not going on a date. He follows the manor on Facebook and liked one of my garden DIY projects Sophie featured. He asked if I'd mind helping him with his."

"You expect me to believe that a woman who is a gazillionaire does DIY projects?"

"I'm not a gazillionaire, and yes, I enjoy doing DIY projects. I don't know why you have such a skewed perception of people with money, but it's annoying. So please keep your opinions to yourself. And just FYI, I'm no longer your girlfriend." She turned to walk off.

"All right, I'm sorry for being a jerk. Please don't break up with me. If not for me, for the sake of the good people of Harmony Harbor. My patients today were actually there to see me as a doctor and not marriage material. Just give me a couple more weeks."

"Fine. But only because Sherry and Kerry indirectly quit because of me."

"Thank you. We have an audience." He nodded at the side window. "I should probably kiss you." There wasn't anyone in the window; he just wanted an excuse to kiss her. He tried to convince himself the reason for that wasn't because he'd been scared when he saw what he thought was the dog eating her face. Or that it had been the kind of fear you feel for someone who means a lot to you.

"No, you shouldn't."

"You don't have to be so cross." He grinned when she gave him a look, and then he and put his arm around her. "So when did you plan on telling me we were going to be next-door neighbors?"

She lifted a shoulder. "I didn't know if the owner would accept the offer. Everything happened really fast once she did."

For some reason, Liv didn't seem too happy about that. He wasn't sure if it was because she now owned a home in Harmony Harbor or if it had something to do with her proximity to him. Which wouldn't bode well for his next question if that was the case. "Since you admit you are indirectly responsible for the clinic being short one receptionist and a nurse, any chance you'd play secretary for me?"

Chapter Sixteen

♥

Olivia crossed the schoolyard to pick up George. It was the last day before summer vacation began. Olivia spotted her on the playground. With her enthusiastic, pint-sized audience cheering her on from below, George, in her lemon-yellow shorts set, traversed the top of the monkey bars with the grace and ease of an experienced tightrope walker. Still, the sight of her up there caused Olivia's heart to double bump against her ribs. Which, she had to admit, was an improvement over what her reaction would have been two weeks before. Thank goodness for self-help books.

George spotted her. "Livy, watch!" She did a backflip off the bars, landing perfectly in the sand on her two feet, red lights flashing on her sneakers. Her friends cheered while Olivia worked on breathing again.

Ms. Ryan, George's teacher, turned as Olivia approached. "I swear, I don't know how you don't have gray hair."

"I do. You just can't see it amongst the blond." Olivia smiled. She liked George's teacher. The thirtysomething redhead was passionate about her job and genuinely liked kids. She'd been a big help to Olivia and George over the past few weeks. As they'd discovered, George hadn't gone to school and was behind the other children.

When George had first started at Harmony Harbor Elementary, there had been talk about holding her back next year. If Ms. Ryan and the principal felt it was in George's best interest to do so, then they'd have to make the best of it. But she and George had been spending time after school and on weekends working on her numbers and letters, so Olivia was hopeful she'd pass. Mostly because there'd been so much change in George's life, and she'd started to bond with the kids in her class.

Ms. Ryan laughed. "Good thing you weren't here five minutes ago. She was walking up there on her hands. Have you thought about putting her in gymnastics?"

"She's registered for the fall, but there's a couple of summer camps I'm looking into." That was the nice thing about working as an events planner for the manor; George could come with Olivia to Greystone or she could work from home. But until she found someone to replace Sherry and Kerry, she was working nine to five at the clinic. Olivia thought she'd have to bring George with her tomorrow, but last night a teenager who lived on Primrose Lane had arrived at her door to offer to babysit courtesy of Julia.

Olivia glanced at Ms. Ryan. "Are you going to make me wait until I open her report card?"

"You passed. Good job, Mom." Ms. Ryan's laughter trailed off. "Olivia, did I say something wrong?"

"No, not all." She surreptitiously wiped at the corner of her eye. "Don't mind me. It's just that I didn't expect to be someone's mom again. Until now, I didn't realize I was. But I guess I am," she said with a watery smile as she looked at George chasing after her friends, her face glowing with laughter and good health.

Somehow, despite all odds, George had worked her way into Olivia's heart. Death—her son's and husband's—had changed Olivia. She wasn't the same woman she'd been before the loss. But slowly, thanks to her friends, George, and even Finn, she was realizing that was neither good or bad, it just was. Despite the pain that would lessen but never fully go away, she could still have a good life.

"You're doing a great job, Olivia. She's adjusting nicely. I've noticed a big difference since you moved into the house on Primrose Lane. And it doesn't hurt that Mia's so popular and has taken George under her wing. By the way, I hear congratulations are in order."

"Do you mean about the Michaelson wedding? It was quite the coup to—"

"No, silly, your wedding." Ms. Ryan grimaced at what was probably Olivia's stunned expression. "Sorry, was it supposed to be a secret? Mia and George have been telling everyone they're going to be cousins."

The only way they'd be cousins was if Olivia married Finn. Moving next door had been bad enough, but working with Finn—or how he liked to put it, *for* him—was bad on a whole other level of bad. And not just because it put ideas in George's head. Olivia had had a few of her own this past week.

She'd suspected Finn would have a wonderful bedside

manner, be warm and genial with his patients, and now she had firsthand proof he was that and more. The man was an exceptional doctor. He had a gift, a sixth sense. He'd accurately diagnosed every patient before the results of their tests had even come in to prove him right. But for all the man had going for him, Finn Gallagher was surprisingly humble.

The direction of her thoughts annoyed her. He was not perfect. For one, he was the most disorganized man she had ever met. He was messy too. And he…was gorgeous and sweet and looked so good in his button-down shirts with the sleeves rolled up to show his muscular forearms and the glasses that made him…Fig Newton, she needed to find him a nurse and receptionist ASAP.

"Olivia, is everything okay?"

"Yes, yes, sorry. When you mentioned the wedding, I started to think about the one at the manor next weekend. Hazard of the job, I guess. George, sweetheart, it's time to leave." She waved her over.

"So congratulations aren't in order then?"

"No, Finn and I are just good friends. You know what kids are like."

"Oh, but I thought I heard you were dating."

She laughed like it was all a big misunderstanding. Given George and Mia's schoolyard gossip, it was past time Olivia and Finn ended their fake relationship. It was confusing for George…and for Olivia. "You know what small towns are like. A hotbed of rumor and innuendo."

"I have some girlfriends who will be very happy to hear that," George's teacher said, and then her smile turned upside down. "Did I say something wrong?"

"No, why? Did I make a face?" *Of course, you did,* she berated herself, *and that jealous twinge you got in your chest is just more proof you need to stop spending so much time with the man.* Ms. Ryan gave her an odd look. Olivia had to say something. "If I did, it's because we've just gotten patient waiting times under control, and I'd hate to see us go back to standing room only. You know, Finn bikes every morning on the boardwalk. Maybe they could catch up with him there."

"Thanks for the tip. I'll let them know." She turned to smile at George. "Thanks again for my cupcake flowerpot, George. I hope you have a wonderful summer. I look forward to seeing you in September."

George swallowed hard and gave Ms. Ryan a wobbly smile. "'Kay. But if I practice my reading and numbers over the summer, can you maybe put me in my friend's class later?"

Olivia crouched in front of her and adjusted the backpack straps on her shoulders. "You passed, George. All that hard work you did paid off."

She blinked her big blue eyes and then threw her arms around Olivia and held on tight. It was the first time George had hugged her, and Olivia found herself blinking her eyes too. She'd forgotten how it felt to be held by a child. Olivia cleared her throat before she became undone in the middle of the playground. "Okay, now say goodbye to your friends." It took a few minutes before they were able to get away. Other parents had arrived and numbers were exchanged and playdates arranged.

"What do you say we have a celebration?" Olivia

asked, taking George's hand as they crossed the road to where she'd parked the Range Rover.

"After we've finished work?"

George had been coming back to the clinic with her after school. Finn had set up a small table and chair for her in his office. Before speaking with Ms. Ryan, Olivia had every intention of going back to work. "No, today's special. We can't work on special days. We have to celebrate."

The clinic closed at five, and Dr. Bishop was in today too. Surely between the two of them, they could handle things. Besides, it wasn't as if she was on the payroll. She didn't owe Finn an explanation if she decided to leave early. She pulled out her phone and texted him that she wouldn't be back and then opened the rear door for George. "Where would you like to go?"

"Aren't we going home to get Pete, Wolfie, and Finn?" George asked, because apparently, it wasn't a party without the bunny, dog, and Olivia's fake boyfriend. Another sign that she had to get a handle on this sooner rather than later.

"I thought we'd go to the manor. Maybe we'll have a picnic on the beach."

Finn had been in a bad mood since three o'clock yesterday afternoon. By six that evening, he was ticked the hell off, and his mood hadn't improved. In fact, it had gotten worse. He'd been out for his early morning bike ride, enjoying the sun on his face, the sound of the waves hitting the rugged shoreline below him, and the birds flitting from the leafy branches overhanging the path when he was accosted by two women in two separate incidents.

Okay, so maybe *accosted* was too strong a word. Propositioned was more of an apt description. And why did the women think he was fair game and know where to find him? Because his girlfriend—his fake girlfriend, his erstwhile receptionist, his supposed friend, and sort-of neighbor—had ratted him out.

And she'd been the one to put him in a bad mood to begin with. A mood that had steadily grown into a giant-sized ticked-off ball in his chest since she'd blown off work as easily as she'd blown off his repeated texts. And then, to make matters worse, he'd discovered she and George had gone to the manor and celebrated George's passing kindergarten without him.

He banged into the clinic, letting the door slam behind him. So much for his dramatic entrance. It didn't faze Liv. She didn't even look up from the computer screen. He saw the reason why as he crossed the empty waiting room. She had earbuds in. He stopped in front of the reception desk and stood there waiting for her to acknowledge him.

While he did, he kind of checked her out. It was a bad habit that had started last week, and no matter how hard he tried, he couldn't seem to shake it. Her don't-mess-with-me vibe got to him every time.

She'd taken to wearing her hair pulled back in a sleek knot that went with the classy sleeveless tops she wore tucked into her straight-cut skirts that she paired with sexy heels. Today she wore siren red from head to toe.

She glanced up and gave him a raised-eyebrow look.

He gave her one of his own and crossed his arms. Mostly to stop himself from reaching over and shoving his hands into her hair and messing it up, and then maybe he'd take her face and kiss the red lipstick right off her mouth. Whoa, where the hell had that come from?

She took out her earbuds. "What's up with you?" she asked in a snotty, Ivy League voice.

Oh, she did not just go there. "What's up with me?" He parked his ass on the edge of her desk. "I think the better question would be, what's up with you?"

She lifted a shoulder and returned her gaze to the computer screen. "If you're cross because I didn't come back to work yesterday, I'm sorry, but I had things to do. Besides, this isn't a paid position. I'm doing this out of the goodness of my heart."

"Even volunteers honor their commitment, Liv."

"That's not fair."

"Neither was not responding to my texts. I was worried about you, and then I found out you were celebrating George passing kindergarten without me." He realized then he wasn't just ticked off; he was hurt. Liv wasn't the only one invested in the kid. He'd been helping George with her homework too.

"Who told you?"

"You were at the manor. Did you really think I wouldn't find out?"

She trapped her bottom lip between her teeth, releasing it to say, "I'm sorry. If it makes you feel better, George was disappointed you weren't there."

"But you weren't. You didn't want me there." Dammit, he sounded like a ten-year-old who'd just been told Santa wasn't real.

"No, and trust me, when I tell you why, you'll be glad

I didn't. George and Mia have been telling people we're getting married." She gave him a look. "See, I knew exactly how you'd react. But don't worry, I took care of it."

She read him right. Just the mention of his name and marriage in the same sentence caused him to break out in a cold sweat.

"Let me guess, you were the one who told everyone we broke up. And then you decided to share my morning routine, on what, Instagram? Is there anything else you shared? You're not giving out my cell number, are you?"

"No, and all I did was mention your morning ride to George's teacher. For your benefit, I might add. I did it so you wouldn't be inundated at the clinic. And I'm pretty sure I found you a receptionist and nurse."

"When you make up your mind, you don't fool around, do you?" He was disappointed. He wouldn't share that with Liv, but he was. He'd gotten used to seeing her every day. He liked having her around. He might tell himself it was because the woman had scary-good organizational skills and had organized not only the clinic, but him too. It was more than that, and he knew it.

He'd been fooling himself. He was developing feelings for Liv that went way beyond friendship. But Liv had George and a crapload of baggage. He wasn't ready for any of it. He might want Liv in his bed, but he didn't want everything else that went along with having her there. She'd want more from him. Way more than he was able or wanted to give.

"I have my job at the manor and George. Add in the time I spend here, and it's a lot to juggle."

He stood up. "You're right, and both Doc Bishop and I

appreciated you filling in, Liv. You've been a big help. Is George in my office?"

"No, she's with Emma at the beach. Her new babysitter," she said when he cocked his head at the unfamiliar name, and then added, "Emma's a certified lifeguard trainer."

He didn't know if she told him that to reassure herself or him. Surprisingly, it did make him feel better. Liv wasn't the only one who had become important to him; so had George. Liv was right. The sooner they put a stop to this, the better. For all of them. Someone was going to get hurt.

"Okay, you should go join them or take a couple of hours to yourself. You've earned it, Liv." He held out his hand. "Thanks again for everything."

"You want me to leave?" She looked around the reception area. "But I have Ava and Dorothy coming for an interview at ten."

"Our Ava? To work here? But I thought she loved being head chef at the manor. And who's Dorothy?"

"Dorothy's a retired nurse. She's dating Ava's dad and was best friends with her mother. They're very close and would work well together. And while Ava loves working at the manor, she used to love nursing. She's been doing a couple of classes online." Liv shrugged self-consciously. "I thought working here would be a good opportunity for her to decide what she wants to do."

"It's a great idea. Doc Bishop's coming in shortly, so he can handle the interviews. Looks like we're all set thanks to you." He stuck out his hand again, practically forcing the words through his clenched teeth. He was even more irritated than when he woke up this morning. "I guess I'll see you around."

"Oh, I…So this is it? This is goodbye?" she said, slowly coming to her feet. His fingers closed around hers. She looked up at him, her whiskey-colored eyes shiny.

"Yeah, it's probably for the best." Jesus, what was going on with him? His throat was so tight it was a struggle just to get the words out. Who was he kidding? He didn't want to end this now. He didn't want to picture what his days would be like without Liv in them. And that was it, the reason he had to say goodbye before he did something he'd regret like fall in love with her. "I'm only here for a couple more months, Liv. It's not fair to George, and—"

She blinked and then nodded, tugging on her hand to get him to let go. He hadn't realized he was holding on so tightly. "Of course, you're right. Thank you for everything you've done for me and George. You've been a good friend, a truly lovely friend," she said, and stretched up on her toes to kiss his cheek.

He swore in his head, fighting the urge to take her in his arms and say to hell with it. To hell with— The door to the clinic opened. Finn frowned. It was Stanley.

Liv slowly lowered on her heels and turned to face the older man. "Stanley, what are you doing here? What's wrong?"

"I'm sorry, Livy. I tried to talk them out of it."

"Who? You tried to talk who out of what?"

"Celeste and Walter are suing for custody of George."

Chapter Seventeen

♥

Olivia stared at Stanley. It was like her body couldn't process two emotional hits at once. She couldn't say goodbye to Finn and lose George at the same time. It wasn't fair. Was this how her life was destined to be from now on? She'd find her happy only to have it ripped away?

If it was, she didn't know if she could take it. Maybe it would have been better for both her and George if she'd just walked away from her in-laws' house that day. Maybe it would have been better if she'd stayed far, far away from the man who just then placed a warm and heavy hand on her shoulder, giving it a comforting squeeze.

"Don't worry, we won't let them take George from you, Liv. You're her legal guardian. Nathan's parents don't have a leg to stand on, do they, Stanley?"

She heard the words uttered in Finn's deep voice, but she wasn't able to completely process them because her mind was currently occupied with her thoughts of moments before. They'd been like random puzzle pieces but were now melding together to form a clear image in her mind. In the center of the picture were George's and Finn's smiling faces.

They were Olivia's happy. No, that wasn't quite right. They were the reason she was able to find it again. They gave her back the ability to feel and know happiness. For so long, life had played out for her in black and white, but now shades of warm, vibrant color seeped into her days.

How had she not noticed that the smiles and laughter that she'd faked for so long, that she'd felt only on the surface, had become real and bone deep? She'd never expected to be truly happy again. To have those moments of pure joy that set your heart and mind on fire.

Maybe that's why she hadn't recognized the emotion for what it was. It had been creeping up on her slowly, quietly. Like George, Finn had found a way past the thick, ropy scars that had developed with each battle Cooper had lost until they fused together to form a hard, impenetrable shell. So now that she knew how she felt about them both, what was she going to do?

She squared her shoulders and lifted her chin. Finn grinned. "George is rubbing off on you." He kneaded her shoulder before he looked at Stanley and repeated his earlier question. "The Sutherlands don't have a chance, do they?"

Dr. Bishop walked into the clinic, turning to hold the door open for two patients.

"It might be best if we have some privacy," Stanley said.

"Take Stan to Doc Bishop's office, Liv. I'll be right there." As though Finn registered her surprise that he planned to sit in on their meeting, he said, "You're not dealing with this on your own. If I hadn't called Nathan's parents, this wouldn't have happened. You have to let me help."

"I want you to be part of this, Finn. But not because I blame you. You have nothing to feel guilty about. You were doing what you thought was best for me and George. Celeste and Walter would have eventually found out she was here."

"Thank you," he said, looking relieved, and then he went to speak to Dr. Bishop.

"I'm sorry, Livy. I should have known how far Celeste and Walter would go once word got out about George," Stanley said as they made their way down the hall.

"I haven't told anyone from my past about George, Stanley. I'm sure Anna wouldn't have said—"

"When you stopped by your house that day with George, the Langstons and Ashbys saw you. They remarked on how much the little girl you were with looked like Nathan and Cooper. Obviously, Celeste assumed you were moving back to Boston, and word would eventually get out, so she gave her version of the story before you did."

Olivia sighed and opened the door to Dr. Bishop's office. Large with a sitting area, it was a better choice than Finn's cramped, messy space. No matter how often Olivia organized it, he managed to turn it upside down within a day. "I should have known what was behind this. They don't want George. This is all about saving face, presenting themselves as the dutiful grandparents."

"There is that, but there's more to it, Livy," Stanley said as she closed the door. He took a seat in the plaid armchair.

She noted his ill-at-ease expression as she sat across from him on the small, brown leather couch. "Ah, I see, so they believe I'm unstable, an unfit parent," she said, repeating words they'd said to her in the past.

If they were going to talk about this, she was glad Finn wasn't there. She didn't want him to know what she'd done. It would change how he looked at her. She didn't want to see the judgment in his eyes.

Stanley made an uncomfortable sound in his throat. "I'm afraid so. But there were mitigating circumstances, and it was two years ago, so I don't think we have to worry about that if you decide to fight them on this, Livy."

"What do you mean, if I decide to fight them? Of course I plan to, Stanley. George is mine."

There was a touch of self-satisfaction in the smile that creased his face. "Does that mean Nathan and I are no longer the horrible, callous bastards you thought we were last month?"

"Just because I've come to love George doesn't mean you two somehow become the heroes of the story, Stanley." Though she wouldn't admit it to him, she no longer saw them as the villains either. It seemed that lately she was looking at the world and the people in it through a different set of lenses. Ones that weren't colored by pain and sorrow.

"You don't know how happy I am that she's found a place in your heart, Livy. I know Nathan would feel the same."

"And Isabella, I wonder how she would feel?" Olivia had been making a concerted effort to regularly mention both of George's parents to her.

She wanted the little girl to feel comfortable talking about them. And she never wanted George to feel that she was trying to replace them, especially her mother. Just as Olivia made sure George never felt like she was using her as a replacement for Cooper. As though George was using her own psychological ploys against Olivia, she brought up Cooper almost daily. Olivia found that the pain wasn't so all encompassing when she talked about him now. It seemed she and George were healing together.

Stanley shrugged. "I didn't know Isabella that well. Her family were missionaries from France. She grew up in Kenya. Loved the land and its people. It's something she and Nathan…" He trailed off, looking uncomfortable.

"It's all right, Stanley. Having George around has made me examine my relationship with Nathan more closely. Cooper getting sick changed us. Or maybe not so much changed us as showed us who we really were, how we perceived things, how we dealt with things. We hadn't worked for a long time. We didn't function as a team," she said at the same time Finn opened the door and walked in, looking as ridiculously handsome as he always did in the light-blue shirt that matched his beautiful eyes.

Yes, thanks to this ridiculously handsome and wonderful man, Olivia realized just what had been missing in her marriage. She'd fallen out of love with Nathan years before, and now she'd fallen in love with a man who shared many of the same passions as her late husband. And lest she forget, he was younger than her. But right now, none of that mattered. That painful almost-goodbye just before Stanley arrived canceled out her doubts.

"You okay?" Finn asked.

Despite a riot of feelings exploding inside her, she nodded as he sat beside her on the couch. Admitting her feelings for Finn, even if it was just to herself, made her feel awkward and uncomfortable around him now. As if he could see through her calm and collected act, her friendship mask, and would hightail it back out the door. Because if ever there was a man who was afraid to open his heart and his arms to love, to let himself be loved, it was the man sitting beside her. She could commiserate. It wasn't that long ago she'd felt exactly the same.

"Liv doesn't have anything to worry about, does she?" he asked Stanley.

"I wish I could tell you that was the case, but I can't. I'm sorry. As soon as I found out what they were up to, I went over and tried to talk them out of it. I almost had Walter convinced, but you know Celeste. She's determined, Livy. She hired a private investigator."

Stunned, Olivia stared at Stanley. Less than five minutes ago, he'd said he wasn't worried about them bringing up the past. The only thing he'd seemed concerned about was whether or not she wanted George. And now it sounded like he thought her in-laws could win. "You think they have a chance to take her from me, don't you?"

"I'm afraid so. They have connections, and Celeste isn't averse to pulling strings."

As Stanley well knew, Olivia didn't like throwing the

weight of her name and money around. But that was the old Olivia. No, she thought at the anxious jitter in her stomach, she was still that Olivia. Except when it came to protecting her family. "In this instance, I'm not averse to pulling a few strings myself. Something you may want to share with Celeste and Walter. Because as you all know, my connections are not merely judges in family court." She wouldn't be so crass as to mention that she had the money to wage a battle they couldn't hope to win.

"I know, and so do they. Or I should say, Walter does. But Celeste has always chosen to believe that you don't have the money or influence that you do. And that's on you, Livy. You've always downplayed your fortune and connections."

Beside her, she felt Finn stiffen and was reminded of previous conversations where he didn't hide his antipathy toward people with money. She glanced at him. "I'm not going to apologize that I have money and that I'm willing to use it to keep George. You weren't there, Finn. You didn't see how Celeste treated her. Walter wasn't much better. It would—"

"Relax. You don't have to convince me. If you've got the connections and the money, I'm all for you using them to keep George."

"You are? But when we talked—"

"I've got a patient in five minutes. So how about you let Stan tell us what we have to do beyond throwing your money and influence around to ensure George stays with you?"

She found herself moving closer, smiling up at him. "Good idea."

He angled his head like he sometimes did when he

thought George was doing something cute and returned her smile.

Her heart skipped a beat when she met his gaze, and then did the same when she turned to Stanley and saw the expression on his face, but for an entirely different reason. "You don't think that will be enough, do you? My goodness, Stanley, what can the private investigator have on me that's so terrible?"

"Plenty, I'm afraid." Stanley leaned over to pull a file from his briefcase. He handed the papers to her. "You live in a small town, Livy. People like to talk. And while I understand your friend, the doc here, was just looking out for you and George, a judge might not see it that way." He handed Olivia what looked like an incident report. The black marks against her were listed in bold print.

"I didn't say you were unstable or unfit, Liv," said Finn, who was reading over her shoulder.

"That may be, but you are Livy's and George's primary physician. Your opinion carries weight. By suggesting Celeste and Walter assume custody of George, you indicated you had grave concerns for her well-being."

"Come on, that's not—"

Stanley raised his hand to interrupt Finn's heated denial. "Let me finish." He looked at Olivia. "By willingly giving George up, even if you didn't go through with it in the end, they'll insinuate that you didn't want or believe you could care for her either."

"If you read farther down, you'll see you have more problems. Like a member of the staff at Greystone Manor saying you regularly leave George unattended while you work and that she was attacked by swans and nearly drowned in the pond. That same employee related another incident at the manor one night where you were heard yelling at George, and she refused to go back inside the manor with you. Both incidents were substantiated by multiple witnesses."

"Now wait a minute," Finn began to protest while Olivia sat there stunned. It felt like the people she thought of as friends were turning against her, but what bothered her even more was that while the report was manipulating the facts, the incidents in question had happened, and she was beginning to question her own abilities as a mother.

"Look, Finn, I understand it's hard not to defend Livy, but just let me get everything on the table first, and then we'll go incident by—"

"There's more?" Olivia asked at almost the same time as Finn.

"I'm afraid so," Stanley said. "You have an enemy at the manor, Livy, and I'd suggest you find out who it is before they damage your reputation further. This same employee said you have a drinking problem. Again, when questioned, this was substantiated by two other witnesses who attended the Mother's Day brunch. Also, questions were raised about your judgment because you've taken into your home a dog that was to be put down for biting George and attacking you."

"It wasn't like that. Wolfie…" She bowed her head when Stanley sighed. "All right, I'm sorry. It's just hard to sit here and listen to all the awful things people are saying behind my back."

"I know. We're just about finished. And I'm sorry, but this is probably going to be harder for you to hear."

Finn put his arm around her. "Come on, this is ridiculous. Liv is a good mother. If you think my opinion carries weight, put me on the stand."

"For everyone's sake, I hope we can keep this out of court. But if it comes to that, believe me, Livy's lawyer will put you on the stand. Because, Finn, it's statements made by you and confirmed by witnesses that provide the best evidence against her. You accused her of being an addict and because of those concerns took her car keys from her. There was also an incident on the docks that was covered up by you, Finn, as well as an incident in front of the clinic where the officer of record withdrew a charge of reckless driving because you pulled in a favor."

Olivia brought a hand to her mouth as the evidence against her piled up. "I'm going to lose her. I'm really going to lose her," she said, afraid she was going to be sick.

"No, no, you're not. They can't force me to testify against you. I'm your doctor."

"You weren't acting in the capacity of her doctor at the time of the incident on the dock or at the time of the traffic violation. The complainant at the manor also attests that you can validate the dog, the drinking, and the pond incidents, and you weren't there as Livy's doctor."

Stanley winced when Finn shot him a furious glare. "I guess you can plead the Fifth or marry her. You can't be forced to testify against your spouse. Actually, that's not a bad idea. It would play in Livy's favor. You're well respected, both a hero and a doctor. And you would provide a father figure for George as well as a stabilizing influence on Livy."

"Stanley, that's a..." She was going to say a completely ludicrous idea, but as she thought about all the evidence piling up against her, she worried that Celeste and Walter would win. But it wasn't only about Olivia losing George. She couldn't stand the thought of George living in a house where she wouldn't receive an iota of the love and attention she deserved.

She glanced at Finn, who was as still as a statue. It was like he thought if he didn't move, they'd forget he was there. His face looked like it had been chiseled out of granite, all except the muscle flexing in his jaw.

She swallowed hard. This wasn't going to be easy. An hour before she'd come to the realization that she loved the man, it would have been easier. Because now her heart was invested in his answer. "Finn…"

He briefly closed his eyes and took a deep breath before shifting to face her. "Liv, don't—"

"Please, Finn. I just need to convince a judge to let me keep her. A year should be enough. It's not like I'm expecting it to be a real marriage. Just real enough to convince everyone that it is."

"Liv, I can't. I—"

"I'll give you a million dollars."

Chapter Eighteen

♥

Liv had been serious. If Finn agreed to marry her and stay with her for eighteen months—Stanley had stuck his legal-eagle nose in and added the extra six—she'd pay him one million dollars. One million dollars to do with as he pleased. Finn had walked out of Dr. Bishop's office to see his patient with the promise that he'd think about it.

For the last five days, that was all he'd done. Think about Liv and George. Had he thought about the million dollars? No, because that just ticked him off. Liv had put him in a difficult position.

Whether she blamed him or not, she could foreseeably lose George because of him. And didn't that just slay him. Most women would have rightly laid into him for the part he played, but not Liv. She was kind and sweet and understanding, and she couldn't lose George. She'd already lost too much. And George? She was thriving now, happy and settled. He couldn't handle the thought of her being taken from Liv. What it would do to the both of them.

So where did that leave him? Stuck in the middle of yes and a definite no. He didn't want to stay in Harmony Harbor for more than a year. He wanted to go back and work in the Congo where what he did actually made a difference. Some of his patients at the clinic might argue that he was making a difference in their lives, but it wasn't the same. He needed the adrenaline rush, the adventure, to test his skills, his boundaries. He needed to be a hero like his brothers.

What he didn't need was to be married to a woman he admired and respected and lusted after…He released an irritated breath at the thought. It wasn't like he lusted after her all the time. Just every once in a while. Like when she wore her classy, expensive clothes and her hair in the sleek knot and her lips were painted cherry red and…Fine, he pretty much lusted after her all the time. Now that he thought about it, that was way worse. Because as much as like could turn to love, so could lust. He both liked and lusted after Liv.

Then there was George. He couldn't play the role of adoptive father to a little girl he could easily love. And there was his answer. He was avoiding Liv because he didn't want to tell her he couldn't do it. Whatever else she needed from him, he'd do. He'd lie on the stand. He'd give her what money he had. But he would not, could not, put himself in the position where he might fall in love with Olivia Davenport.

"Hey, son, glad you made it," said his dad, who was

leaning against Ladder Engine 1 when Finn walked up beside him on Main Street.

"I didn't have a choice. Griff and Liam are whipped. They threatened to carry me in the parade if I didn't come." The parade was part of an annual festival in Harmony Harbor honoring the patron saint of fishermen, St. Peter. It was put on by the Italian American fishing community and had been going strong for more than eighty years.

His dad grinned. "You were safe. They got tagged to carry St. Peter."

Finn debated walking back to the house. Everyone in town would be out, which meant his chances of running into Liv and George were high. Then again, the festival was a big deal, drawing crowds from all over, as evidenced by the hordes of people packed onto the sidewalks, while others gathered on porches that were decorated with bunches of green, white, and red balloons.

As the Navy band led the parade down Main Street to St. Peter's Park at the waterfront, kids with painted faces waved miniature Italian and American flags and laughed at the groups of men dressed in colorful and flamboyant costumes following behind. The costume wearers would be competing in the greasy pole contest later that day. A telephone pole was greased and suspended on a platform over the water with a flag at the end. It was a competition Finn had won in the past.

Sophie's brother Marco, Liam's best friend and a fellow firefighter, walked by wearing an Italian cap and shorts. "Good luck, Marco! Do the house proud," his dad called out.

"You got it, Chief," Marco yelled as he blew kisses to the women in the crowd. He stopped to pose for selfies with a couple of his female fans and called to Finn, "Shame you couldn't compete this year, Doc."

"Careful, I'll be the one looking after you when you do the splits on the pole," Finn shouted back, chuckling when his brother's best friend paled and then gave him the finger.

"Here comes Rosa." His father grimaced as Marco's grandmother, wearing a pink checkered dress and apron, advanced on her grandson. "Looks like he's getting into trouble for giving you the finger."

"Serves him right. Someone should talk to her about cuffing him on the back of the head like that though."

"Marco does, for all the good it does him. Now there's someone I'd like to see Rosa cuff." His father scowled at Doc Bishop, who'd just rounded the corner of South Shore Road. "He's started up the feud again between your grandmother and Rosa. Chief Benson called me yesterday. He's days away from charging both Rosa and your grandmother for public mischief if they don't stop calling in complaints against each other. Your grandmother even tried it on me. Told me I needed to go to DiRossi's deli and put out a fire. She said it was electrical so to just go in there with the hoses blasting."

"Not that I want to get in the middle of this or start something else, but you know that Dorothy and Ava started working at the clinic, right?"

"Yeah, Griff told me about it. I think it's great. Everything's working out, isn't it?"

"Yeah, Ava's doing great. And Doc Bishop's over the moon. He has a crush on Dorothy. He follows her around like a lovesick puppy."

"Dorothy's dating Ava's dad, isn't she?"

"Yeah, but who knows, right? Last I heard you were dating Maggie Stewart." His dad made a face like he didn't know who Finn was talking about. "The beautiful artist who owns the gallery on Main Street, Impressions. The one you spent every day with for two months sitting for your naked painting."

"A lot you know. I wasn't naked in the painting." His father looked away. "Here come your brothers."

Finn hadn't seen the painting, but he'd heard all about it. Maggie had incorporated his mother and sister in the portrait. Not long afterward, things went south between Maggie and his dad.

Finn should be the last one teasing his old man. He was doing the same thing. He wouldn't marry Liv, even if it was in name only, because he was afraid he'd fall in love with her. But unlike his dad and Maggie, he hadn't gone on a real date with Liv. He kind of regretted that now. Which was stupid. It was already hard enough to let her go, and all they'd ever done was kiss a couple of times. As though thinking about her and the last kiss they shared was powerful enough to conjure her out of thin air, his eyes met hers across the street.

She wore a white summer dress, her hair held back from her face by a pair of red-framed sunglasses. Her nose and cheeks were pink, her delicate shoulders red. He fought the urge to cross the road and give her hell for not putting on sunscreen. Then he remembered he'd have to say something if he did. He'd have to tell her he couldn't marry her. So instead he pointed to the sun and her shoulders. She smiled and held up a wide-brimmed white hat with a red floral band.

He found himself scowling at her. Why couldn't the woman be a bitch? He'd been avoiding her for days, and she was smiling at him. She frowned and then gave him a look like, *Oh my God, what is your problem? All I did was smile at you.* And that was another thing that ticked him off—she called him on his jerky behavior, and he liked it.

She lifted a hand, waving at someone with a warm smile on her pretty face. Finn glanced at his father, who was waving at Liv with a grin on his. "God, I'm good."

"Careful, old man. You stick your nose in my business, and I might stick mine in yours," he said, relieved to finally see his brothers approaching carrying the life-sized statue of St. Peter. At least they'd take his father's mind off Liv.

"Your brothers look happy, don't they? Did you ever think you'd see Griff with a son? All the heartbreak he and Ava suffered, and now look at them. Does a body good, it does."

"Are you channeling GG or something?"

"What are you talking about? Can't a father be happy for his sons?"

"Yeah, sure, Dad." Finn waved at his brothers and their wives. He hadn't really registered George wasn't with Liv until he saw her in the parade with Mia. The two girls were swinging their joined hands and waving to the crowd.

George spotted him and broke free. "I missed you." She hugged his legs, and he ruffled her hair. He smiled down at the sweet, upturned face, unable to block an image of her grandparents taking her from Liv. "Come on."

She grabbed him by the hand and tried to drag him onto the road and into the parade.

His throat was so tight that he was surprised he managed to speak. "I've gotta put Miller out." He saw the pinch of disappointment on her face. "How about I catch up with you at the carnival tonight? I'll win you a teddy bear."

"Promise?" she said, as though unsure he would keep his word.

She wouldn't be wrong. He'd been thinking that, after a day of parades, boat races, and the greasy pole competition, Liv would take her home early. He still held out hope and said, "You bet. Now get back in the parade before they leave you behind."

He didn't meet his father's eyes. He could tell how his dad thought things would go by the way he was rocking on his heels and whistling.

Finn was lying on the couch in the living room on Breakwater Way, just about to congratulate himself on earning another reprieve, when a text came in at 8:00 p.m. from Liam. *Get your ass in gear, bro. We're waiting for you at the spinning roller coaster.*

He thought about pretending he was sleeping or in the shower and didn't see the text, but he wouldn't put it past his brothers to come and get him. He grabbed a sweatshirt on the way out the door. It didn't matter that it had been in the low eighties today; the carnival was set up along the waterfront and it was cool at night.

He said hello to the couple next door as he made his way down the street. They were new to the neighborhood. The mom was carrying a giant-size pink dog and pushing a sleeping baby in a stroller while the dad carried what looked to be an exhausted three-year-old. Finn wondered if he could still get lucky. Maybe Liv was on her way home with an exhausted five-year-old. Then he reminded himself it was George. A kid who was a little bit like he used to be.

As he turned the corner, he stopped for a minute to take it all in. The bright lights from the rides that made it look like it was the middle of the day, the smells of cotton candy and corn dogs competing with the briny ocean air. The whirr of the rides, the ding of the bells, the laughter and chatter of happy people having fun.

It brought back memories of all the times he'd gone to the carnival as a kid, as a teenager, as an adult. He looked over and saw the circle of white lights in the distance. Sometimes, like now, the memories were as beautiful as they were painful. He remembered bringing his little sister Riley along with him and his girlfriend and his mom and dad taking a ride on the Ferris wheel.

He walked down the hill and spotted what had to be the spinning roller coaster. Sure enough, he caught sight of his dad taking a turn with George and Mia. Liam was in a car with Lex, and Griff and Ava were in another one. Sophie and Liv stood at the railing waving to the girls.

"The old man looks a little green. Ferris wheel is more his speed," Finn said as he walked toward them.

"Hey, stranger, we haven't seen you in a while," Sophie said, giving him a playful whack.

He rubbed his arm. "You're as bad as your grandmother. How did Marco do in the greasy pole competition?" he asked, hoping to avoid talking about what he had to talk about for a little longer.

"I can't believe there's anyone in Harmony Harbor who doesn't know he won. He's threatening to rent a billboard. But his win isn't the biggest news. Tell him, Olivia."

He looked down at her. "Hi," he said, his voice gruff, probably because the lights were gleaming in her hair and sparkling in her eyes and making him think of things he shouldn't think about.

"Hi," she said back, her smile different than it used to be or maybe he was just imagining things.

Sophie frowned. "Umm, is something wrong with you two? You're looking at each other as if it's the first time you've met."

Great. He didn't know what Sophie was picking up on, but whatever it was, his brothers and father would zero in on it like Miller on a bone. He had to get this over with before they got off the ride. Before he had to look at George and know she might end up being taken from Liv because he wasn't brave enough to take on his fears and let them in his life.

Because as much as he'd convinced himself that a judge would see through the lies, some might believe the case against Liv because she had money, and they'd put themselves in her shoes, a woman who'd been lied to and betrayed and now was raising the child her late husband had with another woman. They wouldn't know that Liv had more compassion and kindness and love to give than half the people on the planet.

"Liv, I gotta talk to you for a minute. Sophie, can you guys look after George? We won't be long." Pulling Liv after him, he didn't give either woman a chance to refuse.

"Finn, what's going on? Slow down." Liv tugged on his hand.

"Sorry," he apologized to her and the man he almost walked into. He needed to find somewhere less crowded, somewhere more private to talk to her. He looked over at the ring of lights. "You wanna go for a ride with me?"

She followed the direction of his gaze. "The Ferris wheel?" She made a face when he nodded. "I don't like heights."

"I promise I won't rock the car. You'll see, it'll be worth it. The view's amazing." Especially now that the sun was starting to set and the sky was streaked with purple and crimson.

"Okay," she said reluctantly.

He led her to the thankfully short line. From where he was standing, he could see his brothers disembarking from the spinning roller coaster. All he'd need was for his family to join them on the Ferris wheel. He helped her into the car. Once they were strapped in, it moved as the operator loaded another couple on.

Finn caught her shiver and peeled off his sweatshirt. "Here you go. It'll be cool when we get to the top."

"I'm beginning to think this was a really bad idea," she said, looking up, he assumed, at the car at the top.

She wasn't alone. He was beginning to think this was a really bad idea for an entirely different reason. "What big news did Sophie want you to tell me about?" He hoped he hadn't just walked into that, but he didn't want to tell Liv he couldn't take her up on her proposition until the ride was going.

She buried her face in her hands and shook her head.

"I still can't believe she did it. I mean, I've seen her in action, so I'm not surprised she could do it. I'm just surprised she got away from me. But you know how fast she is. She—"

He removed her hands from her face. "I can hardly make out what you're saying. You're babbling."

"We were out on one of the boats in the harbor watching the greasy pole competition."

He thought about what Sophie said and the context in which she'd said it. "She didn't."

"She did. The third guy had fallen off the pole, and they were fishing him out of the water, and George says, 'That's easy. Why do they keep falling off?'

"I told her why, and the next thing I know, she's gone. I panicked, and we all started looking for her. Two of the men who'd fallen off the pole dove in to search the water, and then all of a sudden, we hear people yelling, and she's climbing on the platform. She scoots past the next man in line and shimmies her way down the greased pole to grab the flag. She set a record not only for the youngest to win but also for the fastest time."

He started to laugh. "Poor Marco, she ruined his big moment."

"It's not funny."

"Trust me, it's hilarious. I bet Liam loved it."

"Yes, but you're not getting the point. People, cell phones, the moment has been recorded for posterity, and—"

He got it now. "For any judge to see." The Ferris wheel was now turning, making its lazy circles, and they were at the top. It was oddly quiet, the sounds of the carnival and of the ocean fading, everything below them looking small.

"You're right, the view's worth it," Liv said, looking out over the town with a crescent moon hanging above the copper-topped roof of the town hall and the clock tower.

There was a light wind off the ocean and it gently rocked the car. She shivered a little, and he put his arm around her, tucking her in beside him. "You put on sunscreen," he said as a way of distracting her. The scent of coconuts was doing more than distracting him.

"I thought I'd better after the look you gave me at the parade." She had her head on his shoulder, tipping it back to look at him. "Is that the only reason you were mad at me?" She asked the question quietly, as if she knew.

And looking into her big, whiskey-colored eyes that reflected the light from the moon and the stars, he knew he had to do whatever it took to make sure she didn't lose George, even if the thought of what he stood to lose terrified him. "I should have known the moment you dragged me down the hill with you that you were gonna end up being a pain in my ass, Sweet Cheeks."

Her eyes went wide, and she drew back to whisper, "You're going to marry me?"

"No, you're gonna marry me."

She laughed and threw herself in his arms and kissed him. But he'd never know just how good that kiss would have been because she launched herself at him with such force that the car started rocking, and she started screaming, and down below he heard his family cheering, including a little girl with a husky voice.

Chapter Nineteen

♥

The next afternoon, Olivia leaned against the kitchen counter in her home on Primrose Lane, going over the guest list. She'd begun making lists practically from the moment Finn gave her the wonderful news last night. She had lists on her phone, lists of wedding ideas, and pictures of them on her iPad, and at last count, she'd written fifty-five names in the pretty spiral notebook she'd found tucked away in her nightstand. The gold cursive inscription on the pink cover fit perfectly with how she was feeling: *You Can Never Have Too Much Happy*.

Today she was filled with happy. George was happy too. Olivia smiled as she watched the little girl creating her own illustrated list with glitter pens at the table. Her fears, the almost paralyzing panic that she might lose George, had dissolved the moment Finn agreed to her proposal. She just wished she could have been a tad less enthusiastic in displaying her gratitude. If she had been, she might have gotten to enjoy his kiss.

Any hope of a repeat was lost when, in the middle of accepting the family's congratulations under the lights of the Ferris wheel, Finn's dad received a text from Aidan. He'd arrived at the family home on Breakwater Way. From what she'd picked up of the conversation, Aidan wasn't in a happy place. So the Gallagher boys, along with Colin, went back to their childhood home, and the women and kids went their separate ways.

Unlike Liam and Griffin and their significant others, Finn did not kiss Olivia good night. His father did. He sweetly kissed her cheek and welcomed her and George into the family. It was a lovely moment that was only slightly ruined by the look of utter panic that came over Finn's face.

They hadn't discussed it, but she imagined the panic was due to Finn keeping the true reason for their marriage from his family. He wouldn't want them to get attached to the idea only to have their marriage end eighteen months from now. She understood how he felt, and there was a part of her that thought they should come clean. At least to his family.

But the more people who knew, the more likely that Celeste's private investigator would find out. And in the end, Olivia was hoping it would be a moot point. The last thing she had expected was to fall in love with Finn. In her mind, it followed that there was a possibility that he might come to see her as more than a friend. After living together as man and wife for more than a year, surely he'd get over his commitment issues.

The thought made her nervous. She'd sent him a text advising him of the date of their nuptials and hadn't received a response. Ava had told her he was booked solid at the clinic today, so maybe he had to work late. Olivia had texted after five because she didn't want him to worry she was going to become one of those annoying wives who couldn't go a couple of hours without hearing from her man.

But there was a teensy problem with that. She needed to hear from him ASAP because she'd basically booked the priest, flowers, cake, and DJ before realizing she maybe should have consulted him about his plans for next week.

There was a loud knock, more of a banging really, and Wolfie barked and scrambled from under the table. In his excitement to greet the person at the door, he nearly knocked George off her chair.

"I'll get it," George yelled, jumping off the chair and racing after the dog.

From the amount of noise they were making, someone could legitimately believe there were hordes of children and dogs in the not-so-large Cape Cod on Primrose Lane. She wondered if that's why Finn's expression as he entered the house was a cross between ticked off and shell-shocked.

He looked down at George and Wolfie jumping excitedly at his feet and then slowly raised his gaze to Olivia. "Are you flipping insane?"

She wasn't quite sure how to respond and shrugged. "They're just happy to see…" Oh no, excited and happy weren't a good combination. "George, hurry, put Wolfie out—"

Finn's eyebrows drew inward in confusion as he looked down. Then his head shot up, and he jumped back. "Your dog just peed on me!"

She pressed her lips together, trying to stifle an inappropriate laugh, chalking it up to nerves. They weren't married yet, and Finn could back out at any time. "Sorry, he's a little excitable," she said, struggling to keep the laughter at bay.

"You think this is funny?" he said in an exasperated voice. "Why do I even bother to ask? Of course you do, because I'm marrying a loon toon."

"I am not a loon toon," she said, no longer amused.

"Livy's not a loon toon. You're a cranky pants," George said as she wrapped her fingers around Wolfie's collar.

Finn grimaced and crouched down. "I'm sorry. I shouldn't have called Liv a loon toon or insane. I've had a bad day, and"—he narrowed his eyes at Olivia—"I've just found out I'm getting married in…a week."

She mentally filled in his pause with his favorite curse word and winced. "I'm sorry for the short notice, but I can explain."

"Yeah, you can. After I've had a shower and changed." He gingerly removed his shoes and carried them to the front step.

"Oh, sure, okay. I can have supper ready for when you come back if you'd like." She didn't cook, but surely she could have something delivered in time.

He came back inside loaded down with two suitcases and a duffel bag. "I'm not going anywhere. My dad kicked me out. Apparently, he can handle only one son at a time. And since we're getting married in a flipping week, I figured—"

She stared at him. "You're moving in?"

He sighed and put down his bags. "George, would you mind giving me a minute and taking Wolfie outside?"

"Will you play catch with me after?"

"Yeah, but right now I'd like to get out of these pants, so…" He raised his eyebrows.

George cheered, let go of the dog's collar, and ran off calling, "Wolfie!"

As the two of them raced outside, Olivia opened the cupboard under the sink to grab a roll of paper towels, floor cleaner, and two garbage bags. She turned at the same time Finn dropped his chinos. He wore a pair of blue boxers that matched his eyes. Heat flooded her cheeks because there was a part of her that was definitely not thinking about his eyes.

She was wondering how those strong, long, and muscular legs would feel pressed against hers in bed. What he'd look like without the boxers when he walked into the shower. She thought perhaps she'd made an appreciative sound in her throat because Finn said tersely, "If you're done checking me out, I could use one of those bags."

She was about to give him a testy, "You don't have to be so cross," but a glance at his expression stopped her from uttering the remark. She thought perhaps he was embarrassed by his scars.

He had no reason to be. There were three long, purple scars crisscrossing his upper thigh, and two thick, shiny pink scars on his knee, though there may have been more on his calves and shins but they were concealed by a sprinkling of dark hair. He wore a pair of black socks, so she couldn't see the scar on his foot and ankle.

"If you're grumpy because you're self-conscious of your injuries, you're being ridiculous. Most women find scars attractive. They're evidence of your heroics."

He rolled his eyes and then motioned for the garbage bag. "I wasn't a hero. I was just doing my job."

"Right, because running into a hail of bullets to rescue the sick and injured is part of your job description," she said as she laid out the paper towels on the wide-planked hardwood floor. "I…" She trailed off because looking up at him from where she was crouched at his feet gave her a clear view up the leg of his boxers.

"Liv."

She heard the amusement in his voice and bent her head. "Mmm-hmm," she said as she returned to cleaning the floor.

"Look at me."

"I'm a little busy right now. Why don't you go have a shower?"

"That's the plan. I just wanted to know where your bedroom is so I can unpack my bags. Thought you might want to show me which drawers are mine."

"My bedroom?" she asked, a flutter of nerves causing her voice to come out as a squeak and her cheeks to heat.

"Yeah, where else would I sleep?"

"Um. Okay. I just thought…" She threw the paper towels in the garbage bag, stood without looking at him, and murmured, "I'll be with you in a minute. My room's up the stairs on the right. Leave something for me to take up."

She didn't have to look at him to know her offer offended him. She couldn't say that bothered her since she was pretty sure he was amusing himself at her expense. The bedroom thing had to be payback for springing the wedding on him so fast.

After washing her hands, she looked out the open kitchen window to check on George. She'd made a maze for Peter the rabbit and was putting him through his paces. Wolfie lay nearby watching.

Olivia glanced at the entrance before heading upstairs. Of course, Finn hadn't left her anything to take up. She walked into her bedroom and froze. He'd dumped the entire contents of his suitcases and duffel bag on the white down comforter of her king-size bed, half of his clothing landing on the floor. He wasn't here for more than five minutes, and he'd already turned her bedroom into a disaster zone.

The shower was running in her en suite, conjuring an image of him standing naked behind the steamy glass enclosure, his sleek, muscular body covered in soap bubbles. A breathy sigh escaped from between her parted lips as she imagined running her fingers over his broad shoulders, down his…Finn walked out of the bathroom. Naked.

A choking sound sputtered from her mouth. "You're naked. You're naked in my bedroom. You just walked into my bedroom naked."

"You're gonna have to learn to share, Sweet Cheeks. It's my bedroom now too." He gave her one of his annoyingly sexy grins and sauntered past her to…

She slapped a hand over her eyes as he bent to retrieve something from his suitcase by the closet.

"Should have known you'd be a prude, Princess." Apparently teasing her was his entertainment for the day.

A draft of cool air brushed past her, indicating he'd just walked by. She lowered her hand in time to get a full-frontal view as he closed the bathroom door with a cocky grin on his face. It wasn't lost on her that he had *a lot* to be cocky about, but still…

She marched to the door and knocked. "It's all right. You don't need to open the door. I just want to…" He opened the door. She kept her eyes glued on the small scar at the corner of his mouth. "I understand you're upset I went ahead and booked everything for the wedding without consulting you, but I—"

"I don't care about the cake, the decorations, the music, who's on the guest list, or if it's outside or inside. All I care—"

She'd planned enough weddings to realize that the majority of grooms just wanted to know when they were supposed to show up. So Finn's reaction shouldn't hurt her feelings. She should just be grateful that he'd agreed to marry her. "Oh, I see. Well, I won't bother you any more about the details. If you can meet me on the beach in front of the manor at five to eight next Monday, I'd appreciate it. Thank you," she said, turning to walk away.

A large hand closed around her wrist. "Liv, I just wasn't expecting all of this or for it to be happening so fast. I thought we'd get married at the courthouse next month or something."

She turned and dropped her eyes to his feet, relieved to note on the way down that he'd draped a towel around his waist. Though she couldn't deny that his bare chest was a sight to behold. His feet were big and beautiful too.

"I know it's not a real wedding, but I think for it to be believable we have to put some effort into it. Besides that, I'm a wedding planner and have a reputation to uphold. And you've never been married before. I wanted to make it nice." She took a steadying breath and lifted her eyes. "But if it's too much for you, I can tone it down. It's really not formal or fussy. I just wanted to make it a fun night for everyone. We'll be celebrating July Fourth as much as our wedding. I can't change the date though. The judge will already be suspicious. I think it'll be more believable if we get married quickly. And we had a cancellation at the manor."

He smiled. It wasn't cocky or sexy or annoying; it was blindly beautiful and warm. "Okay, July Fourth at five to eight on the beach at the manor. Now I'm going to grab a shower, and then you can show me your plans while we're having dinner. How's that sound?"

"Great." She smiled. "Thank you, Finn. I understand how much you hate the idea of getting married, even if it's a pretend wedding. I appreciate the sacrifice you're making for me and George. I truly am grateful."

He curved his hand around her neck and bent to touch his lips to hers. "You know, Princess, I'm beginning to think the fringe benefits might just outweigh the sacrifice."

Finn was having more fun at Liv's expense than he should, but she was such an easy target. "So what you're telling me is that, in one week, I'm marrying a woman who refuses to cook?"

Liv pursed her lips like she was thinking it over and then nodded.

"I don't know; that might be a deal breaker for me, Liv," he lied as he dug into the smoked salmon pasta primavera she'd ordered from DiRossi's. He didn't care if they cooked their dinners or bought them. If all their meals were as good as this one, he'd be a very happy man.

She glanced out the window to where George was playing with one of the neighborhood kids. While Finn had been putting away his clothes, George had eaten. It took him longer than he expected because Liv had cleaned out two drawers of her lingerie and sleepwear and had yet to put them away, which was distracting. Because while the woman's outerwear was boringly classy and expensive, her lingerie and sleepwear was outrageously sexy and expensive.

It also took him longer than expected because Liv, on the pretense she was checking on him, was really making sure everything was neatly folded in his drawers. Since all he'd ever done is throw his clothes in a drawer, folding time added up.

"It's not like you're not getting anything out of the deal, Finn. A million dollars is a substantial amount of money. If you invest it well—"

He slowly lowered his fork from his mouth. "You were serious about the money?"

"I don't joke about money, Finn."

He laughed, pointing his fork at her. "You are seriously hot when you talk like that. Nothing sexier in my book than a smart and capable woman. You sound like you're the head of a Fortune 500 company."

"I leave that to my cousins. I manage the foundation."

"What kind of foundation?" He knew about the company, but he hadn't heard about the foundation.

"We have several charitable organizations under the Davenport umbrella. U.S. and multinational. The one I've been most involved with is Helping Hands."

He stared at her. He'd heard of Helping Hands. "They've got a great reputation, Liv. They're very well respected. I've actually worked with a couple of docs who were sponsored by your organization. They're first class." He sat back in the chair. "Just how involved are you?"

"I'm the CEO."

"Well, I'll be damned, Sweet Cheeks. You are one hell of an impressive woman." And she continued to impress him the more she talked about her vision for the foundation. Her belief that the programs should be initiated by the people of the community for their community. She felt too many NGOs—not-for-profit organizations—went in with their own mandates. They didn't listen to the people they were there to help. Helping Hands' mandate was to give the people a voice and a hand up.

Finn shared some of his concerns about what he'd seen over the years and the changes he thought that could be implemented to make programs work better.

"You know, I could use someone with your experience and expertise at Helping Hands. Even if you just wanted to sit on the board. I think you'd find it interesting."

"I appreciate the offer, Liv, but I need to be on the front line."

"Right, of course. But you won't be going back before our eighteen months are over, will you?"

He could tell by the slight lift of her chin that she was ready to fight him on this. And he didn't want to fight with her. He wanted to enjoy the night and listen to her talk some more about how she was going to save the world. Which is why he said, "I'm not going anywhere until this is settled with George, okay? However long that takes, I'm here for you. For both of you."

She nodded, but he could tell it wasn't the answer she wanted.

"And, Liv, just so we're clear, I won't be taking the million dollars. I'm doing this because I want to. You and George are important to me."

Chapter Twenty

♥

Colleen scowled at the members of the Widows Club who were fastening the pink honeycomb wedding bells above the chair of honor in the sitting room. They were ruining her plans to keep Olivia away from the manor. Colleen dialed back her temper. She was being too hard on them. They had no idea what they were up against.

Nothing seemed to be going her way these days. Especially when it came to her dealings with Jasper. He refused to comply with her plans. He was moping about and ignoring her. She was almost positive it had something to do with Kitty being all in a tizzy over Kyle Bishop.

It's too bad she couldn't sit her daughter-in-law down and let her have a look at the book because it wasn't only the women of Harmony Harbor who had secrets. Kyle had a few of his own. But that was neither here nor there with the evil one still roaming free.

The spot where her heart should be clenched at the thought of the woman out to get her great-grandson's true love.

Colleen had been happier than a clam in a tide pool when Olivia announced she'd bought the house on Primrose Lane and started working at the clinic. It wasn't a problem when she was working on the spa either because she held her meetings with Sophie and the girls on-site at the cottages. But now with the big wedding only days away, she'd be back at the manor. And of course, the Widows Club had to go sticking their noses in things and ensuring she was here today for the shower they had planned.

Colleen walked over to Gabriel's pram and gave it a jiggle. He looked at her with his big blue eyes, giving her a gummy smile. "You aren't afraid of your GG, are you, my little man?"

Unlike George, who would be the answer to Colleen's prayers if only the child could get over her fears. It's too bad she didn't see Colleen as a tree or a big wave or a greasy pole she had to conquer. She'd heard all about the child's latest antics.

"Where would you like the punch, Miss Kitty?" an ingratiating voice asked her daughter-in-law.

Oh, she was good, that one, worming her way into the hearts and minds of Colleen's loved ones and spreading her poison. She'd seen Ivy talking to that man who'd come nosing around about Olivia. A private investigator, she'd since heard. But Ivy had been canny with how she'd gone about it and no one was the wiser.

"On your head," Colleen muttered in response to Ivy's

question about the punch. She walked determinedly through the woman. Ivy shuddered, spilling the punch on the floor.

Kitty and her friends fussed over the maid and the mess. "There's no need to work yourself up. It was just an accident," Kitty said, patting the distraught woman's shoulder.

Ivy had missed her calling. She should have been an actress.

Simon chose that moment to pad into the sitting room. He took one look at Ivy and was about to retreat when she spotted him. Pointing an accusatory finger in his direction, she said, "It was the cat's fault. He got underfoot and tripped me up. He does it all the time. If you're not careful, one of these days he'll kill someone and then their loved ones will sue and put the manor out of business for good. If it were me, I'd get rid of him before that happens."

Unfortunately for Simon's sake, every time Colleen pulled one of her tricks on Ivy, he was there.

"Do you really think so?" Kitty asked, clutching the neck of her light-blue shirtdress.

"Go, Simon, scoot before Ivy paints you as the murderous villain that she is. Hide in the tunnels till we banish her from the manor. Hurry!" Colleen cried when Evelyn Harte agreed with Ivy and advanced on Simon.

"Come here, you," Evelyn said, reaching for Simon. She just missed getting a hold of his tail.

Colleen relaxed when he'd gotten safely away. Though she truly was on her own now. She turned to see what lies the villainous Ivy was feeding Kitty and Ida while Evelyn went chasing after Simon. It wouldn't do her any good. Once he got to the basement, she'd never find him in the tunnels.

Ivy was whining about how she couldn't go back to the kitchen and tell Helga she'd spilled the punch. Supposedly Helga had it in for her. It wouldn't surprise Colleen if that were true. Helga could be a cantankerous old woman. She was also a canny judge of character.

Ida and Kitty, kindly old women that they were, did the girl's bidding and headed to the kitchen with the half-empty punch bowl.

There was a sly smile on Ivy's face as she watched them go, and then she turned with a laugh that made Colleen's hair stand on end. Walking to the chair of honor, Ivy reached out to tug on a bell but her cell phone rang.

She took it out of her pocket. "Nice of you to finally return my calls, Paige. Anything new to report? Well, isn't that a shame. No delays with the spa at Greystone. Yes, I could. I could indeed set them back a bit. What's it worth to you?" The woman listened with a smile twitching her lips.

Colleen would bet her last dollar Ivy was playing Paige. If she was smart, Paige would have nothing to do with this one.

"Sorry, not enough money for me to bother. By the way, Paige, thanks for passing along your boss's number. We had an interesting chat. Seems he's unhappy with your progress and won't be renewing your contract. He's awarding it to me." She lifted her eyes to the ceiling and released a breath through her nose before saying, "Stop yelling or you won't be able to hear my offer. I'll give you twenty-five percent. Better than nothing, don't you think? Whatever. Get back to me."

She disconnected and sucked her teeth. "They say there's one born every day. You won't be getting a dime from me, Townsend. But that's not something you need to know before I've gotten away with what I have planned. It's a toss-up where the blame will land. Either you or the cat." She tugged on the bell. "Ding dong, the bride is gone."

At the sound of women's voices approaching the sitting room, she stuck her phone in her pocket and turned with a pleasant smile, all evidence of crazy gone from her face. She scared the bejaysus out of Colleen. Mia and George ran into the room, followed by the shower guests.

Colleen walked backward through the wall behind the chair of honor. She didn't want to frighten George and ruin the party, but with Ivy's little ditty playing in her head, Colleen wouldn't be more than a foot away from Olivia.

George screamed and pointed at the chair.

Bejaysus, she hadn't been fast enough.

The women converged on George, trying to comfort her. The circle grew around the child as the rest of the Widows Club arrived, including Rosa, who turned her back on Kitty when she returned with a new bowl of punch.

Jesus, Mary, and Joseph, they'd better not start anything now. They had enough to deal with. George's crying had upset baby Gabriel. The child had a pair of lungs on him like his father.

Mia sidled up to the wall. "It's you, isn't it, GG? I

wasn't sure because George kept talking about someone called bad *juju*. Don't worry, I'll talk to her."

"You do that, child. And you do that fast because the clock's ticking down."

Someone noticed Olivia walking into the room. "Surprise! Surprise! Oh, surprise!" was repeated at various octaves.

Olivia offered her thanks with her typical grace and warm smile but it was obvious she was concerned about George.

"She saw the evil spirit again," Kitty said, twisting the neck of her shirtdress between her fingers.

"I see an evil spirit every time I look at you. Do you hear me scream? No," Rosa said to Kitty, and then stuck her Roman nose in the air, her dark curls bouncing around her shoulders as she turned back to George. "Cara, don't cry. I'll get rid of the ghost, *sì*?"

"Stop butting your big nose into my family's affairs," Kitty said, and then her eyes went wide as though she couldn't believe she'd said it. Under any other circumstances, Colleen would have given her daughter-in-law a celebratory pat on the back for standing up to Rosa, but not now. She was worried what form Rosa's payback would take, and knowing Rosa, she wouldn't take the jab lying down.

There was a communal gasp as the Widows Club reacted to what Kitty said. Everyone stepped back as though giving them room. With the glow of anticipation on their bloodthirsty faces, Colleen was surprised the call to "fight, fight, fight," hadn't gone out.

"What? It's true. Finn is my grandson, not Rosa's. He's

marrying Olivia, so George is my step-great-grandchild, not hers. You've always been after what's mine since we were in grade school, and I've had it, I tell you. I have had it!" Kitty stomped her foot and then pressed her fingers to her mouth.

Colleen breathed a sigh of relief when Jasper appeared beside her daughter-in-law. He'd make sure she didn't say anything more. He wouldn't allow the whole sordid mess to come out. They all had too much to lose, Jasper included.

"Miss Kitty, you're overwrought. Perhaps a cup of tea. Ladies, please take a seat, and I'll have the rest of the refreshments brought in." He imperiously snapped his fingers at Ivy, gesturing toward the kitchen while narrowing his eyes at Rosa.

"Eh, don't give me that look, bag of bones. She—"

He made a point of holding Rosa's gaze while giving Olivia a slight bow. "Enjoy your shower, Miss Olivia. If there's anything you need—"

"Thank you, Jasper. If you don't mind, I need, um, some garlic…and a cross. Yes, that should work." Olivia rubbed George's back. "We're going to get rid of your ghost once and for all."

"Quite," Jasper said, holding back a smile.

"You won't find it amusing if they actually get rid of me, now, will you, laddie?" Colleen said.

Ava, Sophie, Kitty, Rosa, and half the other women in the room held up crosses. Jasper nodded. "I'll be back with the garlic."

Colleen heard the chuckle in his voice.

Julia waved her hand to get the women's attention.

"I'm not an expert, but unless your ghost is a vampire, I don't think garlic and crosses will work."

"The cross, it will work. But we need a priest. Someone call Father O'Malley," Rosa said.

"They might just be the literal death of me after all," Colleen murmured.

Thirty minutes later, she remained in the wall despite an entire sitting room of women and children banishing her from the manor with their garlic and crosses. Holding hands, they formed a circle, and Father O'Malley politely asked the ghost to leave. The temptation to jump in the middle of the circle and shout *boo* was almost too much to resist. But for George's sake, she did.

Finally, the shower got under way. George and Mia sat beside the chair of honor, placing the bows from the gifts on a paper plate. Still stuck in the wall, Colleen picked up on their conversation. It sounded like Mia was telling George about her.

Ten minutes later, when Colleen took a careful peek out of the wall, she prayed that was so. Because Ivy, who was ostensibly standing close by to refill drinks and clear away the garbage, cocked her head when George said, "Finn and Livy don't think I know my daddy's parents are trying to take me away, but I do."

Mia patted her hand. "It's okay. We won't let them. You're going to be a Gallagher just like me."

George nodded. "Livy and Finn won't let them take me. I heard them talking when I was playing hide-and-seek with my friend. Livy was going to give Finn a million dollars to marry her, but he said he doesn't want the money because he cares about me and Livy."

"My mommy and daddy said we don't have to worry about the manor anymore. I bet that's because Finn's going to tell Olivia to give the million dollars to Greystone instead of him."

"We're rich, we're rich," the two of them said, laughing and throwing the wrapping paper in the air.

Ivy's face darkened, and she slunk over to the refreshment table. Colleen couldn't see what she was doing. For Olivia's sake, she had to take the risk. She walked out of the wall. George froze, and her eyes rounded. Colleen pressed a finger to her lips. The little girl nodded and tugged on Mia's hand.

They got up. George towed Mia along behind her as she followed Colleen, who pointed to Ivy. She mouthed *bad juju* and made devil ears behind her own head.

Sensing she had an audience, Ivy palmed the vial she had in her hand. "Would you girls like something to drink?" she asked, smiling sweetly at Mia and George.

Colleen shook her head and pointed at her palm and then Ivy's.

"No, the ghost says you're bad." George lifted her chin. "What's in your hand? What are you doing?"

The woman's face changed. "You need help, kid. You're seeing things. If you know what's good for you, you'll get lost. Now. The two of you. Scat."

Colleen walked behind Ivy and placed her hands around her neck and mouthed *Tell her to go.*

"She has her hands around your neck. She's going to kill you if you don't leave Greystone. She's going to murder you dead."

Ivy blanched and touched her neck. Glancing from

side to side, she slowly backed away and then turned and ran.

Colleen smiled at George and gave her a thumbs-up. They made a good team. With the little girl's help, she should be able to keep Olivia safe until she got Jasper to read the book.

The last thing Finn expected to be doing the night before he said *I do* was making wedding keepsakes. It looked like his brothers felt the same. The three of them were giving him the stink eye.

"What? I didn't ask you to come. Your wives volunteered you," he said to Liam and Griff, and then looked at Aidan. "And Dad volunteered you because you're being a moody pain in the ass."

His brother's black hair was long and shaggy, and he'd yet to shave his beard from his last undercover assignment. He looked as dangerous as the biker he'd been impersonating. There'd been changes in his brother's behavior that made Finn wonder if Aidan was more like the man he'd been pretending to be than the one he remembered.

Finn took a swallow of his beer and thought better of complaining. It was a nice night. The air was warm and fragrant, the sounds of crickets and the blinks of fireflies flitting about the yard reminding him of long-ago summer nights. The four of them were together, and that hadn't happened in a while.

They were sitting around the kick-ass fire table Liv had picked out while they drank beer and made up the blue glass bottle keepsakes. It wasn't like it was a difficult job;

all they had to do was add sand, a shell, and a message
from him and Liv, tie some fancy ribbon called *raffia*, and
add a *thank you* charm. But there were a lot of bottles and
their hands were big and the work tedious, so he supposed
he could understand his brothers' death glares.

"That's like the pot–kettle thing, you know?" Liam
said in response, Finn assumed, to him calling Aidan a
moody pain in the ass.

Griff raised an eyebrow at Liam and gave his head a
slight shake before saying, "Don't mind him. He's been
spouting this kind of crap since Mia moved back to Harmony Harbor."

"No, it's not a Mia saying. It's a GG saying. And
you're missing the point. Finn's calling out Aidan for being moody, and he's just as bad." Liam pointed the blue
bottle at him. "Are you getting cold feet?"

"No, I'm not getting cold feet." Not that he planned
to share with his brothers, but he wasn't moody; he was
frustrated.

Frustrated because he'd been sleeping in the same bed
as the woman he was going to marry tomorrow and that's
the only thing he'd been doing, sleeping. Come to think
of it, he'd hardly done that either.

It was frustrating and annoying and, at least once in the
night and once in the morning, extremely uncomfortable,
bordering on painful, and potentially embarrassing. And
apparently, Liv wasn't having the same problem. She was
sweet and relaxed and didn't think twice about parading
around in her sexy lingerie, which she got a shit ton of at
her shower.

"Really? You sound off to me," Griff said.

"Yeah, totally off. Actually, you know what he sounds like to me—"

Oh no, his brother, the recently former DEA agent, read people even better than Griff, which was saying something. Finn had no intention of getting into this with them now. He needed a diversion. "Does it look like Ella Rose is coming to the wedding? Dad said Harper's giving you the runaround."

"Yeah, well, her days of giving me the runaround are almost over. I just want to get myself settled here with a job and a house, and then I'm going to go after shared custody. If that's what Ella Rosa wants."

"What do you mean? She thinks the sun and moon rise around you. She's a total daddy's girl," Liam said, and he'd know better than both Finn and Griff did.

"This last assignment was tough on her, on both of us. Harley says Ella Rose doesn't want to talk to me. She's mad at me." He took a swig of beer and looked away.

"You know what you need? You need to get laid," Griff stated succinctly.

And Finn, who had just sucked back a mouthful of beer, spewed it across the fire. His brothers shifted in their chairs to look at him. "Oh, come on, you have got to be shitting me. You haven't—"

"Shut up," Finn said to Griff.

"This is a joke, right? You and Olivia…You had to…You haven't?"

Finn gave Liam a keep-talking-and-die look. It didn't stop him.

"Okay." Liam nodded. "Your choice of song for tomorrow is starting to make sense now."

"What song is he singing?" Griff asked.

"'Marry You' by Bruno Mars." Liam sang the chorus.

"That is not the song you sing to a woman you...Holy shit, you're not in love with her, are you?" His big brother crossed his arms. "Unless you want me to object at your wedding tomorrow, you better tell us what's going on. And don't even think about lying." Griff gestured to himself and Aidan. "We're the equivalent of human lie detectors."

Olivia had just come home from a last-minute fitting of her wedding dress. Finn's brothers were gone, and she was helping him pack away the wedding keepsakes. She glanced at him as she picked up a bottle. He'd been acting strange, almost remote the past two days.

She looked down at the black trench coat and high heels she was wearing. The man hadn't even noticed she was dressed like a high-class hooker. She'd thought the trench coat would be a dead giveaway. She'd actually hoped he'd take the hint, and she wouldn't have to follow through with her plan.

He was a doctor, for goodness' sake. Did he not know women get as sexually frustrated as men? What if she misread him and that wasn't the reason he was short with her and George this morning? She took a deep breath and squared her shoulders. It was now or never. She couldn't take it anymore.

"Thanks for all your hard work. You guys did an awesome job. I told you DIY projects were fun." Fig Newton, could she sound any more Pollyanna? She should just whip off her trench coat and have done with it.

She cast him a sidelong glance, her hand moving to the

belt. He caught her glance and...returned to packing his box of bottles. That wasn't very encouraging. He was acting as moody as his brother Aidan.

His brother whom Olivia had immediately thought of when she walked into Books and Beans yesterday. Julia had been reading and acting out *Beauty and the Beast* at children's story hour. Aidan would have been perfect in the role of Beast. Although that would mean Julia would be his Belle, and that was not a match Olivia wanted to contemplate. Julia was too sweet for a man like Aidan. And she didn't see Aidan coming out of beast mode anytime soon, if ever.

"So, did your brothers give you a hard time?" she asked, imagining that Aidan probably did. It would explain why Finn was cranky.

"Why? Did they say something to you? If they did, just ignore them. Especially Aidan, he's not himself."

"Neither are you. You've been acting weird since we came back from the rehearsal. What's wrong?" Her heart rolled over in her chest as she realized the most likely cause for his mood. "Are you getting cold feet?"

He fit one side of the cardboard lid under the other and placed the packed box beside the back door. "No, I'm not getting cold feet." He came to stand beside her. He didn't look her in the eyes. He seemed intrigued with the tendril of hair that had escaped from the knot at her nape. The tips of his fingers brushed her cheek as he reached for it, gently twisting it around his finger. Then he lifted his eyes to hers. "I'm not reneging on my promise either, but I think we should renegotiate the terms of our agreement."

With just his fingers in her hair, the heat from his body,

the smell of his cologne, he had her practically vibrating with desire, and he wanted to talk money? "The only terms we had were that I'd pay you a million dollars, but you…you want more?"

He nodded, his mouth tipping up at the corner.

She was glad he found it amusing, because she didn't. A million dollars was a lot of money. "I'm not sure how I feel about that, Finn. I suppose I could give you an extra hundred thousand, but only if I gave it to a charity in your name."

"It's not money I want more of. I want more of you, Liv. I can't go another night without kissing you, touching you, making love to you. So if you're not—"

She glanced around the yard. "How private is it back here? Do you think Dr. Bishop can see us through the back windows?"

"Liv, I'm a patient guy. Some might even go so far as to say laid-back, and I don't often lose my temper, especially with a woman, a woman I'm going to marry tomorrow. But, Sweet Cheeks, I've gotta tell you that you're ticking me off. I'm putting myself out there, telling you I want you, and you want to know if Doc—"

"You are not the only one who is frustrated and ticked off, Finn Gallagher," she said, shrugging out of her trench coat and letting it drop to her feet.

He stared at her, his gaze moving slowly and appreciatively over her body. Her skin warmed and tingled everywhere his eyes touched. He smoothed his hand over her shoulder and down her arm; his fingers briefly touched and caressed her before moving to her waist and drawing her closer.

"You've been teasing me with your barely-there nighties, so I knew you had a beautiful body, Liv. But seeing you like this, you take my breath away." He kissed her eyelids, her nose, her cheeks, then slid his mouth to her ear. "Do you know what it was like to lie beside you without touching you?" As if to make up for lost time, his hands moved over her body. They were big and warm. His touches and caresses making her shiver with anticipation and moan with desire. "I won't be able to get enough of you tonight, tomorrow, or the night after that and the night after that."

She took his face in her hands and kissed him like she'd been dying to. She was on fire. She wanted him, all of him. His body, his heart.

"We've wasted so much time. We've been lying in bed, both of us wanting the other, too afraid to say anything, too afraid to take the risk. I'm not afraid anymore, Finn. I'm not. I love you. Tomorrow when I walk across the beach to you, I'll be walking to the man I love. The man I want to spend the rest of my life with."

"God you're beautiful, Liv, so soft, so sweet." He brought his hands to her face and then slanted his lips over hers, kissing her passionately, deeply.

There was no denying he wanted her. He just didn't love her. And somehow, she had to find a way to be okay with the man she loved wanting to be friends with her. A friend with amazing benefits that would probably make her love him more.

Chapter Twenty-One

♥

There's a reason people say *Be careful what you wish for*. Finn had gotten his wish last night. Making love with the woman he was about to marry was, without a doubt, one of the best nights of his life. Except for that one moment on the patio when Liv professed her love for him. It wasn't even a moment. It was more like a couple of seconds. Because really, how long does it take to say *I love you*?

He looked down at his bare feet in the sand. He was standing under a pergola decorated with gauzy lengths of red, white, and blue fabric fastened to the poles with starfish. The sky at twilight reflected the color scheme. He wasn't an expert on weddings. As a guest, best man, and groomsman, he'd never paid attention to the themes or decor. All he'd cared about was the food, music (something he refused to think about right now), and his date if he had one. But even he could tell that Liv had worked magic to accomplish what she had in a matter of days.

On the wide swath of golf-course-green grass that overlooked the small private beach at Kismet Cove, red, white, and blue paper lanterns hung from wires that were attached to twenty-foot white poles to create a tentlike structure. A black chalkboard in the shape of a surfboard listed the seating arrangements, and oversized pillows at the base of each pole acted as seating for their guests. They'd be eating barbeque while watching the fireworks display.

Just like Liv had promised, the evening would be casual and relaxed. Right down to the untucked white linen shirts and rolled-at-the-cuff chinos that he and his brothers wore. Like him, they were also shoeless and sockless. Unlike him, their feet were no doubt warm. His were frozen.

Last night, his brothers had asked him if he had cold feet. He hadn't then. The reason they were today was because he'd gotten his wish. He'd made love to Liv. A woman who was in love with him. Every day that they were together and he didn't say the words in return would be like shooting an arrow into her heart. He didn't want to hurt her; she'd been hurt enough.

But he couldn't open himself up to that kind of pain again. He'd made a vow to never put himself in that position. And he hadn't. Until last night. Lying with Liv in his arms, kissing her like he dreamed of, touching her like he'd been dying to, he'd felt it. Over the past month, she'd been slowly chipping away at the barrier that covered his heart. Last night, he'd heard and felt the crack as she made her way inside.

"Finn." Liam nudged him.

He looked up to see Liv on his dad's arm, George holding his hand as they made their way to the beach. Liv wore her hair the way Finn liked it—in a sleek knot. It suited her and the wedding dress that softly hugged her willowy frame—the narrow straps sitting low on her shoulders. Simple, classy, exquisite. Other than diamond studs in her ears and the pink string bracelet George had made for her on her wrist, she didn't wear any jewelry.

He cleared the emotion from his throat, but his voice still came out gruff when he asked Liam, "Do you have the ring?"

"This isn't my first rodeo, you know." Liam patted his pockets. "Wait a minute, I don't have the ring. Miller does."

"Right, I forgot." Finn looked up to see his grandmother in a pale blue pantsuit with Miller on a leash coming along the path to the beach. Liv had decided the dog should be part of the ceremony. She credited Miller with bringing them together. A sign that for Liv their friendship had turned into something more. As he'd discovered, he'd missed a few of those signs.

His father, Liv, and George had reached the beach. His dad wore chinos and a white linen shirt like Finn and his brothers. George looked adorable in a white sundress. Liv must have given in because George had on her red light-up sneakers. It had probably been a concession to the little girl when she couldn't wear her Sox baseball cap. Instead, she had curly blue ribbons in her dark hair and a big smile on her face. Liv had a small smile on hers. He thought it was more for her bridesmaids than for him.

Because when she raised her gaze to meet his, he saw something other than happiness. She seemed nervous, unsure, and maybe just a little bit hurt.

Liam nudged him again. "Snap out of it, bro. You're supposed to be singing with us."

Singing? He glanced to his left. Aidan was playing the harmonica while giving him a what-the-hell look. Griff sang "Moon River" with the same look on his face. Finn joined his voice to Griff's and Liam's.

For Liv's sake, he was glad his brothers talked him out of singing "Marry You." But "Moon River," while a nice song, wouldn't be what Liv had hoped for. It wasn't a song that held any meaning for him or her. He hadn't picked it; his grandmother had. He knew that Liv would want something romantic, something from his heart. But that was the one thing he couldn't give her.

Exactly a month from the day he married Liv, Finn realized he'd made a mistake. He was sitting in the warm, soft sand at the beach watching the sun's rays dance across the waves and the golden-haired woman and dark-haired little girl on their surfboards a hundred yards away.

He recognized his mistake the moment Liv finally managed to stay upright on the board for more than a few seconds. She got this incredible look of triumph on her face like she'd conquered Mount Everest. But that wasn't the precise moment he knew. It was just the lead-up.

The moment he knew without a doubt that he was head over heels, no turning back, crazy-in-love with his wife was when a rogue wave took her out and she came up laughing, still looking like she'd won the prize.

That moment of enlightenment felt like a rogue wave had taken him out. It was a new experience for him. He used to be unshakable on his board, a master of the waves. Loving a woman like he loved Liv was uncharted territory. Now what the hell was he supposed to do?

Just ride the wave, a familiar voice in his head said. It was the same voice that had urged him on every adventure. Skydiving, mountain climbing, swimming with sharks, that voice had always been there.

Liv was his adrenaline rush. The thing that made him want to get up every morning and take on a new day. She was it, his everything. He'd never done anything small or safe. He should have known that, when he fell, it'd be like free falling from a mountaintop.

He stood, brushing the sand off his board shorts. He might not be able to ride the waves like he used to or swim from the lighthouse to Twilight Bay, but he sure as hell wasn't going to sit on his ass and let the woman he loved think for one second longer that she was in this alone.

She hadn't taken her love back when he hadn't returned the words. She hadn't laughed them off as a joke or pretended she didn't mean them. She hadn't acted resentful or tried to make him pay in subtle ways. No, that's not something she'd do. Because Liv was brave and amazing, and his. She'd suffered a heartbreaking loss, yet she'd been willing to take the risk, to open her heart to George, to him. Now she'd given him the courage to do the same.

Finn walked to the water's edge, the midafternoon sunshine glinting off the harbor. He shielded his eyes, looking to where he'd last seen Liv and George. He spotted George and laughed. The kid was like his mini-me. Standing on the board like a pro, she appeared to be lecturing Liv, who was once more pulling herself out of the water and onto the board.

He started out. The tide was low, the warm water still lapping around his ankles several yards from shore. It was fairly crowded but not annoyingly so. That was the nice thing about Harmony Harbor. With more than thirty miles of coastline, there was a plethora of sandy beaches and coves to take advantage of, so you never had to worry about fighting for a spot.

Or so he thought until he turned to grab a little girl who'd swallowed a mouthful of water and spotted a guy walking over and dumping a pile of beach towels and a cooler practically on top of theirs.

Finn handed the little girl back to her mother, the smile he'd just given the woman falling when the guy who was horning in on their territory kicked off his sneakers and spewed sand all over their towels. He was really starting to tick Finn off. Instead of swimming out to his woman to tell her he'd seen the light, he had to defend their territory against a man who looked like a mean son of…The guy whipped off his black T-shirt and tossed it on Liv's towel.

Okay, Finn didn't care how mean or ripped the guy was, he…That tattoo looked familiar. So did the beard. But there was no way Aidan would be caught dead wearing his hair in a stubby ponytail, a fedora on his head, and Elton John–style sunglasses. What really threw Finn, though, was the cigarette hanging off the guy's lip.

From a distance, he heard George call, "Mia! Mia!"

He glanced to the right. His niece was scrambling over the grassy sand dune and onto the beach. She tossed her towel and flip-flops at squatter guy. "Thanks, Uncle Aidan! Hi, Uncle Finn!" she called as she raced past him and into the water.

Ava and Sophie came next, followed by Griff and Liam, who were carting blankets, coolers, and beach umbrellas between them. Next came Lexi, who had Gabe strapped to her back, followed by Byron Harte, who was struggling with a deluxe-model stroller. Interesting addition. Finn wondered how his big brother felt about Harte tagging along.

Finn walked over to greet his family. He gave Aidan a chest bump as he plucked the cigarette from his mouth. "No smoking around the kids." Checking to be sure the cigarette was unlit, Finn stuffed it in the pocket of his board shorts and then picked up Liv's towel. "You got sand all over our stuff. You're lucky Mia said your name. I was ready to take you out." He moved away to shake out the towel. "What's with the hat and shades?"

Griff looked up from fitting an umbrella in the sand. "Word on the street is the matchmakers of Harmony Harbor have him in their sights."

"He should be safe. They'll never find him under all that hair," Liam quipped. "Have you ever heard of manscaping, bro?"

Aidan gave Liam the finger, which Sophie must have missed, probably because she was trying to get comfortable on a lawn chair. "It's one of the services we'll be offering at the spa. You can be our first client," she said.

"Thanks, but no thanks. A little too girly for me."

"Have it done and then come tell me how girly it is," Byron said as he dragged the stroller through the sand.

"Yeah, not going to happen." Aidan glanced at the hair-free, golden brown chest Byron's open shirt revealed. "But if you want to take my place, go for it." He picked up the stroller with one hand and walked it over to where Ava was helping Lexi lift Gabe from his carrier.

Finn waited for Motorcycle Man to give a manly grunt as he deposited the stroller in front of the women. Instead, he kind of leaned out like he was looking at something in the water, his brow furrowed, and then he jerked upright. "Jesus, it's a shark!" He took off, spraying Sophie with sand, waving his arms. "Shark! Shark! Everyone out of the water!"

"He can't seriously believe that is a shark," Griff said, sounding thoroughly disgusted as they ran after their brother, who was galloping into the water, pushing kids out of the way.

"Aidan, stop throwing the kids out of the water! It's not a shark! It's a kid's toy!" Finn yelled. At least that's what the iridescent blue fin looked like to him.

"The guy's paranoid. He's seeing danger and bad guys on every corner. Yesterday, he gave Mia's friend Braden the third degree. Then he told the kid he couldn't play with Mia because he's sure Braden's going to end up in prison."

"Baby bro, that's maybe something we needed to know," Griff said to Liam when they reached the water's edge to see Aidan grabbing the *shark* by the tail. "We might have saved him from embarrassing himself and possibly being charged with indecently exposing a mermaid," his brother finished succinctly as Aidan stared at the long length of blue and green iridescent scaled fabric hanging from his hand.

"Mommy, he killed Millie," a little girl wailed, her cries echoed by several other girls and boys.

"I'd say he has a fifty-fifty chance of being the one who is murdered. Look at their faces," Liam said.

Four of the braver souls had waded out to where Aidan was still holding the mermaid's tail, splashing and yelling at him, "You killed Millie the Mermaid!"

Just down from Finn, a couple of kids were complaining about injuries sustained when Aidan tried to *save* them from the mermaid. "I'll take care of the injured kids," Finn said. "You guys take care of the antihero."

"Todd, Trish, Tina, Tara, over here. Look, see, I'm okay," a sweetly feminine voice called out.

They turned to see Julia Landon with just her head and shoulders above the water, wearing a wig of long, cherry-red hair.

"It's Millie the Mermaid! Look! Look! She's alive!" As the cry went up, boys and girls, including the ones who not two minutes ago had been complaining about wounded hands and feet, plowed through the water toward her.

"No, no, don't come any closer. Just, um, stay back, okay?"

Millie the Mermaid's predicament became clear when a blue bikini bottom floated past Aidan.

A tall blonde strode across the sand with a long-range camera hanging around her neck. "I got great shots. Are you going to do the interviews, or am I?" the woman asked Byron, who was stripping off his shirt and toeing off his deck shoes.

"You do remember Julia, our friend? Well, thanks to He-Man over there, she's skinny-dipping and about to be converged upon by her many fans. So let's save the shop talk until after I rescue her, shall we?"

"As if she wants you to see her naked. Give me that." The blonde took his shirt from Byron and slipped off her flip-flops. "I'm coming, Julia. I mean, Millie," she said, waving the shirt like a flag and then walking over to Aidan, who'd scooped the bikini bottom out of the water and was holding it straight-armed away from him.

The woman, whom Finn now recognized as Byron's sister Poppy and co-publisher of the *Harmony Harbor Gazette*, gave Aidan an up-and-down look. "Just FYI, your disguise isn't working. Someone at the manor has been posting what you're wearing and where you'll be on Greystone's Facebook page. But don't worry. When we publish the pictures and story on the front page of the *Gazette* tomorrow, interest in you will probably level off."

Aidan scowled at her, which seemed to be his default expression these days. "I'd think twice before you publish the story and pictures. They could be used as evidence against your friend."

"Oh, please, I'm not that gullible. You're just embarrassed you made an idiot of yourself. What are you going to have her charged with? She was just trying to get into character for her performance. See what it feels like to be a mermaid."

"Really? And I'm the idiot?"

"I'd stop while you're ahead, Gallagher. My sister has

photographic evidence and isn't afraid to use it. You do want a job with the Harmony Harbor Police Department, don't you?" Byron asked.

Finn shared a look with his brothers. He thought Aidan already had the job. From Liam's and Griff's expressions, they were as surprised as he was. But any thought of questioning his brother went out of his head when George, paddling to shore with Mia on her board and Liv coming up behind her, said, "He's a really big shark, but he won't hurt you, Julia."

Finn shared an out-of-the-mouths-of-babes look with Griff and Liam and smiled at George. "You're right, sweetheart. Uncle Aidan is a big guy, but it was an honest mistake. He didn't intentionally try to hurt—"

"I wasn't talking about him. I was talking about the shark over there." She twisted at her waist and pointed to the fins cutting through the water about fifty yards away. "Oh, it's got a friend."

The water churned with thrashing arms and legs, the word *shark* vibrating in the hot summer air as kids stampeded toward shore. "Don't panic! Stay calm!" Finn called out, keeping an eye on Liv and George paddling to shore.

Griff, Liam, and Byron were wading out deeper to calm things down while Aidan stood transfixed in the last spot Finn had seen him. What the…"Aidan…" Finn trailed off when a naked Julia Landon with Lady Godiva hair streaked toward shore.

His brother broke free from his stupor, grabbed the shirt from Poppy, charged after Julia, leaped into the air, and flattened her in the sand to the sound of kids screaming and the clicking shutter of a camera.

* * *

Two hours later, Griffin walked across the sand to where they were unloading the coolers. "George was right," he said.

The Gallaghers had planned to spend the day and evening at the beach and have a family BBQ. Everyone had agreed they weren't going to let a shark sighting spoil their plans. Griffin had gone to talk to a couple of guys from the Coast Guard.

"Two twenty-foot basking sharks. All they're interested in are small fish and zooplankton, not little kids or mermaids," Finn's oldest brother quipped, looking to where George and Mia sat farther down the beach with the other children who'd remained to see Millie the Mermaid and the By-the-Sea Band.

Olivia admired Julia for going ahead with the scheduled performance after what had transpired. Julia had covered it well, but Olivia was positive she'd been inwardly dying of embarrassment. In her place, Olivia would have been. She glanced at the cause of Julia's embarrassment.

As though Ava, Lexi, and Sophie had been thinking the same thing, they also turned to look at Finn's brother. Aidan looked up from flipping a burger on the small grill a few feet away. "Would you all just get over it? I apologized, okay?"

"Oh, yeah, we heard you. We also heard you calling her a loon toon under your breath when she was leaving. And every time you glance over there, it's as if you're channeling Elvis Presley," Lexi said.

At Aidan's blank look, she did an impression of the King's signature lip curl. Lexi wasn't holding back. Given that Julia was a good friend to all of them, Olivia wasn't totally surprised by Lexi's aggressive defense of Julia, but she thought it might have just as much to do with Byron begging off the BBQ because of work. It had been obvious Byron wasn't a fan of Aidan, and vice versa.

Aidan rolled his eyes. "I get how you're all friends and stick together, but you have to admit there's something off about a grown woman who spends eighty percent of the time pretending to be a character from a book."

"Ah, no. She owns a bookstore with one of the best children's sections in New England. She's amazing with kids and does what she can to encourage their love of reading," Lexi said.

"Yeah, well, that's your perception as a friend. My perception as a cop is she's a bit of a whack-a-doodle. You should keep an eye on her."

Lexi threw a carrot stick at him, and Ava threw a bun. Sophie was at the stage in her pregnancy where it was hard to get in and out of a chair, so she had no access to ammunition. All Olivia had within reach was a fistful of plastic utensils but thought it best not to fling them at Aidan.

"Bro, you better quit while you're ahead. If Harmony Harbor had a competition for most beloved person in town, Julia would win hands down. She's awesome," Liam said as he and Finn carried a picnic table between them.

"Okay, whatever you all say," Aidan muttered, adding under his breath, "Still say she's a loon toon."

Olivia raised an eyebrow at her husband. "I see you're

not the only one who uses the phrase."

He wrapped his arms around her, playfully rocking her back and forth. His bare chest was warm, and he smelled like summer. "I only said it the once, but I take it back. Getting married on July Fourth was a great idea. It will go down in history as the best idea of all time."

Their wedding had been wonderful. Just the other day, she'd been asked by a newly engaged couple from town if they could incorporate elements of her wedding into theirs. They'd seen photos in the *Gazette*.

So she supposed she could understand why her husband said it was the best idea of all time, but something about the remark didn't ring true. He'd been acting strange since the shark sighting—the real one. Not in a loon toon sort of way; he was just way more touchy-feely than usual, and several times she'd turned to catch him staring at her.

She pulled back. "What is going on with you? You've been acting weird."

"How so?"

"I don't know, just more—"

He smiled and stroked her cheek. "I had something important I wanted to tell you, but then the family arrived. I thought I'd wait until we got home and were alone." He glanced at the women getting the food on the table as Liam and Griffin critiqued Aidan's barbecuing. "But I think I should tell you here, with everyone around." He gave her a quick kiss. "Just give me a sec," he said, and headed to where Julia was doing her reading.

True to his word, he returned almost immediately carrying a guitar with Mia and George in tow.

"What? You're making us sing for our supper?" Liam asked.

"No, but I want all of you to take a seat." Finn patted the bench closest to where he stood. "You sit here, Liv." Once everyone was settled in and looking at him expectantly, he began tightening the strings. "You remember the song I sang to you as you walked down the aisle on our wedding day?"

She smiled and nodded, wondering if she'd been able to cover her disappointment as well as she had on their wedding day. After Griffin and his brothers had serenaded Ava with the romantically sentimental "I Swear" by John Michael Montgomery at her wedding, Olivia had hoped for something equally touching at hers.

Instead, she got "Moon River." It was the one point in the wedding where she'd actually wondered if she was making a mistake. It had been blatantly obvious that her husband didn't have any romantic feelings for her. If his song choice and his failure to join in the singing right away hadn't made it obvious, the terrified look on his face had.

His lips twitched. "I can see that you do. When my brothers heard what I initially planned to sing that day, they felt a lot like I imagine you did, Liv. They wanted to know what I was doing marrying a woman I wasn't in love with."

"Finn," she gasped. Why was he doing this to her? She didn't understand. "Not here, please, not in front of—" She was going to say George, but he placed a finger on her lips.

"It's not what you think. Just let me finish. You'll see. It'll be good, Princess. Better than good, it's gonna be amazing." He looked at her as though begging her to stay and be okay.

She nodded and clasped her hands in her lap, forcing a smile for George, who looked worried. Sophie, who sat beside her on the bench, rubbed her shoulder.

"If we were getting married today, this is the song I'd sing to you, Liv. And I'd mean every word." He sang "Die a Happy Man" by Thomas Rhett. And it was as romantically sentimental as she could have wished for.

He sang the words like he meant them, like he loved her as much as the lyrics implied. In some ways, it wasn't a surprise. He may not have said the words to her before today, but there had been times over the past couple of weeks that she'd wondered, because of how he looked at her, how he touched her and made love to her, if he was beginning to have more than just friendly feelings for her.

As he sang the final chorus, everyone whooped and cheered, including George.

Griffin raised a glass. "About time you finally figured it out. We were gonna give you another week."

Finn rested the guitar against the picnic table. "Seriously, you're trying to tell me you guys knew I was in love with Liv before I did?"

"Yep, we made a video and e-mailed it to each other," Liam said, but Liv wasn't listening to them anymore because Finn had taken her in his arms.

"You love me," she said, with maybe the tiniest hint of a question in her voice, but the love and wonder drowned out the doubt.

"Yeah, I do. Who knows, maybe they're right, because as much as it feels like I've been with you forever, it feels like I've been waiting for you that long too. I love you,

Liv. Thank you for being patient with me, for not giving up on me."

"I couldn't give up on you even if I wanted to. We should thank George. If it wasn't for her, we wouldn't be together, and I'm so happy that we are."

"We would have found each other eventually. We were meant to be, Liv."

"You're such a romantic."

"I'll show you just how romantic if we can get Mia to invite George for a sleepover."

They barely made it into the house without ripping each other's clothes off. Finn kicked the door closed, flipped the lock, and then picked Liv up. She wrapped her legs around him. His hands went into her hair. Hers went into his. They both groaned when their lips finally met…and then again when her phone buzzed in her beach bag.

"You have to get it."

It wasn't a question, but still, she heard the hint of one. "I know," she said, acknowledging both his frustration and the fact that phones needed to be answered with George at a sleepover.

The call went to voice mail.

Finn curved his hand around her neck and drew her close to plant a kiss on her mouth as though to remind her of what was to come. "Call them back, and I'll take Wolfie out."

She nodded, doing her best not to reveal her panic. At the nape of her neck, her hair was standing on end. It was Stanley. A text came in. She swallowed before reading it, preparing herself.

It might be good news. Celeste and Walter could have given up their bid for custody. They'd refused to go to mediation. Their court date had been set for September. Maybe it had been moved up. She needed to know. She forced herself to look.

Livy, call me. It's urgent.

Finn followed Wolfie back inside, glancing at her as he closed the door behind him. "Everything okay, babe?"

"Everything's wonderful." And if only for tonight, it was going to stay that way.

Chapter Twenty-Two

♥

Finn was upstairs in bed enjoying a leisurely morning with his wife when Wolfie began barking and racing from one end of the main floor to the other. "What the hell? I took him out last night at eleven. He should be able to hold it till"—he looked at his watch—"ten."

Rolling off the bed, Finn went to grab his board shorts and T-shirt off the floor. They weren't there. He got up and walked to the chair where Liv had left them neatly folded. He returned to the bed as he pulled the T-shirt over his head, leaning in to kiss his naked wife. "Don't move, I'll be back in five minutes."

He planned to take advantage of their kid-free house. "Okay, dog, let's…," he began as he reached the bottom of the stairs. Wolfie didn't race over to him as expected because the dog was barking at something out the front window.

Finn went over to take a look, and then wished he hadn't. A silver Audi was parked in front of the house. Stanley was here, and from the looks of it, he wasn't alone. There was a dark-haired woman in the car.

Sunday seemed an odd time for a visit from a court-appointed social worker, but they often made them without warning. Though it didn't explain why Stanley was here...unless it was bad news. Or good, he quickly amended. After last night, the only thing he'd accept was good news.

He heard Liv coming down the stairs and turned. She'd put on a robe. Glancing from Wolfie to Finn, she bowed her head, her fingers whitening around the wooden railing. "It's Stanley, isn't it?"

She didn't sound completely surprised. Upset, worried, but not entirely surprised. "You were expecting him?"

"He was the one who called last night. He texted that he needed to speak to me. He said it was urgent." She raised her gaze. "I just wanted last night to be perfect. I just wanted to be able to pretend that everything was wonderful for one more night."

He walked over and framed her face with his hands, ducking to meet her eyes. "Everything's going to be okay. We've talked about this, remember? We keep fighting until we eventually win."

"I love you," she whispered. "I don't know what I'd do without you."

"You'd do the same thing—you'd fight. Only now you don't have to fight alone. You won't be alone again, Liv. I'm here for you, always."

There was the sound of a door slamming, and then another one. Finn let Liv go. "There's a woman with Stanley. It might be a court-appointed social worker, so you should probably get dressed," he said as he walked to the window. "Dammit, Liam's just pulled up with George. She must have wanted to come home early."

"We should have talked to her about this, Finn. Warned her—" Liv began as she ran to the door. They reached it at the same time, opening it to hear George call, "Mama! Mama!"

Liv looked up at him with a tremulous smile, her eyes swimming in tears. "I didn't think anyone would call me mama again."

He put his arm around her and kissed the top of the head, lifting his hand to greet his brother. But Liam had turned to watch George run to Stanley's car, hurtling herself into the arms of the dark-haired woman.

From where she sat with her cheek pressed to her partially open bedroom door, Olivia could hear George's mother speaking as her melodic, accented voice floated up the stairs from the kitchen where she, George, Finn, and Stanley were gathered.

Olivia had excused herself only moments before to get dressed. She'd felt like she was going into shock. She'd needed a moment before meeting the woman who'd stolen her husband and now was going to steal the little girl she'd come to love. But just as Olivia had turned blindly to run into the house, George had spotted her and Finn and had dragged her beautiful mother across the front lawn to meet them.

It was all Olivia could do to remain standing. Without the support of Finn's arms around her, she would have dropped to her knees. It was her worst nightmare playing out before her. She couldn't fight George's mother for custody of her. A brittle laugh escaped from her at the thought. George had a mother, a young, beautiful mother who loved her. She didn't need Olivia anymore.

She bowed her head, pressing her fingers to her lips to hold back the sobs that were piling up one after another in her throat. She had to stop thinking about herself and think about George. It must feel like the greatest gift, a miracle, to the little girl. Her mother had returned from the dead. And it wasn't like Olivia would never see George again.

At least she hoped George's mother would allow Olivia to see her. Isabella hadn't been able to look Olivia in the eyes. She was deferential, almost shy with her. With the men, she'd been outgoing and bubbly. Though it could have been nerves. She appeared slightly malnourished, but other than that, she'd fared well in the hands of her captors. As Olivia had heard from her spot by the door, Isabella didn't blame the rebels for kidnapping her. She'd spent her time in the remote camp treating their injuries and illnesses. Two weeks ago, she'd saved their leader's life. In exchange, she was granted her freedom.

Olivia got up and went into the bathroom to splash cold water on her face.

There was a knock on her bedroom door. "Livy?"

"Come in, Stanley." She quickly wiped her face with a damp cloth before reentering her bedroom.

Stanley was sitting on the side of her unmade bed. He

looked up at her and shook his head and then patted the mattress. He put his arm around her when she sat beside him. "Goddammit, Livy, I'm sorry. I wish I'd never gotten in touch with you that day."

"I won't lie to you. It feels awful and terribly unfair, and that makes me feel horribly selfish. But you were right. I needed her, Stanley. I needed George. And because of her, I found Finn." She wiped at her eyes. "Do you think Isabella would be open to George visiting us once in a while?"

He nodded and took her hand. "She didn't know, Livy. She didn't know you and Nathan were still married. It was George who pushed for them to get married two years ago. Isabella's offered to have their marriage annulled. She'll do whatever you want her to do."

"No, I took care of everything the night you told me about Isabella and Georgina, remember? I'd like to give Isabella the town house. In trust for George, of course. If she needs anything—financially, I mean—I'd like to help until she gets on her feet. I'm sure there'll be an opening for her at Mass General. If not, I can pull—"

Stanley gently squeezed her hand, his expression pained. "Livy, she's going back to Kenya. She and George fly out tomorrow morning."

"Tomorrow? But that's so soon. I thought...I thought... Stanley, would you mind giving me a moment? I need to get dressed."

It'd taken ten minutes in a hot shower followed by a thirty-minute conversation in her head while blow-drying her hair, putting on her makeup, and donning a white top over a pair of pink capris for Olivia to reach the point where she felt she could talk to George and Isabella without breaking down. She wanted to organize a going-away party for George and hoped Isabella would be open to letting her stay with them one more night. Olivia was giving herself a mental pep talk when Isabella's lilting voice floated up the stairs.

"I'm not trying to steal you away from DWB, honest. But the work we're doing in underserved communities with HIV and AIDS is groundbreaking, Finn. We're making a difference. It will be hard for Georgina to leave all of you. She'd be so happy if she thought you would join our team, wouldn't you, darling?"

"Why don't we talk about that later, Isabella? George wants you and Stanley to meet her bunny. She made the maze herself." The back door opened, and their voices faded.

Olivia felt sick. Her heart raced, and her legs went weak. She leaned against the wall, slowly lowering herself onto the stairs. She didn't know how long she'd sat there before Finn appeared.

He took the stairs two at a time to reach her side. "Hey, sweetheart, hey, it's going to be okay."

The back door squeaked open. "Come see my room. Me and Livy decorated it."

George's voice broke Olivia from her stupor. "I...I have to go. I want to arrange a goodbye party for George. I'm going to talk to...Julia. She'll help me." She lurched to her feet.

"No, Liv, you're in no shape to drive. Come on, just stay. We'll talk." He took her face between his hands, his eyes searching hers. "You promised, remember? You promised to talk to me if you get overwhelmed."

George was talking to her mother, their voices coming closer. "I can't. I can't talk right now. I can't breathe. I...I won't be long."

Finn called after her as she ran from the house, her car keys in hand. She couldn't stay. It was happening all over again. Isabella was taking Finn from her just like she'd taken Nathan. She was young and pretty. She was a doctor who shared his passion, and she had George, a little girl Finn had come to love too. They were all leaving her. Everyone always left her.

It was like the Range Rover had a mind of its own, and she found herself driving under the stone arch of Greystone Manor. She'd found solace here: a new life, a new love. For a few months, she'd found her happy. And now here she was, devastated, lost, and alone again. She'd come full circle. She hadn't been looking to start over that long-ago September night. Just like today, she'd been running away.

Closing the Range Rover's door, she locked her purse inside. She needed some time to be alone and to think. She wouldn't let either Finn or George leave without saying goodbye. But goodbyes were devastating, heart-breaking, and she'd need her strength to get through this one.

She turned at the sound of the waves hitting the rocks at Kismet Cove, reminded of the day George had arrived. The beach had been the little girl's introduction to Harmony Harbor, the manor, and Finn. She'd feel close to them there. She'd sit on the rocks and watch the waves roll into shore. She'd figure out how to say goodbye and how to go on.

She took the path down to the beach and found a place nestled between two large boulders where she wouldn't be obvious to anyone looking out the manor's windows. The warmth of the rocks and the sun beating down on her head took away the chill that had seeped into her body upon hearing what Isabella said to Finn. Her breathing slowed, taking on the rhythmic ebb and flow of the waves.

Now that the panic was leaving her, she could think rationally. She should have talked to Finn. She shouldn't have run out on him like that. On George either. She'd take a few more minutes and go home. She felt the weight of someone's stare and glanced over her shoulder. There was a woman walking along the path behind her. Olivia recognized her. She'd worked at the manor. Ivy, she thought her name was. She wasn't sure if she was looking at her or looking out to sea, but Olivia smiled just the same.

Colleen banged on the window in the tower room. "Olivia, run! Run, Olivia!" she cried. Ivy was right behind her and had picked up a rock. Colleen threw herself against the window in the tower room. "Bejaysus, let me out! Free me from the manor so I can save Olivia, please. If it means I'll be stuck roaming the grounds of Greystone forevermore, I'm willing to make the sacrifice. Please, Lord." She squeezed her eyes shut as Ivy brought the rock down on the back of Olivia's head.

Colleen was crying, but there were no tears.

Meow.

"She's done what she set out to, Simon. She's killed her. She's killed Olivia."

There was a thump and then…*Meow. Meow.*

"Can't you see my heart is broken, Simon? I can't..."
He was sitting on the window seat, bumping his head
against the glass, trying to get her attention. She prepared
herself before leaning out to look. "Where's she taking
her? She must be alive. If Olivia was dead, Ivy'd let the
tide take her out to sea. Hurry, Simon. Help me. We need
Jasper to get the book."

She raced through the manor in search of Jasper. She
finally found him polishing the entryway table. "It's
Olivia, lad. She needs us. Jasper!" she shouted, but he
didn't look up, squirting the polish onto the dark wood.
She howled her panic and frustration, pushing at the vase
of irises.

"Stop it this instant, Madame," Jasper said, grabbing
the vase and hugging it against his chest.

"You're worried about your flowers when Olivia's life
is on the line? You can save her, my boy. But the only way
you can is if I can make you understand what's happening
right beneath your nose. You need to read the book. It's
there; the clue is there. In Patty's story."

It was no use. Colleen followed Jasper around for more
than an hour and hadn't been able to get through to him.
She was practically hoarse from nattering at him, and
what limited ability she had to move things about was
even more limited. She was using too much of her energy. She had to conserve it in hopes that Jasper would
finally relent. Simon had given up twenty minutes ago,
but Colleen couldn't. She couldn't give up on Olivia.

She felt a surge of hope when Finn entered the manor.
The lad looked upset. She prayed he was here because he
knew something was amiss.

Colleen followed him into the study.

"Sophie, have you seen Liv?"

"No, is she okay? Liam told me about George's mother showing up. I was going to give Olivia some space before calling to check on her. Is there anything we can do?"

"Oh, you poor child, Olivia. I don't know why some suffer so much and some not at all. And now Ivy has you."

"She's not good, Sophie. I'm worried about her. But she's here somewhere. Her Range Rover's in the lot, and her purse is inside."

"Maybe she's in the tower room or went to talk to Lexi or Ava." Sophie pushed back from her desk and took out her phone. "Call your brothers. I'll call everyone I know."

"She mentioned going to see Julia about helping throw together a goodbye party for George. I called Julia. She says Liv never showed."

"I'm happy for George and her mom, but my God, poor Olivia. This has to be devastating for her, Finn."

And for Finn. The thought hit Colleen like a ton of bricks and nearly brought her to her knees. Finn had finally come home and found a woman he could love. He'd let her into his heart, and now there was a very good chance he would lose her. And then they'd lose him. This time they'd lose him forever.

Chapter Twenty-Three

♥

Colleen paced behind Jasper in the ballroom. They knew now. They knew Olivia was missing. Finn was beside himself.

"Sure, I have hundreds of pictures of her, tons of them." Finn angrily scrolled through his phone, raising it for the detective and Chief Benson to see. "But what does that have to do with anything? You're wasting time. My wife is missing. Everyone in town knows her. They don't need a picture."

Word had quickly spread, and people from town had gathered at the manor to offer their help in searching for Olivia. Members of the Widows Club were coming through the doors of the ballroom now, along with Olivia's friends, Julia, and the rest of the business owners on Main Street.

Aidan, Griffin, and Liam turned at the sound of Finn's

raised voice and moved quickly to his side. Aidan put a hand on his brother's shoulder. "They're just doing their job, Finn. We're going to find her, okay?"

Colin, who'd been comforting Kitty, looked over at his boys. He said something to Kitty and then walked over to Chief Benson and his detective. Resting his hand on Finn's other shoulder, he spoke to his old friend. Chief Benson and his detective nodded before moving away.

"All right, son. We're going to find Olivia. You're not going to lose her."

His face stricken, Finn raised his hand. "Don't, don't even go there. I can't think—"

"Finn, calm down. You won't be any good to Olivia if you lose it. Liam and Sophie filled me in about George and her mother, so what I need you to do is tell me everything Olivia said and did from the point they arrived and when she left," Aidan said.

Knowing Olivia as well as she did, Colleen had a difficult time listening to Finn relay the information Aidan asked for. Heartache and fear was mixed with bitter frustration that they couldn't hear her yelling in their ears, screaming the answers at the top of her lungs. She was nearly exhausted and not one of them had heard her. And the one man who could help her was so intent on ensuring Kitty was all right that he either didn't feel her tugging on his sleeve and pushing at him or he was ignoring her.

While Colleen had been ruminating in her head, Finn had said something that made Aidan narrow his eyes at Julia Landon. If Colleen's heart were still beating, it would have stopped. They couldn't afford for Julia's secret to come out now.

"You all thought I was overreacting yesterday, but I've been doing some investigating into Julia Landon. She has close ties to the mayor, who you may remember was working with Paige Townsend. But that's not even the biggest red flag. The woman gave Mistletoe Cottage to Mia. She gave a kid she barely knew a property that's valued at close to two hundred grand. Who does that? I'll tell you who does, Ava and Griff's *fairy godmother*. Surprised, right? So now maybe you'll understand why, when you tell me the person Olivia was going to see was none other than our family's stalker, that I'm going to walk right over there and haul the woman down to the station for questioning."

"Come on, Aidan. You can't do that. She's…Aidan." Liam went after his brother who strode across the ballroom to where Julia was talking to the girls.

Colleen had been counting on Aidan to somehow figure out foul play was involved. He'd always been a canny lad. But he'd made a right hash of it.

Colleen glanced at Simon, who was sitting at her feet. He was her last hope. "You've never let me down in the past, Simon. I need you now. Olivia needs you. Go to Patty's, the mauve Victorian that looks like a gingerbread house. It's a run-down old place just up from the cottage they're renovating for the spa. See if Ivy's holding Olivia there. If she is, you need to bring me something. A piece of mail, something with the address.

"It's a lot to ask of you, I know. But you're a canny cat. I believe in you, Simon. You can do this. Give Jasper one last scratch on your way out, will you? There's a good lad," she said when he gave her what looked like a clipped nod. He padded his way to Jasper, gave him a couple of head butts, and then got a piece of his pant leg between his teeth and tugged.

If that didn't get his attention…"Shoo now, I'm busy. Can't you see the family's in a state, Madame? They need me," he said, and bent to pat Simon. No doubt so people thought he was talking to the cat.

"They need you all right, you daft lad. They need you to read my book, not be mooning over my daughter-in-law. Look, the Widows Club is with her now. See, Rosa's hugging her. They've put their feud aside." They always did in time of trouble.

His hands clasped behind his back, Jasper rocked on his heels. "All right, Madame. It appears you are the only member of the family I can be of some use to."

Colleen sent up a prayer of thanks and another one for Olivia's safety as she followed Jasper to his room on the second floor. "Hang on, Olivia. Help is on the way."

But Colleen's belief that everything would be all right as soon as Jasper read the book and shared his findings with the family turned out to be wrong. Horribly so. Though she couldn't completely lay the entire blame at Jasper's feet. After all, she'd been the one who wrote down Olivia's deepest, darkest secret. And Colleen had used too much of her energy today. So when Jasper turned to Olivia's page, Colleen was unable to turn the pages to the day Patty had tea at the manor.

Jasper closed the book and bowed his head. "I pray that we're not too late, Madame. For both Olivia's and Master Finn's sake." He looked like he'd aged ten years when he returned the book to his safe.

302   DEBBIE MASON

Terrified for Olivia, Colleen was beside herself that she'd been unable to steer Jasper in the right direction. So she hadn't given much thought to why he was walking across the ballroom. Until she saw that he was heading straight for Finn. "No, you daft lad! Not Olivia's secret. Don't tell her secret! You'll throw everyone off. They'll start looking at it as a suicide, not a case of foul play."

And that's exactly what happened.

Olivia came to on a battered oak floor. She smelled floor polish, mothballs, and mildew. She tried to lift her head and groaned when the dark, wood-paneled room spun around her. She was in a house; that much she recognized. How did she...

Her mind felt like it was covered in a thick, syrupy fog, but it slowly cleared. She remembered the sound of the waves, the warmth of the sun and rocks. She'd been at Kismet Cove, and then she remembered why. Her heart ached, and a tear trickled down her cheek. She went to wipe it away. She couldn't. Her hands and ankles were bound tightly together. Panic rose up in her throat, a piece of silver tape across her mouth keeping it there. She'd been kidnapped.

There was a thumping sound and grunting coming from behind her. She rolled to her other side. Fighting against a wave of nausea and the searing pain in her head, she closed her eyes. *Calm down,* she told herself. *Panicking won't get you out of this. Breathe past the pain. Breathe past the fear.* When the pain dulled and the nausea passed, she opened her eyes and found herself staring into the panicked gaze of Paige Townsend. She was bound and gagged too.

A woman's angry voice came from a room off the one where they were being held. The words were muffled until she started to yell, "Your hands are as dirty as mine. I did what you wanted me to but were too afraid to ask." It went quiet for a moment. "I find that hard to believe when the woman you hired to do your bidding burned down the Gallaghers' carriage house last December."

Olivia's gaze shot to Paige. The other woman bowed her blond head and slowly shook it. The eyes she raised to Olivia were pleading. They could deal with the woman's accusation later, but right now they had to get out of here.

Olivia nudged her head toward her own hands and then rolled slowly and carefully to her side, her back to Paige. While Paige worked on untying the rope around Olivia's wrists, Olivia worked on getting the tape off her mouth. She got a small piece at the corner to lift. Closing her eyes, she blocked out the woman ranting in the next room and pressed her mouth and the tape to the floor. She jerked her head up and hard to the right. The movement caused a searing pain behind her eyes, and she was afraid she was going to throw up. She thought of Finn and George and tried once again and then again. On the fourth try, she ripped the tape off her mouth.

The woman was still ranting, but it sounded like it was to herself now. There was a loud crash. Glass shattered. All Olivia could think was that she didn't want to face that woman bound and helpless. She tested her restraints but they hadn't loosened. She turned to face Paige and found herself looking instead into a pair of bright blue eyes. "Simon," she cried.

Seeing someone familiar, even if he was only a cat,

caused Olivia's eyes to fill with tears and her heart with hope. He dropped what looked like an envelope and then licked her face with his sandpapery tongue before he got to work chewing through the rope binding her hands together.

She grimaced, whispered *sorry* to Paige, and then leaned in to pull the tape from the woman's face with her teeth.

Paige's eyes watered, but she didn't make a sound when the tape was ripped from her mouth.

"Who is that woman and what does she want from us?" Olivia whispered.

"She was Patty O'Hurley's paid companion, Ivy. She worked at the manor. I think she killed Patty for her house. She's going to kill you." There was another crash from the other room, and Paige shot a frantic glance over her shoulder. Returning her gaze to Olivia, she talked faster. "She's got it all twisted up in her head. There's a clause that prohibits the O'Hurley home from being sold unless a Gallagher no longer owns the manor and its lands. Ivy thinks that if she gets rid of you, the Gallaghers will have to sell out, and then she can sell the house she inherited from Patty." Paige gave her another pleading look. "She's going to kill me too. I tried to stop her. I offered her fifty thousand dollars to leave Harmony Harbor. I told her, if she didn't go, I'd tell the police about the threats she'd made against you."

Paige shook her head, tears spilling onto her cheeks. "I didn't know she was crazy. I should have just gone to the police, but then I'd have to tell them everything, about the carriage house...The fire was an accident, Olivia. I didn't know all of you were staying there that night. I just wanted to give the Gallaghers a scare. Make them think about what could happen if a fire started in the manor."

Olivia barely processed everything Paige was saying. She was stuck on the revelation that Ivy wanted her dead. Just as panic once again threatened to overtake her, Simon nudged her. Her hands were free. Her small cry of relief and gratitude was cut short when the door flew open and bounced against the wall.

Ivy sent a hate-filled glare their way. She spotted Simon, startled, and then snarled. She turned and ran back into the room that Olivia now saw was a kitchen. Simon looked from the kitchen and back to Olivia. He padded to her. Rubbing his cheek against Olivia's, he purred. His eyes held hers for one brief moment, and then he picked up the envelope and ran from the room. His tail disappeared around the door just as Ivy reappeared with a knife in her hand. "Devil cat," she cried, chasing after Simon.

Paige stared at Olivia and whimpered, "She's going to kill us."

"Don't panic. We're going to get out of this." She leaned over to quickly untie Paige's hands while searching the living room for a weapon. She made a list of them in her mind; poker by the fireplace, seven feet away; lamp on a small table to her right, two feet away. The rope fell from Paige's hands. "Untie your feet, Paige."

She glanced at the other woman, she was pale, her hands shaking. Afraid Paige was going into shock, Olivia whispered in a firm, confident voice that she planned to get them out of there. She kept talking while untying the ropes binding her own feet together.

"She's coming back. She's coming back," Paige said, her voice warbling as it rose.

Ivy stormed into the room, waving the knife. "Where is he? Where have you hidden him?"

"He's gone, Ivy. He's just a cat," Olivia said while surreptitiously testing the rope at her ankles. She hadn't had time to completely untie the rope, but she'd managed to loosen it. She glanced at Paige's feet. They were still tightly bound. Olivia's first thought had been to run. It looked like she would have to stay and fight.

"What do you know, Miss Richy Rich?" Ivy snarled, ranting about a ghost at the manor.

While she ranted about the ghost and the Gallaghers and Patty O'Hurley's children, Ivy paced from the kitchen to the window in the living room. Olivia took advantage of Ivy's distraction to inch her way back and to the right, at the same time pushing against the rope with her feet.

When she was within reaching distance of the lamp and reasonably sure she could kick off the rope around her ankles, Olivia drew Ivy's attention back to her. "I don't know why you're doing this, Ivy, but I have money. I'll give you whatever you want. All you have to do is let me and Paige go."

She snarled, stabbing the knife in Paige's direction. "If it weren't for her, I wouldn't be in this mess. She's not going anywhere." Ivy crossed her arms, sucked on her teeth, and nodded. "But you and me, we could work out a deal. Two million. I want two million, a new identity, and a house. I want a house in…somewhere warm, somewhere no one will…" Something came over her face, and her eyes narrowed. "You'll tell them. You'll tell the Gallaghers. I have to get rid of you and just bide my time. Yeah, that's what I have to do. Get rid of—"

Olivia grabbed the lamp, staggered to her feet, and worked on kicking off the rope as Ivy ran toward her. Olivia swung the lamp, knocking the knife out of Ivy's hand. It clattered onto the floor inches from Paige. "Paige," she cried, but the woman was curled in a ball, rocking. Olivia dove for the knife, her fingers closing around the handle just as Ivy jumped onto her back. The force of the blow flattened Olivia on the floor, knocking the breath from her lungs. Ivy slammed her head into the back of Olivia's. Olivia cried out. It felt like her head was splitting in two. The room spun, pinpricks of light exploding in front of her eyes.

Ivy grunted, breathing hard. Her hand closed over Olivia's. Olivia tightened her fingers around the handle and gritted her teeth, determined not to let Ivy get the knife. She thought of Finn and George, and it gave her a sudden burst of strength. She pushed up off the floor, flipping Ivy onto her back.

Olivia scrambled away, but Ivy recovered quickly and lunged, grabbing her by the hair. She dragged her backward. The second blow to her head had weakened Olivia, but she still had the knife. She slashed the blade in the air.

"Bitch!" Ivy bared her teeth when the knife caught her arm. She threw herself at Olivia, and they struggled for the knife. Olivia tried to push Ivy off her, and in doing so, her grip on the knife slipped. Ivy grabbed the knife and plunged the blade into Olivia's side.

As Olivia fell back onto the floor, she heard Paige

screaming. Olivia thought how unfair life was. Two years before, she would have given anything to die. And now that she had everything to live for, it didn't look like she would survive. But she couldn't go without letting Finn know how much she loved him.

She had to say goodbye, to him and George, the little girl who she'd come to think of as her own. She didn't want them to suffer. She wanted them to be able to let go and go on. The thought that they'd let their life and future be overshadowed by grief was as painful as the thought of leaving them behind. She knew now that Cooper would have felt the same. He would have wanted her to be happy.

Olivia brought her finger to the wound in her side and then, on the battered floor, began to write a love letter to Finn and to George.

Chapter Twenty-Four

♥

I'm sorry, Master Finn, but I thought you should know. In case—"

"In case what, Jeeves? In case Liv tried to kill herself? Look, look at their faces." He gestured to Griff, Liam, and his dad. "They're wondering too. And you know what will happen now? Instead of searching for my wife, searching for the person who took her, they're going to be looking for a body."

"Son, Jasper was only trying to help."

"But it doesn't help. None of you know what Liv suffered when she lost her son."

Finn took a deep breath, bowed his head, and nodded. "I'm sorry, I know you do, Dad. Our family has suffered, too, but there's a difference. We had each other. Liv didn't have anyone. She'd lost her parents a few years before, and because she'd spent every minute of every waking hour caring for her son and searching for a cure, she'd lost her friends too. Her husband wasn't there when Cooper died. And Liv, who fought so hard to keep her son alive, was shamed and blamed for prolonging his suffering by her husband and his parents. She lost the most important person in her life, and she had no one to turn to, Dad. She was in pain, she was burned out, and she—"

He swore and wiped his arm across his eyes. "Dammit, you know her now. You know the person she is. She wouldn't take her own life. She wouldn't leave me. She loves me. And as much as she loves George, she would be happy that George didn't lose her mother."

"Finn." Griff lifted his chin.

He turned to see Stanley, George, and Isabella staring at him. Both mother and daughter were crying. "I'm so sorry. I didn't know. I didn't know," Isabella sobbed.

George angrily scrubbed at her face and lifted her chin. "You're stupid. You're all stupid. Livy wouldn't do that. Livy wouldn't hurt herself 'cause she was sad. She—" George broke off, staring into space, and then she nodded. Her brow furrowed as though she was concentrating.

"What's wrong? What's happening to my daughter?" Isabella cried.

"I'm sure she's just upset. Master Finn, I can see to the little one," Jasper said, nodding at George's half-hysterical mother while he guided the little girl off to the side.

Finn frowned. George seemed oblivious to where she was. "Stan." It took a minute for Finn to get the lawyer's attention. When he did, Finn gestured at Isabella and then he walked to where Jasper was crouched beside George.

Finn was relieved to see George appeared to be fully alert now. She nodded at something Jasper said to her and then took the old man's hand.

"Master Finn, the little miss believes she knows who would wish Olivia harm."

George glanced up at Jasper and then looked at Finn. "Ivy did it. She hit Livy and took her. She's bad *juju*. Ivy's bad *juju*. We have to save Livy."

"Ivy's your ghost?" Finn asked George, confused.

"She's not a ghost, Master Finn," Jasper said, answering for George. "Ivy's been working in housekeeping for the past couple of months, but she hasn't shown up for work since Olivia's shower. There's something familiar about her, but I can't place her."

"I'll check the employment records," Sophie said, and hurried from the ballroom.

Jasper closed his eyes and shook his head. Finn thought he heard him mutter, "I'm trying, Madame. I'm trying."

Meow. Simon dropped an envelope at Finn's feet. He picked it up. "Patty O'Hurley."

"Yes, yes, that's who it is. Ivy was Mrs. O'Hurley's paid companion." Jasper glanced at Simon. "I believe that's where we'll find Olivia, Master Finn." He pointed at the address on the envelope.

Everyone turned to run for the doors. "No, George, you stay with your mom. I'll bring Liv back, I promise."

Finn raced through the manor and into the parking lot. A black Jeep screeched to a stop beside him, and the passenger door swung open. Finn jumped inside, followed by Griff and his dad.

Griff gave them an update as he put on his seat belt.

"I just talked to Aidan—cops are on their way. They got a phone call just before mine. Some guy saying that both Ivy and Paige Townsend had worked for him, but he'd been unaware to what lengths they would go to secure the estate. He said Ivy has both Paige and Olivia and was going to…" Griff trailed off.

Liam cursed and jerked the wheel, the Jeep's tires squealing. "Hang on. We're going off-road. It'll cut the time in half."

They reached the Victorian in under five minutes. In the distance, they heard the sound of sirens. Finn jumped out of the Jeep before it had come to a complete stop. "For Chrissakes, Finn." He shot Griff a look as he ran up the steps.

"Okay, okay, I'd do the same but the point is not to get yourself killed so you can save your wife," Griff said as Finn tried the door. It was locked. Griff kicked it in.

They heard Ivy before they saw her. "You're too late! They're dead!" And then she came running at them with her knife raised. A bullet whizzed between Finn and Griff and hit Ivy between the eyes. She dropped two feet in front of them.

Aidan lowered his gun. "Go. She came out of the room to the right. Ambulance is on the way."

Heart pounding, Finn sprinted down the hall. He saw Olivia the moment he stepped into the room. She was lying in a pool of blood. He didn't remember crossing the room or kneeling beside her or taking her cold hand in his. Her finger was bloody. She'd written his name. She'd written to him and to George. She loved them. She wanted them to go on. To live, love, laugh, and be happy.

"Finn! Snap out of it. She's alive. She's got a pulse," Griff said.

Liam ran in with a first aid kit. Their father was kneeling beside Paige. He looked at them and shook his head.

"You've got this, bro. You've got this," Liam said. "Tell us what you need us to do."

He kissed Liv and whispered in her ear, "I love you, Princess. Keep fighting. Keep fighting for me, for us." He opened the kit and quickly pulled on gloves. "Make her comfortable, get something for under her head. Griff, talk to her." And then Finn did what he did best—he worked on saving a life.

The smells and sounds were familiar. Without opening her eyes, Olivia knew where she was. She'd spent too much time in hospitals not to. And while she admired the men and women who worked there, she'd grown to hate hospitals. But today, waking up in one felt like the most wondrous of gifts. As was the ridiculously gorgeous man holding her hand. He'd fallen asleep with his head on her thigh. She slipped her hand out from his to stroke his beard-stubbled face.

His eyes slowly opened, and he lifted his head. "You're awake," he said, as if he thought he was dreaming.

"Yes, thanks to you. I heard you, you know. I heard you telling me to fight." She stroked his hair. "Thank you for saving me."

"Thank you for fighting." He took her hand and kissed her palm. "I read what you wrote." He rubbed his face, his eyes shiny. "I don't even want to think about losing you, but if we'd been five minutes later...Your words, your last thoughts, they would have meant something, Liv. I would have tried to honor them." He smiled. "They made me think about a lot of things. How I've dealt with losing Mom and Riley. They helped, Liv. Thank you."

"I'm glad." She lifted his hand to her face, rubbing it against her cheek. "I'm sorry I ran out on you, Finn. I should have talked to you about how I was feeling. But when I heard Isabella asking you to come to Kenya, it felt like—"

"Liv, I'm not going to Kenya. I'm staying right here with you. I've let DWB know I won't be coming back."

"No, please don't do that because of me. You'll end up resenting me. We'll work it out."

"I loved the work I did with DWB. I'm proud of what we accomplished, but I was running, Liv. I was using my work to avoid coming home and dealing with the pain of losing Mom and Riley. I think it's about time I gave back to my own community. And if that board of director's job is still open at Helping Hands, I'd like to throw my name in the ring."

"There's always a place for you on the board."

The door to her room opened. "Okay, there's something seriously wrong with you two. Olivia barely escapes death, and the moment she wakes up, you two are talking about work?" Liam said, coming into the room with his brothers and father.

Finn narrowed his eyes. "Were you listening outside the door?"

"Uh, yeah, we didn't want to interrupt anything."

Olivia thought maybe she should remind them she was recovering from a knife wound to the side and it was highly unlikely she and Finn would be doing much more than kissing and cuddling for a few weeks. But before she had a chance to say anything, George and her mother poked their heads into the room.

"Is it okay if we come in?" Isabella asked.

"Yes, of—" She laughed when George strode into the room like no one had better try and stop her. Olivia worked to hide her wince. It looked like laughing was out for a while too. Finn got up and kissed her. "I'll get you something for the pain." He motioned for his brothers and father to follow him.

George came around the bed with a flowerpot decorated with rainbow-colored handprints. Inside the pot was a yellow primrose. One that had no doubt come from their garden. "I made it for you," George said, putting the flowerpot on the side table.

"It's beautiful, George. I love it, and I love you," she said, holding out her arms to the little girl.

"I love you too, Livy," she said, stretching up to kiss Olivia's cheek. She dropped back down on her light-up shoes. "I saved you."

"You did?" Olivia held back a smile. George really was a lot like her father. "I thought Finn saved me."

"Yeah, but he wouldn't have gotten there in time if I hadn't told him about Ivy." Olivia didn't get a chance to find out how George had known it was Ivy, because the little girl filled her in on the rest of the news. She heard about Paige. Ivy had severed an artery, and Paige had died before Finn, his brothers, and father had arrived. She also learned that Aidan had shot and killed Ivy.

Isabella grimaced. "I'm sorry. George, Livy is just awake. Maybe we should wait—"

"There's more?" Olivia asked, trying to keep the alarm from her voice.

"Yep, good news," George said, hopping up onto the side of the bed.

"Georgina, be careful!"

"It's okay. I'm fine, Isabella." Olivia smiled and then looked at George. "So, what's the good news?"

"Me."

She laughed, and then winced. "I agree, you are a very special little girl, but—"

"No, silly, you get me. I'm going to live with you during school and live with Mama on the holidays."

Olivia looked at Isabella. "I don't know what to say. Are you sure?"

"It's what she wants. She's made a home here. She has friends, she loves her school, and her dog, and bunny, and she loves you and Finn. It would be selfish of me to take all that away from her. Unless you don't want her."

George scowled at her mother. "She loves me. Of course she wants me."

"She's right, I absolutely do. But are you very sure, Isabella? I don't want anything other than George to be influencing your decision."

Nathan's other wife held her gaze. "I promise, it's not." She held out her hand to George. "Livy needs her rest. We'll come back tomorrow." She waited at the door while George said goodbye and told Olivia how to care for the plant. Then George scooted under Isabella's arm and out the door. "Nathan made a lot of mistakes, Livy, but she isn't one of them. And entrusting her to your care wasn't either. He knew you'd fight for her, just like you fought for your son. Thank you. Thank you for not holding what Nathan, and what I unknowingly, did to you, against George."

"Hey, Princess, what's with the tears?" Finn said as he walked into her room five minutes later. He came around the bed and carefully sat on the side. "Are you in pain?"

She nodded.

"Okay, just give me a minute, and we'll take care of that."

She sniffed. "It's not the kind of pain a pill can take care of." She told him about her visit with George and Isabella.

"Your ex might have been an asshole, but he had great taste in women. And he raised a pretty awesome kid."

"She is, and now she's partially ours."

"Yeah, so I'm thinking maybe we should plant plastic flowers." He laughed, lifting his chin at the flowerpot. "Just so you know, it took her five tries before she found the one she liked."

"Do you know the meaning of primrose?"

"No, do you?"

"Of course I do. I'm a wedding planner." She smiled at his what-does-that-have-to-do-with-anything look. "Primrose means I can't live without you."

He smoothed her hair from her face and gently kissed her forehead. "You and I know better though. Because while I can live without you, and you can live without me, I don't want to, and I thank God I don't have to, Liv."

Her wholehearted agreement was lost in his kiss.

"Okay, you two lovebirds. I just have to check on the patient, and then I'll let you get back to it."

They both looked over to see Dr. Bishop smiling at them from the door.

"She's married to a doctor. I think you know him. Your partner at the clinic, ring a bell?"

He waved a dismissive hand at Finn. "Yes, which is why she's my patient and not yours. Though I will commend you on an excellent piece of emergency fieldwork, my boy. Well done, and you'll both be pleased to know everything's a-okay with the little one."

"What happened to George?" Olivia asked.

The older man laughed. "Not that little one. That one." He pointed at her stomach.

"I'm…pregnant? She's pregnant?" Olivia and Finn asked at almost the same time, looking at each other.

As though Dr. Bishop had staged the whole thing, Finn's entire family walked in the room, including George, Isabella, and Stanley, at the precise moment he said, "Yes, we'll be welcoming another baby Gallagher next spring."

Hidden in Greystone Manor is a book containing *all* of the dark secrets of Harmony Harbor...including Ava DiRossi's. No one—especially her ex-husband, Griffin Gallagher—can ever discover the secrets that tore her life apart years ago. Only now Griffin is back in town. Still handsome. Still angry with her for leaving him. And still not aware that Ava never stopped loving him...

An excerpt from

Starlight Bridge

follows.

Chapter One

♥

Ava DiRossi didn't believe in fairy tales and happily-ever-afters, but right about now, she'd sell her soul for a fairy godmother.

As the elevator shuddered and creaked on its way up to the north tower, Ava removed her black work shoe. The sole had come loose, flapping when she walked. She hammered it against the steel frame of the service cart in hopes it would hold out until the end of her shift. After several good whacks, she stopped to examine the seam. Satisfied the shoe wouldn't fall apart before she got home, she slipped it back onto her foot.

Obviously she didn't need a fairy godmother to take care of her footwear or to provide her with fancy gowns. And Prince Charming? She'd had one of her own. A long time ago. Only he'd turned out to be more princely and charming than she deserved, and she'd ended their fairy-tale marriage. But there was something a fairy godmother could help her with. If Ava had one, she'd ask her to turn back the clock to three months earlier. Her life had been so simple then.

She loved Greystone Manor. It had been her refuge, her sanctuary. She'd been left alone, free to do as she pleased as long as the guest rooms were well and properly cleaned. And they were, because Ava wouldn't have it any other way. She made sure each room sparkled and shone.

But everything had changed the day Colleen Gallagher died and Ava's cousin Sophie had become manager of the manor. It seemed like every time Ava turned around, her cousin was there with a new scheme to improve Greystone's bottom line. One that invariably required Ava's help and was designed to push her out of her comfort zone.

The elevator jerked to a stop. Without thinking, Ava pushed the service cart toward the now-open doors. A jarring pain shot up her arm, and she sucked in a breath through her teeth. That's what she got for letting thoughts of fairy godmothers fill her head. She used her good arm and her hip to push the heavy cart into the deserted hall. As though in judgment of what she was about to do, long-dead Gallaghers looked down at her from the portraits in gilded frames that lined the stone walls.

"I'm not any happier about it than you are," Ava told the portrait of William Gallagher, the family's patriarch. He looked like the pirate he'd been reputed to be. "But Colleen would understand. She'd want me to find her memoirs."

Until the private viewing at the manor three days after Colleen had passed, no one had believed that she'd actually written her memoirs. But during the wake, in a recorded message for the Widows Club—of which Ava was a member, the token divorcée—Colleen had held up the book, proving that it did indeed exist. And not only had Colleen written about her life and her secrets, but she'd also recorded each and every one of theirs. Just before Colleen announced where she'd hidden the book, static filled the screen and the videotape was damaged beyond repair.

There were secrets in the book that Ava couldn't afford to have come to light. Secrets she'd confessed to Colleen in a weak moment. Secrets the Gallagher matriarch had promised to take to her grave.

Oh, now, you have a head full of fanciful thoughts today, don't you, Ava my girl?

"Yes, thanks to you and Sophie, my head seems to be full of them these days. And I can tell you I was much happier without them," Ava said as she parked the cart under William's portrait, then sighed when she realized she was talking aloud. Talking to her ex-husband's great-grandmother, who'd died more than two months ago.

It wasn't the first time Ava had caught herself doing so. She wasn't worried she was going crazy though. Her newly acquired habit was a result of stress and exhaustion. There wasn't much she could do about being so tired she could hardly think straight, but she could alleviate part of her stress by finding the book that would reveal the truth about her and that night and the man she'd allowed to ruin her life.

In case someone happened upon her in Colleen's room, Ava tossed two sponges in a bucket and made her way to the walnut-studded door, sliding her passkey into the lock. Colleen had lost her battle with her son Ronan, a historian, over the entry upgrade. She never did like change. If Colleen had gotten her way, Greystone Manor, which had been built in the early nineteenth century and modeled after a medieval castle, would have stayed exactly the same.

Meow.

Ava jumped, pressing a hand to her chest as a black cat wound his way between her legs. Simon, who'd arrived at the manor a week before Colleen died, raised his blue eyes and meowed again. Placing the bucket on the hardwood floor, Ava crouched to scratch behind his ears.

"You miss her, too, don't you?" she said to the cat, realizing that was most likely the reason she'd been talking to a dead woman. She missed Colleen. Ava had worked for her ex-husband's family for more than a decade.

Simon purred, rubbing his head against her leg. She gave him a final pat. "You can come with me, but you have to stay quiet."

Ava picked up the bucket and straightened to open the door. As she did, a sweet, floral scent wafted past her nose. She frowned at the fresh bouquet of pink, yellow, and white roses in a crystal vase on the nightstand beside the canopied bed. Odd. Who would…Jasper, she decided. The older man had been with the Gallaghers for as long as she could remember. He'd been Colleen's right-hand man and confidant. Skinny as a rail with stiff, upper-crust manners, he was a pain in Ava's *culo*.

Her gaze lifted from the roses to the Gothic-style leaded windows that overlooked the gardens. Sleet pelted the windowpanes, and the barren trees swayed in the cold mid-January winds. She wrapped her gray sweater around her while casting a longing glance at the fireplace with a three-tiered wrought-iron candelabra standing in front of it. The fireplace was more for show than heat. So no matter that she could practically see her breath in the room; now wasn't the time to put it to the test and risk an actual fire.

She eyed the hundreds of books lining the walls of the sitting area. More were stacked haphazardly on the antique tables on either side of a well-worn, gold damask love seat with additional piles creating small towers on the hardwood floor. A cluttered white desk with feminine lines sat in the center of the room with a view of the dark, turbulent sea through the French doors that led onto a stone balcony.

The room looked exactly the same as the night she'd searched it with her cousin, her Auntie Rosa, and the rest of the Widows Club. As far as Ava knew, no one had found the book. Though not for lack of trying. It had to be here, somewhere in this room.

She set the bucket beside the fireplace and walked the perimeter, lifting the heavy, antique-gold drapes and peeking under the oil paintings in search of a safe or secret compartment. Simon meowed from where he stretched out on the back of the love seat, once again drawing Ava's attention to the shelves of books behind him.

They'd been looking for a brown, leather-bound book the night they'd first searched the room—aptly named *The Secret Keeper of Harmony Harbor*. Ava wondered if Colleen had hidden it within another book. She wouldn't be surprised if she had. Colleen had been a cagey old lady.

As Ava catalogued the sheer volume of books, she realized she'd be here longer than she had anticipated. Unconsciously, her hand went to her bruised arm; she couldn't be late again. She reached in her pocket for her earbuds and turned on her iPod. Fitting the buds in her ears, she got to it, leafing through one book at a time. Alone with her music—aside from Simon—Ava felt some of the day's tensions leave her. She liked repetitive, mindless work. She found it calming. Well, it was usually calming. With the book on the loose, it was somewhat less so today.

Someone tapped her shoulder, and she jumped, dropping the book she'd just taken off the shelf. She whirled around, pressing a hand to her chest. "You practically gave me a heart attack."

"Sorry." Sophie grimaced. Ava's cousin wore her uniform of a white blouse and black pencil skirt. "I called out, but you mustn't have heard me. What are you listening to?" She pulled the bud from Ava's ear and held it to hers. "It's loud"—Sophie made a face—"and depressing."

"'Mad World' by Gary Jules. It's not depressing. It's beautiful." Ava reached into the pocket of her black uniform dress and turned off the iPod, then bent to pick up the book she'd dropped. "I, um, was looking for something to read."

Sophie removed the black-framed glasses that held back her long, chestnut-brown hair and put them on, leaning forward to look at the book. She raised an eyebrow. "*Finnegans Wake* by James Joyce. Interesting choice."

"I thought so. It was one of Colleen's favorites."

"You miss her, don't you?" Sophie said with a sympathetic smile.

It wasn't that long ago that her cousin had been as anxious to find Colleen's memoirs as Ava. A fire in Sophie's LA apartment left her and her daughter, Mia, homeless, forcing them to move back to Harmony Harbor. For years, Sophie had kept the true identity of Mia's father a secret. But just a month after arriving home, the truth came out. It had been a difficult time for Sophie and Liam, but in the end, their love for each other prevailed.

So Sophie would understand Ava's need to find the book only too well and would no doubt offer her help. But there'd be a price to pay. Sophie would want to know her secret, and it was a secret Ava would take to her grave. "*Sì*, I do."

Sophie rested her hip against the back of the love seat, absently petting Simon. "Do you think I'm horrible for renting out Colleen's suite?"

Her cousin had announced her plans last night. It was the reason Ava was searching the room. While there was a part of her that didn't want Colleen's private space invaded, she understood why Sophie felt she had to do so.

Within a day of her cousin announcing plans for a bridal show at Greystone, their major competitor, the Bridgeport Marquis, announced plans for their own bridal show. Yesterday, the Marquis's bridal suite had been featured in the *Harmony Harbor Gazette*.

"You know, if Colleen were here, she'd have suggested it herself, Sophie. The bridal suite at the Marquis can't compete with this." Ava lifted her hand to the French doors. "Look at the views."

Sophie nibbled on her thumbnail and nodded. "I know, but maybe I overreacted. The old bridal suite has an ocean view too. It's just not as big as Colleen's. I'll have Dana stage them both. If she thinks the old bridal suite shows just as well, we'll feature it in the *Gazette*. That way we won't have to pack Colleen's things away."

Dana Templeton was a long-term guest at the manor. She'd also become a close friend to both Ava and Sophie. The woman had exquisite taste…and a secret. She was probably as anxious to find Colleen's memoirs as Ava.

"Next on the list is updating the restaurant menu," Sophie added with a look in her golden-brown eyes that was all too familiar.

"It's getting late. I should probably get going," Ava said in hopes of avoiding another conversation about the restaurant. She turned to pick up the books she'd piled on the floor. She adored Sophie, admired the woman she'd become, but her cousin had an almost obsessive need to fix things, including the people she loved. Over the past two months, it had become apparent that Ava was her new pet project.

"You're not walking home. I'll give you a ride. It'll give us a chance to talk about the restaurant," Sophie said brightly.

Ava bowed her head and sighed. Her cousin was like a dog with a bone. "Sophie, no matter how often you ask, my answer will be the same. I can't. My father—"

"Please, just think about it? You're an incredibly talented chef. No, don't wave me off. You are. You know how important the bridal show is for us. I can't have Helga handling the food. I need you, Ava. Greystone needs you."

"No, what you need is a well-trained and experienced chef, and that's not me. I want to save Greystone as much as you do, Sophie, but I can't take over the restaurant. I'll do anything else but that."

"What if I talk to Uncle Gino? I'm sure he'd—"

Fingers of fear crawled up Ava's spine at the thought of Sophie talking to her father. She drew the sleeve of her sweater over her hand, fisting it around the gray wool. "No. *Capisci?*" The words came out more forcefully than she intended, and in Italian. When she was nervous or upset, she slipped back into the language she'd grown up hearing at home.

"No, I don't understand," Sophie said with equal force and a stubborn jut of her chin. "You helped out before, so I don't know why you won't help out again."

There were times when her cousin reminded Ava of her Auntie Rosa, Sophie's mule-headed grandmother. This was one of them. "Because you were desperate." Ava held up a hand when Sophie opened her mouth. "Find someone else. I'm not interested. I'm a maid, Sophie. Not a chef."

"What happened to you, Ava? What happened to the girl I remember?"

Ava had once loved to cook—it had been her passion. But she was no longer the girl her cousin remembered. She didn't want to be. "She grew up. Now, do you think I can get back to my job?"

Sophie made a face. "Fine. Griffin will be arriving within the hour unless his plane was delayed by the weather. It should be enough time for the room to warm up. There's extra firewood in the lobby. I'll go—"

"Griffin...Griffin's staying here? In this room?" Her ex-husband rarely came back to Harmony Harbor. In the past ten years, Ava had only seen him a handful of times. Though that may have been because he'd gone out of his way to avoid her. Granted, she had done the same. But she hadn't been able to avoid him when he'd come home for Colleen's funeral or for Liam and Sophie's wedding.

"I thought I told you he was coming home." Sophie lifted a shoulder as though it had slipped her mind, but Ava saw the hint of a smile playing on her lips. "We needed some extra muscle to help get the ballroom ready for the bridal show. You have to admit Griffin fits the bill."

She wouldn't let her mind go to just how well her ex fit the we-need-muscle bill or allow herself to think about the potential consequences of her tenacious cousin playing matchmaker. Ava would worry about that later. Right now, she was more terrified at the thought of Griffin staying in a room that quite possibly held a book that contained her deepest, darkest secret.

"What's wrong?" Sophie touched Ava's bruised forearm, her brow furrowed with concern. "It's not like when he came home for Colleen's funeral. His ex won't be with him if that's what you're worried about."

At the light pressure of Sophie's hand on her bruised arm, Ava clenched her teeth to stifle a groan and reached for the bucket. "Nothing's wrong. I just have a lot to do before he arrives. I'll get to it now." She prayed her cousin took the hint and left, because for the first time in more than a decade, Ava had no intention of doing her job. She was going to find Colleen's book instead. Or at the very least, ensure that Griffin didn't.

Sophie looked over the room. "I promised Mia and Liam I'd be home for supper, but if you need me to stay—"

"Thank you, but no. I'll get done faster without you."

"Um, are you forgetting I used to work as a maid? I was actually pretty good at—"

Would she never leave? Ava took matters into her own hands and carefully steered her cousin toward the door. "Yes, I'm sure you were the Maid of LA, but I am the Maid of Harmony Harbor, so you can go now. Give Mia a kiss for me."

Sophie laughed. "Okay, okay, I'm leaving. But call me when you're finished, and I'll give you a ride home."

"*Ciao,*" Ava said, and closed the door. Heart racing, she pressed her back against it. Simon sat in front of…the fireplace. The one place none of them had thought to look. Ava raced across the room. She knelt on the floor to move the heavy wrought-iron candelabra, careful not to knock off the candles as she pushed it to the side. Ignoring the pain in her arm, she scrutinized the brick facing for a sign it had been tampered with. When she didn't find any, she ran her fingers along the dark oak frame and mantel.

Simon meowed and padded into the fireplace. He sat on the logs and looked up. Ava stuck her head inside and did the same. It was too dark to see much of anything. She was typically prepared for whatever might come up on the job, but she didn't carry a flashlight, and she didn't have her cell phone. Her father had broken it two weeks before in another fit of temper.

She skimmed her right hand up and down the wall where Simon was staring. Two of the bricks were loose.

She pushed her finger between them, touching what felt like soft leather. She held her breath as she tried to lift it and the edges of paper brushed against her finger. It was a book. Her pulse kicked up with excitement, her shoulders sagging with relief.

Her relief was short-lived. No matter how hard she tugged on the upper brick with her uninjured arm, it refused to budge. Gritting her teeth, she tried using both hands. Her bruised arm protested the movement, but she refused to give up and breathed through the pain.

Fifteen minutes later, she stopped to regroup. There had to be another way. Her hands were blackened with soot, the tips of her fingers raw, and the bricks had barely moved. She looked around the room for something to wedge between them and spied the poker.

"We're in business, Simon. This should do—"

"Tell Grams I'll see her in a bit."

Her gaze shot to the door. She'd recognize that voice anywhere. Griffin was here. Now. Outside the door. She shot to her feet, shoving the candelabra in front of the fireplace.

Meow.

She'd trapped Simon. She grabbed the cat, put him on the floor, and scooped up the bucket and sponges while frantically searching for somewhere to hide. The balcony. She didn't care if she froze to death; she couldn't let him find her here.

As she turned to run, Ava heard the beep of the passkey. She wouldn't make it. She spun around and ran the short distance to the bathroom. Her breath coming in panicked puffs, she stepped inside the bathtub and carefully inched the crimson and gold shower curtain across the rod. She sagged against the tile wall, praying his *in a bit* meant he'd drop his bags off and leave.

If it had been anyone other than Griffin, she'd pretend to be cleaning the room. But she remembered all too clearly the humiliation of being discovered by Griffin and his ex-wife the last time they'd stayed at the manor. He'd looked at Ava like he hadn't known who she was, and his wife had asked for fresh towels, acting as though Ava hadn't done her job.

And then there was the book. She couldn't leave without it.

"How did you get in here?"

Her gaze jerked to the curtain, her heart beating double time. She let out the breath she'd been holding when the bed creaked. Simon. Griffin was talking to the cat. "Better question would be, what have you been up to? Your paws are black. Off the bed, buddy."

Her toes curled in her shoes, a warm, fluttery sensation settling low in her stomach in response to the slow drawl of Griffin's deep voice. He always spoke in that low, unhurried tone. Even when he was angry or when he was whispering how much he loved her or when he was talking her out of her temper. Only then there'd been a hint of laughter too. Her temper used to amuse him. He had a long fuse; she had a short one. She used to, at least.

Her lips curved at the memories; then her wistful smile faded when the consequences of what he'd just said penetrated her lovesick brain. Simon's paws were dirty. All she'd need was for Griffin to start looking for the source. She had to…

There was the rasp of a zipper, then the light thud of

something hitting the floor. At the sound of heavy foot-falls approaching the bathroom, Ava's eyes went wide, and she pressed her back against the tiled wall. A bare, muscled arm reached past the curtain, a large hand turning on the water. The cold spray from the showerhead hit her in the face, and a small, shocked squeak escaped before she could contain it.

Griffin whipped back the shower curtain. His thick, toffee-colored hair glistened under the fluorescent light, his dazzling, deep blue eyes wide in surprise. She opened her mouth to say something, but the words got stuck in her throat as her eyes drifted down his body. He was completely and gloriously naked. And even more beautiful than she remembered.

About the Author

DEBBIE MASON is the bestselling author of the Christmas, Colorado, and the Harmony Harbor series. Her books have been praised for their "likable characters, clever dialogue, and juicy plots" (*RT Book Reviews*). When she isn't writing or reading, Debbie enjoys spending time with her very own real-life hero, their three wonderful children and son-in-law, two adorable grandbabies, and a yappy Yorkie named Bella.

You can learn more at:
AuthorDebbieMason.com
Twitter @AuthorDebMason
Facebook.com

Fall in Love with Forever Romance

PRIMROSE LANE
By Debbie Mason

"[The Harmony Harbor series is] heartfelt and delightful!"
—RaeAnne Thayne, *New York Times* bestselling author

Finn Gallagher returns for a visit to Harmony Harbor only to find that the town's matchmakers have other plans. Because it's high time that wedding planner Olivia Davenport gets to plan her own nuptials. And finding true love is the best reason of all for Finn to move home for good.

Fall in Love with Forever Romance

COMEBACK COWBOY
By Sara Richardson

In the *New York Times* bestselling tradition of Jennifer Ryan and Maisey Yates comes the second book in Sara Richardson's Rocky Mountain Riders series. When Naomi's high school sweetheart comes riding back to town, this self-sufficient single mom feels something she hasn't felt in years: a red-hot unbridled need for the handsome cowboy who left her behind. As much as Naomi's tried, a woman never forgets her first cowboy...

Fall in Love with Forever Romance

ON THE PLUS SIDE
By Alison Bliss

Thanks to her bangin' curves, Valerie Carmichael has always turned heads—with the exception of seriously sexy Logan Mathis. But Valerie is determined to get Logan's attention, even if it means telling a teeny little lie to get a job at his bar…Logan can't remember a time when Valerie didn't fuel all his hottest fantasies. Now the she-devil is working behind his bar and tempting him every damn night. But no one warned them that sometimes the smallest secrets have the biggest consequences…

Fall in Love with Forever Romance

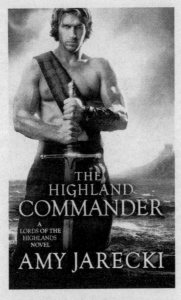

THE HIGHLAND COMMANDER
By Amy Jarecki

As the illegitimate daughter of a Scottish earl, Lady Magdalen Keith is not usually one to partake in lavish masquerade balls. Yet one officer sweeps her off her feet with dashing good looks that cannot be disguised by a mere mask...Navy lieutenant Aiden Murray has spent too many months at sea to be immune to this lovely beauty. But when he discovers Maddie's true identity—and learns that her father is accused of treason—will the brawny Scot risk his life to follow his heart?